CRUZATTE

AND

MARIA

Also by Peter Bowen

The Stick Game
Long Son
Thunder Horse
Notches
Wolf, No Wolf
Specimen Song
Coyote Wind

Kelly and the Three-toed Horse
Imperial Kelly
Kelly Blue
Yellowstone Kelly

CRUZATTE

MARIA

A Gabriel Du Pré Mystery

PETER BOWEN

ST. MARTIN'S MINOTAUR
NEW YORK

www.minotaurbooks.com

ISBN 0-312-26253-1

First Edition: March 2001

10 9 8 7 6 5 4 3 2 1

. . . For the tribe of Martin—
Bill, Laura, John, Brian, and Pooker Bear . . .

CRUZATTE

AND

MARIA

CHAPTER 1

Du Pré limped into the Toussaint Saloon. He slid up on a stool, wincing.

"What the hell happened to you?" said Susan Klein, not looking up from her knitting.

"Shoeing horses," said Du Pré. "One of them he don't like it so good."

Susan nodded.

"How bad?" she said.

"There is this sound," said Du Pré, "when his hock hit my ribs. Like when you crunch carrots, your teeth."

"Coughing any blood?" asked Susan Klein. She still didn't look up from her knitting.

"No big clots," said Du Pré.

Susan nodded.

"You want sympathy or a drink?" said Susan. She frowned at the wool in her hands.

1

"Both," said Du Pré.

Susan put her knitting down on the bartop. She went to the well and put ice in a tall glass with whiskey and water.

She pushed the drink over to Du Pré.

"You pore ol' son of a bitch," she said, looking at him mournfully.

Du Pré nodded.

He drank.

Susan went back to her stool and sat.

Click click click went her needles.

"Harvey Wallace called for you," said Susan. "He said he will call back."

"I am dead, tell him, ver' sad, but the funeral is tomorrow," said Du Pré.

Harvey Fucking Weasel Fat Wallace, Du Pré thought, Blackfeet FBI Agent, never calls me with any good news.

"That would be telling an untruth," said Susan Klein.

"OK," said Du Pré, "I will tell him I am dead. Ow." He rubbed his ribs.

The door opened and a couple of ranchers came in laughing. They they took the drinks to the pool table and the balls thundered out of the belly of the table. A rancher racked them and the other broke; balls clacked.

"Shit," said one of the ranchers.

Du Pré rolled a smoke, and he lit it and blew out a long stream of blue-gray cloud.

"They really grind up dog turds to mix in that stuff?" said Susan Klein.

"Poodle," said Du Pré. "Ver' expensive dogs."

A ball rattled down a pocket.

"Whoeee!" said a rancher.

The telephone rang. Susan Klein didn't stir.

Neither did Du Pré.

The telephone rang and rang and rang. Finally, one of the ranchers went to the pay phone and picked it up.

"Yeah?" he said. He listened.

"Du Pré!" he said. "Fer you."

Du Pré sighed, and he got up and walked slowly toward the old box on the wall by the front door. The rancher who had answered it looked at him.

"Thanks," said Du Pré, "from my heart."

The rancher grinned.

Du Pré lifted the receiver to his ear.

"Yah," he said.

"Du Pré," said Harvey Wallace. "Long time no come to phone. You prick."

"I am dead," said Du Pré. "Ver' sad, you should come, the funeral, it is tomorrow."

"You don't want to talk to me," said Harvey. "I told my boss that you wouldn't. I said, 'Du Pré will tell me to go to hell,' what I said. She said to try my best. Or I'd be out there, in the fucking cactus, eating fried calf nuts and smelling that stinking goddamned sagebrush and all the rest of that shit I couldn't wait to get away from."

"She say all that?" said Du Pré. "She knows you good, huh?"

"Very smart lady," said Harvey. "Scary, actually. Here I am, drawing a fat government paycheck and bennies and all, and the ungrateful bitch wants me to work, too."

"I was kicked, a horse, today," said Du Pré. "And me, I come here to have some nice drinks, sit, smoke a little, get used to my ribs which are not the ribs I woke up with, this morning, they have changed. So maybe you could stop telling me, your work troubles, ask me what it is you want me to do so I can say *go fuck yourself, Harvey* and go back, get used to my ribs."

Harvey sighed.

"We have a problem maybe," said Harvey. "Actually I lied. My boss actually did not say a word to me. Nobody has. But, well, I don't have very much to do, you know, this being government work, and so I read the newspapers, lots of newspapers, and I even read some of what folks call newspapers out where you are."

3

"My ribs," said Du Pré. "They are waiting, your punch line."

"For the last three years," said Harvey, "people have been disappearing over there on the Missouri."

"Yah," said Du Pré, "We have this governor, Meagher, he fall in long time ago they don't find him. So he is who I am looking for?"

Harvey sighed.

"I smell trouble," he said. "Look, nine people have just up and flat evaporated in the last three years. They all were going down the river through that White Cliffs area, you know, Fort Benton on—"

"To the dam," said Du Pré.

"Yeah," said Harvey. "They found their boats, floating down in the river, and they found their gear, some of it anyway, but the people they never did find. . . ."

Du Pré sighed. He rubbed his sore ribs.

"Too bad," said Du Pré. "They go down the river covers them, mud and sand, they don't come up. Happens, you know."

"I know," said Harvey, "but I just don't like this."

"So," said Du Pré, "so send one of the Mormons you got, you know, the wing tips the suit, blend in so good, have them ask them questions."

"Very funny," said Harvey. "But there is something else. The local law there doesn't seem to care very much."

"Shit," said Du Pré. "They are lost, the river, but don't know what county they are lost in? They got no money at all, Harvey, is why they do not care. They got maybe a sheriff, two deputies, county big as them states back where you are, they got troubles now, yes."

Harvey sighed.

"Maybe," he said.

"Oh," said Du Pré. "You got no jurisdiction, can't send nobody, so you call me, your good friend Du Pré, him got the broken ribs and he is ver' thirsty, say, Du Pré, you maybe go up there, snoop around for your old friend Harvey, see maybe you can find a crime, one that he likes . . ."

4

Harvey sighed.

"Fuck you, no," said Du Pré.

"I guess," said Harvey, "I'll have to talk to Madelaine."

"Prick," said Du Pré.

"Thing is," said Harvey, "much as I talk about the West and say I hope never to see goddamn prickly pear cactus and smell sage again I don't really mean it. What I am afraid of—"

"They already start a war out here, Harvey," said Du Pré. "They say, the ranchers, you are so bad for *the environment.* I know people get killed here, long time."

"I don't want that," said Harvey.

"Me either," said Du Pré.

"Good," said Harvey. "I knew I could count on you."

"NON!" yelled Du Pré.

"Thing was, well, about the dog . . ." said Harvey.

"My ribs hurt, I need a drink, I say no, non, Harvey, it is nice talking to you always. Go fuck the dog now, be happy," said Du Pré.

"It was this bloodhound," said Harvey.

Susan Klein brought Du Pré his drink. He had some.

"I sent this guy out there, look around a little," said Harvey.

"Wing tips, dark suit," said Du Pré.

"Ranch kid from Wyoming," said Harvey. "Supposed to be looking for a little spread, up on the river."

Du Pré sighed.

"He's there about three days, no motel, so he's got this little motor home, you know," said Harvey.

"Fuck," said Du Pré.

"One morning he's camped down by the river on BLM land, in this little grove of trees. Scratching at the door. My guy figures it is a dog got lost, he opens the door, there's the dog."

Du Pré waited.

"Big bloodhound," said Harvey. "Long face, big ears, and this sign on a string around his neck."

Du Pré muttered curses under his breath.

"Want to know what the sign says?" said Harvey.

Du Pré waited.

"Look on my collar," said Harvey. "So my guy does and there is this little brass plaque there, got the dog's name on it and a phone number."

Du Pré waited.

"My name is Whispering Smith," said Harvey. "That was the dog's name, I mean."

"There is no sign on that dog, look at my collar," said Du Pré.

"No, there wasn't," said Harvey. "But I thought I needed to add that for dramatic effect."

"Son of a bitch," said Du Pré.

"You know who Whispering Smith was?" said Harvey.

"Yes," said Du Pré.

CHAPTER 2

Bart Fascelli was grilling eggplant and tomato halves and garlic cloves, and the rich smell of olive oil and charcoal and garlic rose up in clouds.

He had two legs of lamb in a covered cooker, crusty brown outside, pink inside.

He had baked Italian bread.

Du Pré and Madelaine sat at the big table Du Pré had made from big rough four-by-fours of walnut and butternut. Bart had sketched out the design. He had gotten the wood somewhere, and paid a lot of money for it.

"So who was Whispering Smith?" said Bart.

"Charley Siringo," said Du Pré. "He was a Pinkerton and he broke up cattle rustlers, said his name was Whispering Smith."

"Whispering Smith," said Bart. "Good guy or bad?"

"Depends on whether you are a cattle rustler or a rancher," said Madelaine. "Lots of things just depend."

"That goddamned Harvey," said Du Pré. "Him, want me go up there and see about these people they are missing."

"How many?" said Bart.

"Nine," said Du Pré.

"Maybe they just drowned," said Bart.

Du Pré nodded. He lit a smoke.

The telephone chirred and Bart grabbed it and went back to his cooking. He had the phone to his ear.

"Oh, Maria!" he said. "How are things?"

He listened.

"No shit?" he said.

He listened.

"Yeah," he said. "Of course. No, I told you that I would much rather you read a good book or went to a museum or a concert. Everybody has to work. Your work is educating yourself. So you won't turn out like me."

Bart laughed, and he handed the phone to Du Pré.

"Papa," said Maria, "say something."

"Yah," said Du Pré. "So what you want, me to say?"

"Ah," said Maria, her voice lilting like Du Pré's now. "I just want to hear métchif a little."

"Yah," said Du Pré.

"So how are you?" said Maria.

"Got kicked my ribs hurt that goddamned Harvey is after me and it is snowing outside," said Du Pré. In the last two minutes the sky had blackened and big fat wet flakes of snow were falling hard.

Spring.

Maybe a full-blown blizzard.

Seen one in July once.

"That Bart," said Maria. "He is paying for me to go, school, and anything I want to do, learn more. He is a nice man."

Du Pré grunted.

Maria was holding something back.

"You are coming home," said Du Pré.

"Papa!" said Maria. "You knew. I didn't tell anyone. I didn't tell Madelaine, no one. But you know."

"I am your papa," said Du Pré.

"Yeah," said Maria. "I will be there in two, three weeks."

Du Pré grunted.

"You know how much Bart is paying for me to go to school here?" said Maria. "Forty-seven thousand a year, with everything, my rent on my apartment."

Du Pré whistled. Forty-seven thousand dollars was more than he made in three years, most years.

"Madelaine is there," said Maria.

"Yah," said Du Pré, handing the phone to Madelaine.

Madelaine walked off with it, away from the cooking and the men.

Du Pré looked at Bart.

"Forty-seven thousand dollars a *year*?" said Du Pré.

"Out of the question," said Bart. "You aren't worth that much."

"That is what you are paying, so Maria can go, that fancy school," said Du Pré.

"That's different," said Bart. "She *is* worth that."

"Jesus," said Du Pré.

"I thought you wanted a raise," said Bart. "Out of the question."

"I don't work for you," said Du Pré.

Bart thought about that for a moment.

"God is merciful," said Bart.

Him give me money from time to time and I make furniture for him, I finish out his house for him. Packets of hundreds, right from the bank. I have more money in my pocket sometimes than any Métis ever had.

Du Pré looked at his friend.

"You are a prick," said Du Pré, "but thank you anyway."

Bart waved airily.

"How much are you worth?" said Du Pré, grinning.

He had never asked Bart that before.

9

Bart looked at him.

"There's a magazine," he said. "*Forbes*. They said I was worth two point seven billion dollars."

"Oh," said Du Pré.

"But I am sure it is a lot more than that," said Bart.

"Oh," said Du Pré, "that Maria, she is coming home."

Bart smiled sunnily.

"Good," he said. "I'll get her a ride."

Du Pré shook his head.

"Let them fly, the regular plane," he said.

"Aw, come on," said Bart.

Du Pré thought about it.

For one thing, there wasn't a regular plane to this part of Montana.

The roads were full of frost boils.

The drive to Billings would be hell.

"Fly them from Billings maybe," said Du Pré.

"Done," said Bart.

"Ok," said Du Pré. "Me, I do not want my daughter spoiled."

"Maria," said Bart, "would be insulted if I spoiled her. You know . . . well, like so much it's too easy for me."

Du Pré nodded.

So damn easy for you it kill you pret' near, Du Pré thought.

Bart's red face, bloated with drink and misery, Bart's shaking hands, his convulsive vomiting.

I remember all that.

Hasn't had a drink, years.

Good.

"It's a pleasure for me to help Maria," said Bart. "She will go out into the world and do something good. She's a person with so much light in her."

Du Pré made himself another ditchwater highball.

"What is eating on you, Du Pré?" said Bart.

Du Pré looked at him.

"Harvey," said Du Pré. "Him want me, go over to the Missouri, the Bear Paw country. People are missing there."

Bart nodded.

Du Pré drank.

"Harvey send a spy," said Du Pré. "They know right away, send him the dog."

"I get all that," said Bart. "Why does Harvey think you can do this when his guy couldn't?"

Du Pré shook his head.

"Me I do not know."

Lots of people are not telling me everything, Du Pré thought.

"I won a big ranch there," said Bart. "Bought it to save it, if I can. God, the cattle business is terrible now. The Van Der Meer place. Outbid two insurance companies and some computer millionaire. Why the hell people want a cattle ranch when they get money I don't know."

Du Pré laughed. Bart owned a dozen in the West, huge places.

My friend he digs ditches and foundations with his backhoe, his dragline, his dozer. He likes the work, gets all dirty, days end there is a hole in the ground wasn't there before.

Jesus.

Madelaine came back, grinning.

Du Pré looked at her.

She shook her head.

Lots of people not telling me everything, thought Du Pré.

"Dinner's ready," said Bart.

CHAPTER 3

Du Pré looked up at the sky and nodded.

"See them," said Madelaine, "over there?"

The plane was a silver glint to the southwest.

If that was the plane.

"She not been here a long time," said Madelaine. "Good to see that Maria."

Du Pré rolled a cigarette.

My Maria she come back here from that English school she has been studying at, probably tell me she is marrying somebody. I smile, I pray for him.

"Du Pré," said Madelaine, "she is not getting married."

Du Pré looked at her.

"Sometimes you think damn loud, Du Pré," said Madelaine. "She talks to me, you know. Women things. You are just her father."

Yah, thought Du Pré, me, I know that. My wife die, Jacqueline and Maria they are small. They take care of me good. Some of the things they cook for me, they almost take care of me altogether, but I eat them and smile.

Long time gone now.

The plane was descending, a twin-engined prop type, blue and white.

The pilot set the airplane down on the dirt runway softly and the blur of the propellers darkened and the engine noise wound down.

A band of sheep ran past Du Pré and Madelaine.

The plane was slowing but still going fairly fast.

Cow looks for a place to hide, Du Pré thought, sheep, look for a place to *die*.

Little Marisa shot past on her horse, laughing. She turned the pony deftly and the sheep stopped cold, milled, and retreated.

Du Pré turned. Most of Jacqueline's mob of children were there, faces full of glee.

Aunty Maria, she is ver' popular here, Du Pré thought. They play a few awful jokes on her, so she knows that they love her.

"Scary bunch, them," said Madelaine. "Pilot maybe turn round, fly away."

Alcide was carrying the pet owl. The Great Gray was looking at the sheep, yellow eyes sleepy.

The plane rolled to a stop and the pilot stopped the engines and the propellors slowed and the door of the plane opened down, making a short ladder to the ground.

A big blue duffel bag flew out. Another. A third.

The children passed Du Pré and Madelaine in a body, shrieking.

"Good," said Du Pré. "She bring a lot of bribes. Maybe my Maria she live till sundown."

Maria came out of the door, smiling, and she got to the ground and the kids surrounded her. Alcide trotted in late, burdened by the owl. Five dogs followed. The sheep bunched in alarm.

13

Maria waved at Du Pré and Madelaine, when she got an arm free for a few seconds. She was lifting Berne to kiss her while little Pallas hugged her waist.

"Them kids they like her," said Madelaine.

A tall young man, dark-haired, wearing glasses, poked his head out of the plane. He said something to Maria. She said something back. He came down the steps, gingerly.

The children all looked at him.

"We got to save him," said Du Pré, stepping forward.

Madelaine snorted and she followed.

"Papa!" said Maria. "Madelaine! You got a cattle prod maybe?"

Pallas had left the mob and she approached the young man, who was standing nervously at the bottom of the steps.

The little girl was looking up at him, very grave.

"I am Du Pré," said Du Pré.

"Mr. Du Pré," said the young man. "Glad to meet you. This must be Madelaine. I'm Ben . . . Ben Burke."

"You my auntie's boyfriend?" said Pallas. She had her little fists on her hips.

"Uh, yes," said Ben, puzzled.

"You be good to her I cut your balls off," said Pallas.

"Pallas!" said Madelaine, "I paddle your butt. You apologize."

"I am very sorry and will cut your balls off . . ." said Pallas.

"Nothing much to do, that one," said Du Pré. "My advice, don't piss her off."

"Believe me," said Ben Burke, "I won't." He was shaking with laughter.

"That Maria, she warn you?" said Madelaine.

"Her description," said Ben, "was insufficient."

"Don't show no weakness," said Madelaine. "Them kids smell it, they bunch up and charge."

Little Pallas was still standing there.

"I guess you're OK," she said.

Ben bowed to her. He reached into the plane and brought out

14

a battered canvas-and-leather suitcase, and then some newer luggage, of a honey-colored morocco.

The pilot came out, yawning, and she lit a cigarette.

"Good morning," she said.

"You want some breakfast?" said Madelaine. "We are all going to eat now at my place."

"Sure," said the pilot. "I have some time."

Du Pré picked up the luggage and Ben got his bag. The children lifted the duffel bags, full of their presents. They went toward Du Pré's old cruiser and Raymond's pickup truck.

Ben got in the back of the pickup, and he took the duffel bags from the children. Then they all piled in, pushing and laughing.

"I drive fast," said Raymond, sticking his head out of the cab, "maybe some of them fly out."

Ben sat on a duffel and Pallas and Alcide sat next to him. The owl on Alcide's shoulder closed its eyes.

It was a couple miles to Madelaine's, and Du Pré and Raymond parked and the kids got down and Maria got out of the cab of the pickup and Madelaine and the pilot went on in while the children surrounded Maria.

"Papa," said Maria, "this is Ben."

Du Pré nodded. Maria shrugged off many little hands and she came and hugged him for a long time. Ben stood waiting.

"It is good to be back," said Maria.

She has some little tears, Du Pré thought. It is her home, one of them anyway.

They all went inside then, the children bounding through the door with the duffel bags, and they opened them in the living room and they picked up presents and looked at the names of the packages, all wrapped in bright tissue papers.

The rightful owners began to rip the packages open.

"You want a drink maybe," said Du Pré to Ben. He nodded toward the back door. "Next fifteen minutes be very dangerous in here."

The smell of baking and frying sausages billowed out of the kitchen.

"You want a beer?" said Du Pré. "Some whiskey maybe? We got some wine, too, not ver' good."

"A beer would be good," said Ben.

Du Pré wriggled into the kitchen and got one out of the fridge and he wriggled back out and they went out in the back. Happy cries came from the house.

Ben sighed when he held the beer. He opened it and drank about half of it in one draught.

Du Pré held out his flask and Ben had a stout nip from that.

"Tell me," said Ben, "how have you lived so long?"

Du Pré laughed.

"You got to whack them right off," he said. "Across the nose is good."

"Uh-huh," said Ben. "Like you did at the airfield."

"It is a pasture," said Du Pré. "Got a nice orange windsock on it, cost about fifty bucks."

Ben laughed. He looked at the Wolf Mountains blue in the distance.

"How far away are they?" he asked.

"Thirty miles maybe," said Du Pré.

Ben nodded. He looked at them again.

"Beautiful," he said.

Du Pré passed him the flask. He rolled a cigarette and offered it and Ben took it. Ben pulled a lighter from his pocket and waited until Du Pré had rolled another and he flicked the lighter and lit Du Pré's smoke and then his.

Goddamn, Du Pré thought, he drink whiskey, smoke some. Bet he even eats meat.

"You come now eat!" said Madelaine, out the kitchen window.

Ben began to drop his cigarette.

"No," said Du Pré. "We got important business here, then we eat."

They smoked, had another snort, nodded, and went in.

Madelaine handed them plates piled high with scrambled eggs and frybread and chokecherry jam and sausages. She tucked forks in their pockets.

"Go on out," she said. "I come right after."

Ben and Du Pré went back outside.

They sat at the picnic table.

They waited until Madelaine came with a tray, carrying her food and a pot of coffee and cups.

Madelaine sat down and they ate.

"You are a brave man," said Madelaine, looking at Ben.

"Oh, no," said Ben. "I stuck my finger into the cabin and told the pilot to go on or else."

Ben sipped some coffee.

"She told me to fuck off," he said, "but I tried to run, and nobody can take that from me."

CHAPTER 4

"I tried to call a couple friends," said Maria, "but no one is home."

Du Pré grunted. Madelaine looked off toward the Wolf Mountains, snow-crowned, alpenglow blazing on the peaks.

Ben was looking at the country, drinking it in.

They were walking toward the Toussaint Saloon. There were cars and trucks filling the field and park across the way. It was ten o'clock at night, the June chill setting in.

They got to the Toussaint Saloon and Du Pré held the door open and he came in last. The place was utterly dark.

"Where is Susan?" said Maria. "What is this?"

Something rustled in the back of the room. More rustling to each side.

The lights came up slowly. Someone was turning the rheostat in the hall that went to the kitchen.

Maria looked around. There were big blue tarps over piles of stuff all over the room.

"Ah," she said. "Now I get it."

Susan Klein came out of the back, grinning.

Whoops sounded from under the tarps, and the people hidden there began to come out and hug Maria.

One tarp remained lumpy, and there was laughter coming from inside it. Everybody had gotten out but Bart and Father Van Den Heuvel.

Susan Klein dashed out from behind the bar.

"Stand still, goddammit," she yelled. She began to pull, and in a moment the two men were blinking in the light. Father Van Den Heuvel had a bandage on the left side of his head. He had shut it in the car door again.

Maria ran to Bart and hugged him. He beamed.

Du Pré went in back and got his fiddle, and he came out and got on the little stage with Nepthele and Bassman, who were ready. Du Pré ran the bow over the strings and swiftly tuned the fiddle and they began to play "Baptiste's Lament."

Maria was crying, her eyes sparkling.

Bart bowed and took her arm and they went to the dance floor and after a minute Bart nodded at Ben, who cut in, and then other couples began to dance, too.

Susan Klein was shoving drinks over the bar, and a couple of women were bringing out platters of food and setting them on a trestle table pushed against the wall.

Men kept cutting in to dance with Maria. Du Pré and Nepthele and Bassman cranked up the tempo. The old wooden building boomed and creaked.

By the time that Du Pré and Nepthele and Bassman quit for a break everyone was glowing and laughing.

Du Pré set his fiddle on top of the old piano. He closed the rawhide case.

"Du Pré," said Madelaine. She held out a tall glass of whiskey and water and ice. Du Pré drained it. He nodded.

"I play better the next time," he said.

19

"You play good this first time," said Madelaine. "You one of those never happy with what you do."

Du Pré laughed, and he slapped his face lightly. It was true. When he did a song he was always thinking of ways to make it sound better. So he never played a song the same way twice.

Sometimes that worked out and sometimes it did not.

People were serving themselves food and chattering and making groups at the tables.

Du Pré rolled a cigarette and lit it.

"She say how long she will be here?" said Madelaine.

Du Pré shook his head. Little Métis girl goes away, good schools, comes back not very often. Mostly, they don't come back at all for ten years, then they do. Come home then.

Du Pré laughed.

Madelaine looked at him.

Du Pré shook his head. He was thinking of Maria and the stolen guns and the day he had killed the killer Lucky. With a stone. Maria had swiped the guns from the Sheriff's Department, lost them in the computer. While she is at that tony Eastern school, in Massachusetts, a state so pissy they throw you in jail a year for *having* a handgun.

Maria came to them then, holding a glass of red wine. Ben stood with her.

"I be here a while," said Maria. "Not Toussaint so much, but in Montana. I am going to be a journalist."

Du Pré nodded. Be a journalist, have your own whorehouse, open a restaurant. I am a father, I say how nice, be a smart father.

"So I have this assignment from a big magazine, called *Crossings*," said Maria. "I am going along with a film crew on the Missouri. They are doing a program on Lewis and Clark, their expedition."

Du Pré laughed.

"Papa . . . ?" said Maria.

"Some your ancestors along on that," said Du Pré. Catfoot had said one of his great-great-great-grandfathers was Pierre Cruzatte, a Métis riverman and voyageur who played the fiddle for the men in camp. Another grandfather had been Jean-Baptiste Toussaint Charbonneau, son of Sacajawea and the worthless interpreter Charbonneau.

Catfoot was a good singer knew all the old songs, so he was probably right about all that.

"Which ones?" said Maria.

"Cruzatte, Sacajawea, Charbonneau, and Pomp," said Du Pré. "Catfoot said anyway."

"Jesus," said Ben.

"Yeah," said Du Pré, "us Métis we are everywhere but mostly forgotten."

"I don't think I tell the film crew this," said Maria.

Du Pré shrugged.

"Papa . . ." said Maria. She was about to ask him for something.

Du Pré's sixth, seventh, eighth, and eleventh senses crackled.

My daughter she wants something, Du Pré thought, and she know I will not want to do it.

"I see the film crew in New York," said Maria. "They need somebody who knows about that stuff, you know . . ."

Du Pré shook his head. No. NO. NOOOOO!

"So they ask me because I am from here if I know anyone maybe be a consultant," said Maria.

"Consultant," said Du Pré.

"Expert," said Maria.

"Bullshit," said Du Pré. "I am an old man; I do not need to keep a bunch of fools alive, the river. It is a nice river anyway. Killed a lot of Métis, kill a lot of idiots."

"Papa," said Maria, "it is important."

Ben was looking faintly ill.

Jesus Christ, thought Du Pré. He is one of them.

"Maria," said Du Pré, "what is this about maybe you tell me."

Maria looked at the floor.

Madelaine was laughing so hard she choked.

"You are fucked, Du Pré," she said.

Yah, Du Pré thought.

"Who is making this film?" said Du Pré.

"It is for public television," said Maria.

"OK," said Du Pré. "You are writing for this magazine, and Ben he is working on this for *public television*."

Maria nodded.

"The Missouri it is mostly dams now," said Maria, "but the White Cliffs are still there."

Du Pré sighed.

"That is a place that maybe it is not smart to go to now," said Du Pré. "People down there are pret' mad at them dumb environmentalists, always attacking them for being ranchers."

Mad enough to tear down the Eye of the Needle, a rock arch that had stood high above the brown Missouri for ages.

Go away, flatlanders, there is nothing for you here.

"It could be a good film," said Maria.

Du Pré looked at his empty glass.

"You got him," said Madelaine. She took Du Pré's empty glass.

"What you want me to do, when I am a *consultant?*" said Du Pré.

"Play the music, Papa, and you know how to make a pirogue."

"I make you a little pirogue long time ago," said Du Pré. "Only one that I ever make."

"The expedition had a small white pirogue and a larger red one," said Ben.

Du Pré nodded. Yes, they did. Chopped out of big cottonwood trunks, sealed with fat.

"Lewis and Clark hired four Métis," said Ben, "because they were rivermen."

Du Pré nodded. One of them shoot Lewis in the ass, too, think he was an elk. So us Métis got a song about that.

"The Lewis and Clark Expedition is our great national epic," said Ben. He seemed to really believe that.

Du Pré sighed.

"Your big chance," he said, looking from Maria to Ben and back.

"I'm assistant director," said Ben.

"Oh, good," said Du Pré. Madelaine came back with her wine and a fresh glass for Du Pré.

Maria had a little smile tugging at her lips.

"Yah," said Du Pré, "I do it."

"Thank you, Papa," said Maria. She threw her arms around him.

Du Pré hugged her.

I am fucked, he thought.

The crowd got quiet suddenly. They were looking at the front door.

Benetsee was standing there, with his sidekick Pelon a little behind him.

The old shaman was dressed in worn clothes and running shoes. He had a dirty red kerchief wound round his head.

"Benetsee!" yelled Maria, running to the old man.

"Shit," said Du Pré.

CHAPTER 5

Du Pré sat on the old stump near the sweat lodge. The sun was high and hot. He rolled a cigarette and looked off toward the Wolf Mountains, shimmering in the heat haze.

The pair of golden eagles who lived on the butte that jutted up from a spur of rock that ran from Jessup Mountain were high above, flying for the hell of it. This early in the year there was no need to hunt. Winterkill lay everywhere, a harvest of carrion.

Benetsee and Maria were in the sweat lodge. They were singing. Benetsee's voice was powerful and young, strong in the old songs.

Pelon was splitting some wood for the stove in the cabin. The nights were still chilly. Spring had come late.

"How long does this take?" said Ben. He looked at the sweat lodge.

Du Pré shrugged.

Ben had wanted to sweat with Benetsee and Maria but the old man had said no, he would have to wait and do it with Pelon.

"Do you know why he had just Maria for this?" said Ben.

Du Pré nodded. Because she has something to hear in there, by herself.

Du Pré shook his head at Ben's raised and questioning eyebrow.

"I been putting up with that old fart, years," said Du Pré. "It is best not to ask questions, them answers come when they will."

"Huh?" said Ben.

"Benetsee is a joker," said Du Pré. "You look interested he will set you up, right now. You wait, it will all turn out."

Ben nodded, unsatisfied.

Pelon thudded the maul into a big round of bull pine and he left the woodmaking and wandered over to Du Pré, who rolled him a smoke.

"That miserable old goat," said Pelon, "will tie knots in your head and then piss on 'em so they stay good and tight."

Ben looked from Du Pré to Pelon.

"I thought he was a holy man," he said.

"Oh," said Du Pré and Pelon together, "he is, he is . . ."

They both laughed.

"I see," said Ben.

"Holiness is not a very serious business," said Pelon, "and it is a very serious business indeed. I misspeak. It is not a *solemn* business."

The singing got louder, and there seemed to be more voices than there were people in the sweat lodge.

Pelon smoked.

"How did you . . . come here?" said Ben.

"That old bastard found me and told me to come," said Pelon. "And a good thing it was, too."

Pelon dropped his butt, and he squashed it with his heel and went back to the woodpile.

"You could tell me more but you won't," said Ben.

Du Pré nodded.

"I could tell you a lot and it wouldn't mean shit," said Du Pré. "You want to know about Benetsee, you ask him."

"He's intimidating," said Ben.

"Yah," said Du Pré.

The flap of the sweat lodge opened and Maria dashed out clutching a towel to cover herself. She leaped into the pool of water the creek made and yelped at the cold.

That water was snow yesterday, Du Pré thought.

Maria clambered out and stood shivering.

"Jesus Christ," she said.

Du Pré nodded.

Ben took her clothes over to her. Maria went behind a willow to dry and dress.

Benetsee came out of the lodge, wearing a loincloth, and he walked slowly to the pool and stepped in and disappeared.

Maria walked out from behind the willow, dressed in jeans and boots and a soft white shirt. Her wet black hair hung on one shoulder.

Du Pré stood up.

"I will sweat now," said Pelon. "You can come, too." Du Pré shook his head, then nodded at Ben.

"Sure," said Pelon. "Let me show you how to build the stone fire."

Pelon picked up an armload of split wood, small stuff that would catch and burn hot and quick. He went to the fire pit and began to build a stack, very carefully, quickly setting the wood in, for there were still coals from the earlier fire.

Then he took a shovel and carried the sweat lodge stones to the fire pit, and he set them atop the ricked wood. Little yellow tongues of flame were already flickering and reaching up hungrily.

The fire was soon blazing.

"Go fill this," said Pelon, handing Ben a small bucket.

Ben walked to the pool and he dipped out water. A kingfisher flew past.

Ben turned around.

"He's not here," he said. He pointed.

"Who?" said Pelon.

"The old man," said Ben.

Pelon sighed and went back to watching the fire heat the stones.

Ben came with the bucket.

"So where did he go?" said Ben.

"That kingfisher, him," said Maria. She was smiling.

"Oh," said Ben.

He looked at Du Pré and Pelon and Maria.

"He sneaked off," said Ben.

They all laughed at him.

Benetsee came out of the cabin, wearing new clothes and clean new running shoes. His red bandanna blazed in the sun.

Ben goggled.

"How did he . . . ?" he stammered.

"Go and sweat," said Maria, "and don't think so much."

Ben nodded, but he looked uneasy.

The rick of wood collapsed into glowing coals, and the stones lay down upon the heat. They were getting white in places, almost hot enough.

"Take off your clothes, get in the lodge," said Pelon.

Ben went behind the willow. He came out in a moment wearing a towel around his waist. He walked gingerly, his bare feet unused to ground.

Pelon carried the first stone to the lodge and put it in the pit, and then the other six.

I haul those rocks here, Du Pré thought. Driving around with Benetsee, he had loaded many such rocks, all a reddish close-grained stone that didn't come from the Wolf Mountains. I haul about two hundred of the suckers, they disappear.

Pelon slipped out of his clothes and into the lodge and he pulled the flap down after him. Tendrils of steam came out of the sides of the door.

"Poor Ben," said Maria. "Hell of a place for a good Episcopalian to be."

Du Pré laughed.

Benetsee came up to them and grinned, and Du Pré sighed and rolled Benetsee a smoke. Then Du Pré opened a jug of the awful screwtop wine Benetsee liked, and he filled a quart jar with the pink gassy fluid.

Benetsee drained the wine in one long swallow. He smacked his lips and grinned, showing only old brown stubs of teeth.

"I think you were pret' hopeless," said Benetsee to Du Pré, "but you turn out all right."

Du Pré nodded.

"It is that good woman of yours," said Benetsee. "You are shit without her."

Du Pré nodded.

"But you still pret' hopeless," said Benetsee. "So Pelon is in there with that Ben whiteskin. He not near so hopeless as you, Du Pré."

"Old bastard," said Du Pré. "You be nice I don't bring you no tobacco, none of that horse piss you like."

Benetsee laughed, almost soundlessly.

"No damn fun picking on him no more," he said to Maria. "He don't get mad, kick stuff around the yard."

"Did you do that, Papa?" said Maria.

Du Pré nodded. Damn right I did this old bastard about drive me crazy his damn riddles.

"Pelon even more hopeless than Du Pré here," said Benetsee, "but he work hard, not like this lazy Du Pré."

Du Pré sighed. He fished a flask out of his pocket and had a shot of whiskey.

"OK," said Benetsee, looking hard at Maria, "you remember where this is?"

Maria nodded.

"You don't forget," said Benetsee.

Maria shook her head.

"You only see it once, you don't see it it change you know."

Maria nodded.

Riddles, thought Du Pré, always his damn riddles.

Benetsee held out the jar, and Du Pré poured more wine in it.

The flap to the sweat lodge flew open and Ben came out, gasping, his white skin flushed red. He blinked at the light, and then he ran toward the pool and fell in. Water shot up.

Du Pré walked over, and he put the flap back down and pressed it tight.

Inside Pelon began to sing.

Du Pré laughed.

CHAPTER 6

Du Pré lay in the bed smoking, looking up at the dent in the ceiling plaster he had been meaning to fix for some years.

Madelaine had her head on his shoulder.

Du Pré blew out smoke.

Madelaine lifted her head.

"Du Pré," she said, "it was not us talking, you know, Maria and I we talk about how maybe you could be an advisor to this movie. But I never spoke to Harvey."

Du Pré nodded.

"Him," said Du Pré, "he figure it out himself. Knows about this movie, knows about my music, they are trying to make the movie so it is like it was. Not that many Métis fiddlers here, Montana."

Madelaine laughed.

"Harvey, he is not so dumb," she said.

Du Pré nodded.

"But I don't do it anyway," he said.

"OK, Du Pré," said Madelaine.

"Fuck him," said Du Pré.

"OK," said Madelaine.

It was the middle of the afternoon and so they got up and they dressed and went out into the cold spring weather.

Du Pré looked at the Wolf Mountains, blazing white on the peaks, with bluish lines and patches where the wind wore the snow off the rock.

"I want to see Susan," said Madelaine, "so maybe we go down there, you have a drink, smoke, then we go out to Jacqueline and Raymond's, it is Alcide's birthday."

Du Pré nodded.

Got about a birthday, every month, all them kids.

They walked up the dirt street.

Mrs. Beamis was out in her yard looking sadly at the brown leaves in her flower beds. She was very old and she never spoke to anyone.

Madelaine waved, and Mrs. Beamis lifted a hand, barely.

"She maybe needs to go someplace soon," said Madelaine. "Her family, they are all living, the Coast. I don't know who to call."

Madelaine, Du Pré thought, feed the world, bandage it, find a nice place for an old lady to die in.

There were five cars in the lot next to the Toussaint Saloon. One of them was a very old Land Rover, scarred and repainted and patched.

Du Pré stopped to look at it.

"I leave you here," said Madelaine, "looking at that old piece of shit."

"It is maybe a 1950," said Du Pré. "They are great things."

Not like the silly SUVs Land Rover was making now, along with everyone else. Mercedes-Benz. Maybe Ferrari they start in soon.

Madelaine went on in.

Du Pré walked around the old Land Rover. Old it might be, but the tires were new, big radials with road treads. The back of the Rover had several old aluminum suitcases and locking boxes in it. There was a sleeping bag, a simple cheap one that you could throw in the washer.

Maryland license plates.

Guy drives this in Maryland, he loves it a lot, thought Du Pré.

On a hunch, Du Pré got down flat and looked at the shock absorbers.

Very big, very expensive, and adjustable. Gas shocks.

He got up and dusted his pants off.

"Like the old beast," said a voice. It was soft and faintly British.

Du Pré turned.

A white-haired man stood there, leaning on a cane.

He was dressed in worn clothes, the many-pocketed jacket a photographer carries gear in.

He had trifocals on.

He moved down the steps, swinging his right leg, stiff at the knee.

"Bill Rupe," he said, holding out his hand. Du Pré took it. The man's grip was firm.

"Du Pré."

"The fiddler," said Bill Rupe. "Wonderful music. I have some of your work, the Smithsonian records anyway. Are there more?"

Du Pré nodded.

Bill Rupe went to the old Rover and he reached in and he got some tapes.

Du Pré's.

"Du Pré!" said Madelaine, from the doorway. "You come, you got a phone call, it is Harvey."

"I am dead tell him," said Du Pré.

"You tell him," said Madelaine.

Du Pré nodded at Bill Rupe and went up the steps. He took the pay phone up on its cable and stuck it to his ear.

"No," said Du Pré.

"Du Pré," said Harvey, "I need your help here, my friend."

"I am retired," said Du Pré.

"Thing about it is two more disappeared, there," said Harvey. "They were a photographer and a writer, going down the river, high water. They knew what they were doing. They'd been all over the world running rivers and doing articles."

Du Pré grunted.

"They were due out days ago," said Harvey.

Du Pré grunted.

Harvey was drumming something on his desk.

"They weren't the sort to get into trouble," said Harvey.

Du Pré sighed.

Madelaine brought him a drink and kissed him on the cheek.

"OK," said Harvey, "it's personal."

"So you come," said Du Pré.

"Listen to me," said Harvey, "just listen to me."

Du Pré drank.

"Yah," he said.

"I was in Nam," said Harvey. "Young kid, eighteen, Air Cav, we went in to bail out the Marines who'd gotten stuck at Khe Sanh."

Du Pré sipped more of his drink.

"There was a hell of a firefight," said Harvey, "and I was shooting and screaming along with everyone else. You know how it is."

"Yah," said Du Pré, remembering shooting some people, not in Vietnam.

"There was a photographer there, got one shot, became very famous, you saw it, everybody saw it. The one of the medic lifting the wounded soldier just when the shell exploded and tore the soldier's chest open, both of them bewildered."

"Ya," said Du Pré.

That photograph, all that horror, ver' good. The damn stupid war went on for six more years or so. The photograph of the little girl who had just been napalmed and the one of the soldier dying

33

while the medic looks on helplessly, probably the most famous shots of the war.

"Photographer got the picture," said Harvey, "he also got some of the shell fragments. I was maybe fifteen feet away. I got pressure dressings on the photographer's wounds. Didn't look like he would make it. He was flown out, and the surgeons saved him. He would not let go of his camera."

Du Pré swirled the last of his drink in the glass.

"You son of a bitch," said Du Pré. "You jack around, long time, ask nice, whine, be an asshole, talk to my Madelaine, all I know you talk to my Maria."

"You've got to do this," said Harvey. "I know how bad things are out there now."

Du Pré looked at Madelaine and raised his glass.

She nodded.

"All right," said Du Pré. "Maybe I see this now, you are so hard on me, do this. I did not want to. See maybe I have the story I am telling you now."

Harvey sighed with relief.

"You are there, this photographer, he thinks you maybe save his life. He is a decent guy, tracks you down, thanks you."

"Yup," said Harvey.

"You are friends," said Du Pré.

"Yup," said Harvey.

"Guy has a son," said Du Pré. "He becomes a photographer, like his old man."

"Yup," said Harvey.

"Old man is Bill Rupe," said Du Pré.

Harvey sighed.

"He's there already," said Harvey.

"Yah," said Du Pré. "Got this old Land Rover."

"Yeah," said Harvey.

"What is his son's name?" said Du Pré.

"Jack," said Harvey.

"Shit," said Du Pré. "This is not good Harvey."

"Du Pré," said Harvey, "you got to see if you can keep it from getting any worse."

"All right," said Du Pré.

He slammed the phone back in the cradle.

Madelaine handed him another drink.

Du Pré walked outside to the lost son's father.

CHAPTER 7

Bill Rupe drove expertly, dodging the potholes with little movements of one hand on the steering wheel. The old Rover rumbled and clanked and smelled of hot motor oil.

Du Pré would point, and Rupe would turn.

They came to the long rutted drive that led up to Benetsee's cabin, and Rupe slowed to a crawl, smart enough to approach clumps of grass with caution. There could be a rock in them nicely placed to rip out the oil pan or transmission.

Rupe pulled up by the cabin and shut off the Rover.

He looked at the old cabin, with its sagging porch and firewood ricked on one end and a broken old chair by the door.

Benetsee appeared in the doorway, in his old worn clothes and dirty running shoes and his red kerchief tied round his head. He grinned.

Du Pré and Rupe got out. Rupe took his cane from the Rover and walked toward the old man.

Benetsee came down the steps so Rupe wouldn't have to go up them.

"Benetsee, Bill Rupe," said Du Pré, nodding at each in turn.

The old medicine person and the old photographer shook hands and looked at each other directly.

"We sit out back," said Benetsee. "You bring wine, maybe?"

"I bring wine," said Du Pré. "I was not going to, but Madelaine she run out we are leaving, got wine in a bag. Wine in the bag is in a box. An udder got this one teat. Tobacco, too."

"Good woman," said Benetsee.

The two old men walked around the cabin.

Du Pré fished the box of wine out and the sacks of tobacco and he followed. When he went by the porch he grabbed a fruit jar sitting near the post.

Benetsee and Rupe found places to sit not far from the sweat lodge, and Du Pré broached the wine box and he filled the fruit jar and he handed it to the old man.

The horrible wine bubbled and fizzed.

Benetsee drank it down.

He held out the jar. Du Pré filled it again and handed it to the old man, who handed it to Bill Rupe.

Bill Rupe drank the jar without pausing. He handed the jar back to Du Pré. Du Pré filled it.

"Now I got two of you," said Du Pré. "My ass aches good now. Now I roll cigarettes for you two old bastards."

"Of course," said Benetsee and Bill Rupe.

So far they had not said one word to each other, but then they did not have to.

Du Pré walked to the back porch and he got another jar and he came back and filled it and then the two old men clinked glass and drank.

Du Pré had a snort from his flask.

He sat on a stump.

He rolled smokes, two of them, and he lit them and handed them to the old men, and they smoked.

37

Du Pré sank into his hunting dream, letting his mind fix on a moving butterfly. He had seen the butterfly when he was eight, and been hypnotized by its beauty and the beat of its wings. Ever since when he needed to sit absolutely still he thought of the black-and-yellow swallowtail and he could see it for many hours.

He was wholly aware of the world around him, and could wake the moment a deer or elk came into range.

"My son is lost," said Bill Rupe. "He is dead, I am sure of that."

Benetsee nodded.

"I want to know why he was killed," said Bill Rupe. "I want to know who did it. I want to speak with them."

Benetsee nodded.

"Will you help me?" said Rupe.

Benetsee sat still and silent for a long time.

"Du Pré will help you," he said finally. "Him good man. I don't tell him that his head get fat."

Du Pré heard it but let it pass. He watched the butterfly.

"I think I know why he was killed," said Bill Rupe, "but it was a mistake. Isn't that always what happens? The wrong people get killed, the wrong things get done, violence and rage are barren of hope and use."

Benetsee began to sing, his old voice strong, in Cree.

Du Pré watched the butterfly, flapping its beautiful wings in the sunlight, he heard the old man's song.

make us strong for the people . . . make us strong for the people
make us see into the earth
there is earth in the hearts of the people

Another answered.

Pelon, Benetsee's apprentice, was in the willows by the creek.

A willow flute began lilting, a Celtic melody.

Métis melody.

Benetsee stopped singing.

There were tears streaming down Bill Rupe's cheeks.

Rupe shook his head. He took a kerchief from his pocket and wiped his face.

Du Pré watched the butterfly.

Rupe got stiffly up. He pushed his cane and began to walk back up the little rise that they had come down.

Du Pré watched the butterfly.

"Leave the damn butterfly," said Benetsee. "Roll me a smoke."

Du Pré snatched out of his dream and fumbled for the bag of butterfly. Tobacco.

Du Pré shook his head.

He took out a paper and he put tobacco in it and he rolled it and ran the glue streak across the tip of his tongue and he smoothed the paper.

He handed it to Benetsee.

He held out his lighter, and the old man bent to the flame.

Benetsee inhaled and blew out a long stream of smoke.

"What do I do?" said Du Pré.

Benetsee didn't move or answer for a long time.

"Listen," he said.

Du Pré waited.

"Got a lot of angry people," said Benetsee. "People ver' mad they are on their land now they are being pushed away."

Du Pré nodded.

"Sioux come here push the Crow away, Blackfeet come here push the Shoshone away, Cree push the Sioux, whites come push everybody, not much new," said Benetsee.

Du Pré nodded.

"Which people," said Du Pré. "I am to be strong for which people?"

Benetsee looked at Du Pré for a very long time.

"How many peoples you got their blood in your veins?" said Benetsee, "All people, same blood, red."

Du Pré nodded.

"Him good man that Rupe," said Benetsee. "Him say, I just want to talk, people who killed my son, say, you killed the wrong man. My son want to help you."

Du Pré nodded.

"Bad times," said Benetsee. "Going to get worse, Du Pré. Don't get very smart."

"Shit," said Du Pré.

Benetsee laughed and laughed.

He stood up and he turned and walked to the willows and he was gone in the leafless branches.

Du Pré had another cigarette and then walked back up the path to the Rover.

Bill Rupe was sitting behind the steering wheel.

Du Pré got in.

Rupe started the old Rover and backed the old thing out without turning his head. Just glanced at the mirrors.

They headed back toward Toussaint.

It was getting dark.

They had been at Benetsee's for hours.

Du Pré smiled and shook his head.

A huge yellow-gray coyote ran across the road, leaped a fence, and was gone in the sagebrush.

Du Pré laughed.

Bill Rupe looked at him.

"Your friend is a holy man," said Rupe.

"Pain in the ass," said Du Pré.

"He is that, too," said Rupe. "I saw Jack, saw him clearly, over on the other side of the creek."

Du Pré rubbed his eyes.

"He was good," said Bill Rupe. "He was a good man."

Du Pré said nothing. He looked at the road ahead.

"Mr. Du Pré," said Rupe, "you have to stop this before any more people get killed."

Du Pré nodded.

"They always kill the wrong ones," said Rupe.

CHAPTER 8

"We want *veracity*," said Trey Binder, filmmaker.

Du Pré and Ben and the filmmaker were sitting in a huge motor home. A ruck of cameras and books and magazines heaped against the walls. One magazine cover was framed in gold and had Trey Binder's face on it.

What next? asked the copy stripped over the flattering photograph.

Du Pré nodded.

The motor home was parked next to a bridge over the roiling Missouri, well into spate. Whole trees were floating downstream. The bloated carcass of a dead cow sailed past.

"How long does it take for that river to go down?" asked Trey Binder.

Ben and Trey looked at Du Pré.

"When it wants to," he said finally.

"I mean usually," said Trey.

"Couple of weeks maybe," said Du Pré, "if it don't rain too much."

"Fucking weather," said Trey, "has cost me a lot of money."

Copies of the shooting script of the movie were piled on a small desk. They were bound in black and gold.

"How are you so sure about the pirogues?" said Trey, looking at Du Pré.

Du Pré shrugged. He got up, and he rolled a smoke and went out the door.

What an asshole, Du Pré thought, but then they all are.

Goddamned Maria.

Three months with this asshole I am going to be in a ver' bad mood.

Veracity. Shit.

A pickup truck came down the highway and the driver slowed and then he pulled off and he stopped and he rolled down the window.

"Afternoon," said the driver. He had a gun rack in the cab of his truck with several guns in it.

"Same," said Du Pré.

"Californians?" said the driver, nodding at the motor home.

"Maybe," said Du Pré. "Is there someplace near got a good cheeseburger, maybe beer?"

"Sure," said the driver. "Maudie's. Up there about five miles. Right near the highway, actually, it's on the old road."

Du Pré nodded.

"They are making a movie about Lewis and Clark," he said.

The driver nodded.

"That goddamned bicentennial," he said. "We'll have idiots up the wazoo here. It used to be quiet here, I liked it."

"Yah," said Du Pré. He rolled another smoke and offered it to the man in the pickup. He shook his head.

"Three years I quit," he said, "and I hate it. Wife wouldn't let up on me, you know how it is."

Du Pré laughed.

42

A motorboat roared up the brown river, coming under the bridge.

"Jesus," said the man in the pickup. "They hit one of them half-sunk logs they'll *die*."

The motorboat came out from under the bridge and headed for some slackwater on the far side of the river.

Du Pré and the man in the pickup watched the boat. It was going fast, and whoever was driving it couldn't read water. The slackwater was where the worst of the flotsam lay.

The boat stopped dead and the bow shot up in the air and it hung there for a moment and then fell off to one side. The plunge almost swamped it, but then it righted. It had two outboard motors on the rear transom, and one was set now at a strange angle.

The sodden tree the boat had hit boiled up, black branches and trunk, and it lifted the boat again.

"Shit," said the man in the pickup. He pulled a cell phone from the seat and dialed.

"I'm at Macatee Bridge," he said. "Some idiot just hit a tree in his stinkboat. They aren't drownin' yet, but they should be in about two minutes."

The man in the pickup waited, phone to his ear.

"I know I know," he said. "But it don't look good."

The motorboat spun in the clutch of the dead tree and both circled lazily downstream. One big black branch lay across the gunwales.

"They ain't with you, are they?" said the man in the pickup.

Du Pré shook his head.

"Come on," he said. "We best get to the other side and see if we can fish anyone out."

Du Pré jumped up and he sat on the side of the truck bed and the driver took off for the far side of the bridge. He pulled off on a small gravel margin and reached behind the seat of the pickup and pulled out a long, coiled rope.

Du Pré looked in the truck bed, but there was nothing there that would be at all useful.

43

They ran across the road and looked down.

"Christ," said the man.

The boat and the tree had piled against one of the bridge supports, and a thick wave of brown water was hammering at the boat.

Two people in orange life jackets were holding on to the frame of the windshield and not looking up.

The man built a loop in the rope and he tied it with a bowline and he lowered the rope down toward the trapped people. They weren't looking up. A wind was rising, and the rope moved around in a circle.

"Damn," said the man.

Du Pré ran down to the end of the bridge and found a path that led down to the river. He slid and fell going down, on the loose flat shales peeling away from the mother rock beneath.

The drowned tree was bucking as the current grabbed at it. The boat didn't move.

But it would.

Du Pré yelled, but neither of the people looked toward him. The roar of the water was loud out there.

Du Pré looked up and saw the man with the rope waving. Then the man threw down a coil and Du Pré caught it. The man belayed the rope directly over the trapped boat.

Du Pré calculated quickly and put a couple of knots in the rope for grips.

Then he put one foot in the loop and swung out toward the boat. The wind pushed him downstream, and he had to push away from the concrete piling. He did a lazy loop back to shore and stepped off on a huge rock. He took the loop in his left hand and he hopped back up to the place he had been standing on.

Damn fool stuff. I get hung up out there that tree take me, too, when it goes.

One of the people holding on to the windshield of the motorboat saw Du Pré. He screamed something.

Yeah, I know, Du Pré thought, though he couldn't hear the words.

44

Du Pré tried another swing, aiming upriver some, and this time he went far enough to grab on to a piece of rebar sticking out of the concrete. The boat was right below his feet. It was perhaps five feet from the hands on top of the windshield frame.

Helpohgodohelpohgod said one of the people, a man wearing aviator glasses.

The tree shuddered, and both of the men in the boat screamed.

Du Pré felt a jerk on the rope, and he dropped a good foot.

The two men in the boat were struggling to lift themselves toward him, and water ran out of their heavy clothes.

Another length of rope fell, long enough to reach the people in the boat. Du Pré caught it with his left foot and steadied it until the man in the aviator glasses could grab an end. More of the rope was payed out and the man in the aviator glasses kicked his partner, and then both men grabbed the rope.

Damn, damn, damn, thought Du Pré, I am useless here now.

He pushed himself away and as he did he heard a scream and when he looked toward it he saw the tree rearing up, shuddering.

Du Pré swung as far in as he could and then dropped off and sank deep into the water. The current was strong, and it pulled him fast away. When he broke the surface he was in a strong eddy. He made for the jumbled rocks and grabbed on and held and swung his legs up to deny the river purchase. The current wasn't that powerful.

Du Pré looked and looked and finally he saw a handhold and he grabbed it and held and pulled himself up and then another and in a moment he was out of the water and rolling on to the top of a huge block of rock.

The black tree crashed past, and Du Pré could feel it slam into the rocks he was on.

The boat had disappeared.

Du Pré stood up, water sluicing from his clothes.

An orange boat cushion bobbed on the brown water. A cooler popped up, a blue-and-white one, and it rose three feet out of the water.

"You all right?" said the man who had been up on the bridge.

"Yah," said Du Pré.

"Jesus," said the man. "You got away there just in time. Another two seconds it would have pulled you down, too."

Du Pré nodded. He made his way back to the path where the man was standing.

"Damned brave," said the man.

Du Pré looked over at the brown river and the place where the boat had been. A brown tongue of water curled up from the piling.

"They went down, broke off the rope," said the man.

Du Pré heard sirens.

They struggled back up the path and got to the roadway. Two sheriff's cars were there, and two deputies.

"Buck," said one of the deputies to the man. "What the hell happened?"

"Some damned fools in a speedboat," said Buck.

"River's *closed*," said the deputy.

"No it ain't," said Buck. "It is open for business just like always."

The wind was coming up, and Du Pré was suddenly chilled.

CHAPTER
9

"You are all wet, there, Du Pré," said Madelaine. She put a tall glass of whiskey and soda and ice in front of him. It was her night to run the Toussaint Saloon.

"Yah," said Du Pré, "I been after that veracity for sure."

"Talkin' shit again," said Madelaine. "You gone swimming. Two people drown down there, the Missouri. One of them is named Veracity?"

"It means the truth, I think," said Du Pré.

"What the fuck happened, Du Pré?" said Madelaine.

"Couple of assholes run into a tree with their boat, get piled against the bridge. We try to save them, but it don't work out," said Du Pré.

Ben was sitting next to Du Pré. He had a very lost look on his face.

"Couple of cheeseburgers," said Madelaine. "That fix you two?"

Du Pré nodded.

"Give him one of these, too," he said, lifting his glass.

Madelaine dropped a package of Bull Durham on the bartop and some papers and matches.

"Du Pré," she said, "you kill yourself I will find you and you will be ver' sorry."

Du Pré shrugged.

Madelaine went back to the kitchen.

There was no one else in the bar yet.

"While we were inside talking, me and Binder," said Ben.

Du Pré rolled a cigarette. He lit it and passed it to the young man.

"There were people dying outside," Ben went on.

"Yeah," said Du Pré, "it was that veracity, you know."

"For God's sakes," Ben yelled, "we don't know anything! That's why we need you so badly."

Madelaine came out of the kitchen.

"Du Pré," she said, looking hard at him, "you are picking on Ben. You quit. Maria rip your nuts off she know."

Du Pré nodded.

"Binder's a good filmmaker," said Ben, "he really is."

"OK," said Du Pré. He went around the bar and made a stiff whiskey and water for Ben and pushed it over.

"Thanks," said Ben.

Du Pré nodded. He rolled himself a smoke and lit it.

"I'm lost here," said Ben.

Du Pré nodded.

"Well," said Ben, "will you teach me?"

"What?" said Du Pré.

"About this country."

Du Pré smoked.

"OK," he said.

Maria came in, looking apprehensive. She walked over to Ben and put a hand on his shoulder.

Ben put his hand on hers.

"Papa," said Maria, "what has happened?"

"We go down to see this Trey Binder, he is by Macatee Bridge, a couple people in a speedboat have a wreck and they drown," said Du Pré.

"What they are doing on the river now?" asked Maria.

Du Pré shrugged.

"You are all wet," said Maria, looking at Du Pré.

Du Pré nodded.

"He went in after them," said Ben. "He tried to save them. I was in the motor home talking to Trey."

Du Pré came back around the bar and sat down on his stool.

Maria sighed.

"Ben," she said, "this is not your fault."

"I know," said Ben, "but two people died. Then this other guy who was there said, 'ah fuck them, just some more flatlanders.' "

Du Pré laughed.

Madelaine came out with the platters with the cheeseburgers and the fries and coleslaw on them. She put them down and she put bottles of ketchup and mustard up and then she went to the end of the bar and got napkins and silverware.

"Papa," said Maria, "that guy really say that?"

Du Pré nodded and bit into his cheeseburger.

Ben was looking at his.

"Eat that," said Maria. "Drink your drink, eat that."

Ben slugged down some of the drink.

"The rest," said Maria.

Ben drank the rest of his drink, and Madelaine made him another one.

He had a few bites of his cheeseburger.

"Papa," said Maria, "Quit picking on Ben. You tell him about all that or I fit a chair over your head a few times."

Du Pré laughed.

"OK," he said. He finished his cheeseburger and some fries and rolled another smoke. Maria had pulled up a stool, and she sat between and behind them.

"This is good country," said Du Pré. "I live here all of my life, gone to Germany, the Army, and I travel a little but I live here, my parents live here, long time gone . . . we are raising our kids doing our work, feed our families. Then maybe ten years ago, a lot of people start to come here and they don't know the country, they keep getting lost, we have to go and get them. We don't mind a few, but it goes on all of the time, you know. . . ."

Madelaine lit a cigarette. She pushed the pack across to Maria, who took one and lit it.

"It is a funny time," said Du Pré. "Even worse down on the river, sixty miles away there, lots of people. They come and bitch about the cattle, get lost, want help, throw trash around, they weren't there before now there are a lot of them. Got ver' bad manners."

Ben nodded.

"Those people, that boat, should not have been out there. But down there, that county is huge, got maybe fifteen hundred people in it. They don't got any money, can't keep their schools open hardly, they don't got time and money, chase after those fools."

Ben looked up.

"Lewis and Clark, their expedition come through here, 1805 and 1806," said Du Pré. "So now it is two hundred years, lots of people coming where there weren't people before."

Ben nodded.

"Things change it is hard," said Du Pré.

"Du Pré," said Madelaine. "Better you just say what you mean."

"Down, the White Cliffs there, was this arch, sandstone, up high. Lewis and Clark call it the Eye of the Needle, it is pretty interesting."

"I read about that," said Ben.

"It is not there now, somebody tear it down. They are saying, go away."

"So you think it's a bad idea to make a film," said Ben.

Du Pré nodded.

"It would make more people come."

"There are several films planned," said Ben. "I keep hearing things."

Du Pré sighed.

Oh, that is great, Du Pré thought, whole bunches of people all over that part of the river.

"Trey will do a good job," said Ben.

Madelaine reached across the bar and patted Du Pré's hand.

"You are damn gloomy there, Du Pré, thinking on trouble."

Du Pré had more of his drink.

The door opened and Bart came in, covered in mud.

"Yagh," he said. "Too wet to dig, but I got to do it anyway."

Maria laughed.

"Yah you got to do that," she said.

"Don't pick on me," said Bart.

Du Pré grinned. My friend is probably worth a billion dollars, maybe more, but he like digging with that damn dragline, his backhoe.

"He is making a movie about Lewis and Clark," said Du Pré, nodding at Ben.

"I am a lowly assistant on it," said Ben.

"Where?" said Bart.

"White Cliffs country," said Du Pré.

Bart nodded.

"You talk to any of the ranchers down there?" asked Bart.

Ben shook his head.

"I'm one of them," said Bart.

Du Pré laughed. It was hard to tell what Bart owned, and he often didn't know. He had to ask Foote, that lawyer.

"Where?" said Ben.

"The old Carbonado Land and Cattle Company," said Bart. "North of the river, against the Bear Paws."

Du Pré whistled. He had been on that ranch once a long time ago. Four hundred thousand acres, maybe more.

"I should get Trey," said Ben, "to talk with you. We'll need some road access."

Bart looked at Maria.

She smiled.

51

"Okay," he said.

"You ever been there?" said Du Pré.

Bart nodded.

"Maybe we go down there and look around," said Du Pré.

"Talk to Van Der Meer," said Bart. "He runs it, I think."

"You mean talk to Foote," said Du Pré.

Bart nodded.

"I got an irrigation ditch to dig," said Bart.

CHAPTER 10

Du Pré looked a long time at the gigantic cottonwood. The tree was nearly eight feet thick. The bark was unscarred, so it had never been hit by lightning. The air near it smelled sweet.

Du Pré pulled the lanyard and the chain saw caught and roared. The bar was five feet long, and the teeth glinted in the sun. Du Pré set the saw against the tree down low and made his first cut. Chips streamed from the cut. The saw bit deep and fast.

Du Pré sawed three-quarters of the way through the trunk. He felt a slight movement. The heavy tree was flexing down a little. He pulled the saw out before it got bound up.

He walked around to the other side of the tree and looked up. The branches were trembling, and the leaves danced. There was no wind.

Du Pré set the bar against the tree and cut in again, two inches higher than the first bite. When he got in a foot and a half he stopped, pulled the saw out, and looked up at the tree again. The leaves had quit trembling.

"What are you doing, exactly?" asked Ben.

"Some these trees they are rotten inside," said Du Pré. "You got to be careful. This one is sound. Rot and some branches dance and some don't."

Ben nodded.

Du Pré handed him the chain saw.

"Go back over there," he said. "This tree fall on that saw then it cost a lot of money."

Ben walked away.

Du Pré picked up a metal wedge and a sledgehammer and he set the wedge in the cut and he tapped it home and then he stood back and swung hard. Again. Again. The wedge rammed into the soft wood.

He put in six more, spaced six inches apart.

The tree cracked, loudly.

Du Pré ran away, dropping the sledge on the ground.

"I heard that," said Ben.

The tree cracked again. The topmost branches quivered.

Crack. Shudder. Crack.

Then it was quiet.

"Do we need to drive the wedges in farther?" said Ben.

Du Pré shook his head.

There was a raw, tearing sound, and the top branches shook.

A bang.

The tree began to lean, and then it began to fall. When it crashed to the ground branches flew up and the earth shook a little.

The sap smelled crisp and sweet.

"How old is this tree?" said Ben.

Du Pré shrugged.

"Cottonwoods are like big weeds. They grow fast. We count the rings. I would like to know myself," he said.

They walked to the fallen tree and began counting.

Ben got one hundred and forty-one years, Du Pré one hundred forty-three.

"Seems a short time for something so huge," said Ben.

Du Pré nodded.

He started the big chain saw, went to the first big branch, and cut through the bole. The tree was perhaps six feet through there. When it had fallen it had landed on another dead cottonwood, which bucked up the top. Du Pré cut through easily, and then he walked around to the other side and finished the job. The bole came free of the top, which moved a little and settled.

"That is the easy part," said Du Pré. He went to the toolbox and he got out a screwdriver and wrench and he took the chain off the chain saw and he put another on.

Ben looked at him.

"Got to cut a rip cut," said Du Pré. "Different teeth. The other chain just bind up."

Du Pré handed Ben the pin from a chalk line and he walked down the length of the bole. He motioned to Ben to raise the pin higher. Then to hold. Du Pré pulled the chalk line tight and snapped it. A blue line appeared, broken by the rough bark.

Du Pré started the chain saw and began to cut through the bole lengthwise. It was hard going. When he ran out of gas he refilled the tank and handed the saw to Ben.

It took four hours to split the giant bole in half.

"That is enough," said Du Pré. He began to gather all of the tools. They carried them down to his old cruiser, parked up on the bank above the island the tree had grown upon.

The Missouri curled brown beyond it. Time had filled in the channel and there were only a few inches of still water over the stones.

Du Pré backed and turned and he drove off on the rutted track, up the hill and over and down through a gate that Ben had to jump out for. Charolais cattle grazed on the hills.

They bumped along on the track for miles and finally came to a county road. Ben opened the gate and Du Pré drove through and

Ben put the gate back and they went on toward Maudie's roadhouse.

Du Pré pulled in beside some pickups, and they got out and went in. Some men in worn clothes and boots were playing pool in the back, and others sat at the bar, with beers or drinks. They all looked at Du Pré and Ben, and then they looked away.

The woman behind the bar brought them beers and a basket of popcorn.

Something shadowed the front window, and was gone. A truck or a motor home.

Du Pré sipped his beer.

The front door opened and Trey Binder came in, followed by a pair of young women, his assistants. He stopped for a moment and looked round, then came over to Du Pré and Ben.

"Man," said Binder. "This is the fucking middle of nowhere."

The balls on the pool table clacked and silenced.

The bar had gone dead still.

Trey walked up to the bar and looked back at his assistants.

Du Pré stood up, grabbed Binder by the shoulder, and ran him toward the door so quickly that Binder was through it before he had a chance to speak.

"What . . . ?" he said.

The assistants and Ben came out.

"Get in the motor home and go, now," said Du Pré.

"Why?" said Binder.

"I am tryin' to keep you from bein' killed," said Du Pré. "Go now."

Binder shook his head.

Du Pré pushed him toward the motor home.

"Come *on*," said Ben, grabbing Trey's arm and pushing him through the door. Ben climbed in after him. The assistants followed, scared and confused.

"Get out of here," said Du Pré. "Just go."

Ben started the motor home and pulled out on the highway.

Du Pré rolled a smoke and went back inside the bar and up to the woman.

"I am sorry," said Du Pré. "He got no manners."

"Damn few of them do," she said. "Friends of yours?"

"The kid with me is," said Du Pré.

The door opened and the man who had stopped at the bridge the day the people in the motorboat drowned came in. He was grinning.

"Du Pré!" he said, "you're back!"

Du Pré relaxed.

The balls on the pool table began to clack again.

Buck came to the stool next to Du Pré's and he sat and Du Pré pointed and the woman behind the bar drew a draft and set it in front of Buck. She made change from the five Du Pré put on the top of the bar and she set it in front of Du Pré. He nodded and she made him another drink and she took the money for that.

"Bill," said Buck, looking at a man a few stools down, "horse step on your foot or somethin'?"

"Naw," said Bill. "Some feller come in here to display his bad manners. Spoiled a good day."

Laughter.

Du Pré sighed.

I better to walk out of the door not get thrown through the window, he thought.

This movie, they maybe better make it in California.

"That motor mansion was at the bridge," said Buck. "I take it the driver messed up?"

Du Pré nodded. *Do not cuss in front of the lady behind the bar.*

"Tourists?" said Buck.

Du Pré shook his head.

"Movie people," said Du Pré. "They are going to make a movie about Lewis and Clark."

"Here?" said Buck.

Du Pré nodded.

"I wouldn't do that I was them," said Buck.

Du Pré nodded.

"I really wouldn't," said Buck. "Last bunch through here made a real mess and left. Tore down fences, so it would look more like it did back then. Oh, they'd contracted for the use of the land, but they was supposed to put the fences back and then didn't. You know?"

Du Pré nodded.

He sipped his drink.

CHAPTER
11

Du Pré looked at the adzed holes in the cottonwood logs. He tapped on the side of the pirogue a few places.

"Maybe another inch down," he said.

Ben sighed.

"This is hard goddamned work," he said.

Three other men were working at shaping the logs. The damp wood was soft but stringy, and would cut but not chip off.

Trey Binder was directing a cameraman. The hand tools were the same ones used in the days of Lewis and Clark.

The two pirogues were taking shape. Twenty or so feet long, six wide, flatbottomed and bluntly pointed at each end.

"The red pirogue was this big maybe," said Du Pré, "the white one was maybe sixteen feet and three, three and a half wide."

"How the hell do you know that?" said Ben.

Du Pré laughed.

"Voyageurs sing about the four-man, two-man pirogues. Big ones they carry four paddlers, maybe twenty bales of pelts. Little ones they carry two men, eight bales of pelts. Big ones are hard to handle, the little ones easier. Men in the big pirogue make more money, they are carrying more furs."

"From a *song*," said Ben. "That's all you have to go on?"

Du Pré laughed.

He walked away, leaving Ben chopping and cursing.

"You get him cussing, there," said Du Pré to Binder, "him sound like he is working."

Binder nodded. He motioned and a woman with a sound boom moved toward the pirogue and the shaper in it.

The ground was thick with chips. Hornets flew past, and lighted, drawn by the sweet smell.

Another crew a quarter of a mile away was chopping out copies of the smaller pirogue.

Red bateaux, white bateaux, bunch of men, one woman, Du Pré thought.

Long time gone.

My father, Catfoot, once, he make me a little pirogue, let me use it on the big stock tank, tell me it is like the bigger ones only smaller. Use that cottonwood, seal it off, the outside, with fat or pitch.

Du Pré stepped across the shallow still water and up the bank, and he got into his cruiser and drove off on the track toward the main ranch house. When he got to the last hill he could see Bart's truck parked in front.

Du Pré drove on down to the fence and let himself through and he put the gate back and then he drove on in and parked beside Bart.

A woman opened the door before he had a chance to knock. She was smiling. She had gray hair and dark skin and wore worn denims and scuffed boots.

"Du Pré?" she said. "I'm Lou Van Der Meer. Pleased to meet you. I have heard you play."

Du Pré nodded and mumbled and shook her hand.

She led him to the kitchen where Bart and her husband, Kit, were sitting. There was coffee and pie. Blackberry.

Kit got up and held out his thick rough hand.

Du Pré sat and Lou brought him coffee.

"I hate this," Bart finally said. "It was yours for so long."

Kit laughed.

"Coulda been worse," he said. "Coulda been bought and cut up, or made into one of them private bird-hunting clubs. There's a lot worse things could have happened."

Du Pré nodded. The Van Der Meers had been on this land since 1882, and now they did not own it anymore.

"Thanks for staying on," said Bart. "No one knows this place like you do."

"I'll be able to pay better attention to it now that I don't have to lie awake nights wondering when the bank will repossess it," said Kit. "Cattle business was always chancy. Lately it's been quite predictable, in that you always lose money."

"Nothing lasts forever," said Lou. "The kids are taking it hard. Especially Kelly. She pitched a fit when we told her."

"Took off on her horse," said Kit, "and we didn't see her for a week."

"I got a daughter like that," said Du Pré.

"Where is she?" said Lou.

"She is here," said Du Pré. "She is going to be a journalist. Got an article to do, this Lewis and Clark movie, how it is made."

Kit nodded.

"On the river," he said, "I suppose?"

Du Pré nodded.

"Tell them to be very careful," said Lou, "make sure they get all the permissions they will need. The last bunch through here pissed everyone off so bad it's a damn wonder nobody got shot."

Du Pré nodded.

"I tell them that," he said.

"They sent lawyers first," said Kit, "to lease land, for sixty days, to shoot the movie. They said they wouldn't damage anything, and if they had to remove anything, they would put it back. The money was fairly good, so people signed."

Du Pré nodded, and Bart sighed.

"They behaved right till the last, and then they tore hell out of Buck Keifer's place—he's barely hangin' on anyway—tore out his fences and pulled windmills down. Shot their movie and left."

"Buck was gonna sue, but his lawyer talked him out of it. Said that it would cost more'n it was worth, what with havin' to sue an out-of-state corporation owned by another corporation and so on."

"Don't think Buck slept much," said Kit. "Took on every job he could weldin' and about all night he'd fence."

"What happened here?" said Bart.

"We didn't let 'em in," said Kit. "The money wouldn't have helped that much. They still crapped up my irrigation ditches, did it at night, I think—we didn't find out for a while. Weren't waterin' up for a while."

The door opened and two young men came in, ruddy and wind-burned, and they put their jackets and hats on pegs and carefully wiped their boots.

"Bob . . . Paul," said Lou. "This is Bart Fascelli and Gabriel Du Pré. He's the fiddler."

The young men held out their hands and everybody shook.

"Got the bulls moved," said Paul, "and I'd best go and fix that busted windmill on the Lolly Creek stock tank."

"And I'll get them hydraulics on the well truck," said Bob.

They got coffee and leaned against the kitchen counter.

"I got to get back," said Du Pré, "see they are doing the pirogues OK."

"I'll come," said Bart.

They got their jackets and left.

"See you there maybe," said Du Pré.

Du Pré heard a deep beat of horse hooves.

He turned and looked toward the faint sound.

A stream of horses came over a hill a half mile away. They were running hard, and close.

There was a rider behind them on a big bay, crouched down to cut the wind. Her hat was dancing on its strings behind her, and her long dark hair streamed in the wind.

The horses came down the hill toward the little line of brush at the bottom and they turned and found an opening and they jumped over the little watercourse and pounded up the slope and out of sight for a moment, and then they came over the top and down a wide trail toward a big round corral.

The rider was standing up in her stirrups now, cracking a whip, keeping strays with the herd.

The horses streamed into the round corral and they slowed and turned and the rider pulled her horse up and she slid off and moved the rails across the opening. The horses were still wanting to run, and they tossed their heads and went round and round, still in a body.

The rider got back on her horse and began to walk the bay to cool him down.

"Now," said Bart, "that was something."

Du Pré nodded.

"That must be Kelly," said Bart.

"Ride like that she sure don't want this place sold," said Du Pré.

"The Van Der Meers are going to manage this place long as they want to," said Bart.

"It is not the same," said Du Pré.

"I know," said Bart.

Kelly Van Der Meer was walking the big bay toward the barn. She went by, not a hundred feet away, but she looked straight ahead.

Du Pré got in his cruiser and he started it and turned around and headed back toward the island and the crews making the pirogues.

By the time he got to the gate Bart was right behind him. Du Pré opened it and he drove on through and then he got out and waited for Bart to pass and he closed it back up.

Bart got out of his car.

He looked off toward the Missouri and the bleak hills, the green of the cottonwoods on the bottoms and the islands.

"Feller could get to liking this," said Bart.

A speedboat shot down the river, engines roaring.

"Bastards," said Bart.

Du Pré nodded and got back in his car.

CHAPTER 12

Madelaine was the only person in the Toussaint Saloon when Du
Pré came in. It was early in the afternoon. People were home eating a big dinner after going to church. It was sunny and warm and
green outside.

Madelaine was beading a small bag. She had on some reading
glasses that had slid down her nose.

"Shit," she said, looking over to the side. She glared at the needle. "Bead jump off. I am going blind, my ears can't hear, this old
age is pretty damn tough."

Du Pré snorted. He went behind the bar and he made himself a
tall whiskey and water and he carried it around to the front and he
sat down right across from her.

Madelaine stuck another bead on the needle. She stuck her
tongue out of the corner of her mouth.

"You fuck pret' good for the arthritis," said Du Pré.

Madelaine ignored him.

"Hah!" she said, "got him on there. Yes."

Du Pré rolled a smoke. He lit it and yawned.

"How is that vera-city business doing?" said Madelaine. "I am telling people that Du Pré, he is out making them veracities, damn good at it, too."

Du Pré snorted.

"Something is eating your ass, Du Pré," said Madelaine.

Du Pré had some more of his drink.

"I got a bad feeling, this," he said.

"Bad feeling?" said Madelaine. "Bad that what you are doing is bad? Bad that something bad happen? Or you just maybe get your dick caught your zipper there?"

"Bad happen," said Du Pré. "So far, nine dead people."

Madelaine nodded.

"So you have asked Benetsee yes?" she said.

"No," said Du Pré, "that old fucker he just give me riddles—I am ver' tired of them, you know."

"The future is all riddles, Du Pré," said Madelaine. "It ain't happened yet, is why."

Du Pré nodded.

"Somebody get killed," said Madelaine. She looked up.

Du Pré shrugged.

"You are worried, Maria," said Madelaine.

Du Pré nodded.

"Then you damn well better go see that Benetsee," said Madelaine.

"He is not there," said Du Pré. "Him, that Pelon, they are gone. Been gone. Three days."

Madelaine looked up at the light, and she held the needle up and counted.

She stitched.

"You don't like this movie," said Madelaine.

"No," said Du Pré.

"Bad people making it?" said Madelaine.

"They are all right," said Du Pré.

Madelaine nodded.

"Bad things come of it," she said.

Du Pré nodded.

"Bring a lot of people, the river, and that is not good," said Madelaine.

Du Pré shook his head.

"This place is a place for not ver' many people," said Madelaine. "It is too tough."

"Remember those fools, come here, the wolves?" said Du Pré.

Madelaine nodded.

"Like them, I think," said Du Pré.

"Canada," said Madelaine. "We maybe go there."

Du Pré sighed.

"Lewis and Clark them come up the river there," said Du Pré, "long time gone. Cruzatte he fiddles for them all they dance, go on to the coast. They got that Charbonneau, that Sacajawea. Little Jean-Baptiste that Clark call Pomp. They are looking for something new. Now I am Cruzatte for people, making a movie. I don't know what they are looking for."

"Veracity," said Madelaine. "Means the truth. I looked it up, the dictionary."

"People down there are ver' mad," said Du Pré, "been alone there, long time. They see, everywhere else all them new people come they drive out the old people."

Madelaine nodded. She put another bead on the needle.

"Better I say *no* when Maria she asks me to do this," said Du Pré, looking at the ceiling.

"You never good at saying *no*, your daughters, Du Pré," said Madelaine. "Anyway she talk to me about that. She knows you don't want to do it. But she thinks, Du Pré talks with the film people it will maybe be not so bad. That Lewis and that Clark they hire voyageurs, help them on the rivers. Nobody knows rivers like them. So she is thinking, too, you know."

Du Pré took a peanut from the bowl, and cracked the shell and tossed the meats in his mouth.

"Eye of the Needle," he said.

Madelaine nodded.

"It is there, long time, above the river. Cruzatte carve his initials in it, pret' soft sandstone. I have been beside it, it is pret' big, but I don't see Cruzatte's carving."

"So somebody tears it down, Du Pré," said Madelaine, "somebody says, go away, nothing for you here. It was falling down anyway."

"Lot of trouble to do that," said Du Pré. "They got to haul bars and jacks up, ropes, tear it down, let the tools back down and go away. In one night."

"Blow it down, about three seconds," said Madelaine.

"Yah," said Du Pré. "Carry a stick of dynamite up there it is a lot lighter."

"Shit," said Madelaine. She looked over at the floor and she shrugged and she picked up another tiny bead with the point of the needle.

"Why they don't do that?" said Du Pré.

Madelaine shook her head.

"OK," she said, "I see that."

Du Pré thought of the big sandstone arch that had stood high above the river. Voyageurs call it the Door of the Wind. Some songs got that in them.

"So go there," said Madelaine.

Du Pré looked at her.

"Go there a couple days see what you dream," she said.

Du Pré laughed.

"I got to work this movie," he said.

Madelaine nodded.

She pulled the heavy thread tight.

"Tell them you got to take some time," she said.

"Yah," said Du Pré. "Maybe I am lucky, they fire me."

"You are working, Maria," said Madelaine.

Du Pré laughed.

"OK," he said, "I go and talk to her maybe now."

"She will be here not too long," said Madelaine.

"She call you?" said Du Pré.

Madelaine shook her head. Du Pré had long since stopped wondering how Madelaine knew some things. It was enough that she did.

"You know," said Madelaine, "those film people have a lot of money. Maybe they do something down there that is good."

Du Pré nodded.

The door opened, and Maria and Ben Burke came in. Ben looked pale and bothered. Maria's face was blank.

"You are right," said Du Pré.

Madelaine snorted.

Ben and Maria walked over and took stools on either side of Du Pré.

Madelaine held her needle up to the light.

"Damn," she said. She flicked her wrist. She squinted again.

"Let me see," said Maria, leaning over the bar. She looked at the beadwork.

"Ver' good," she said.

"Old lady like me not got much else to do," said Madelaine. "Bead, listen to people bitch. Du Pré is ver' grouchy."

Maria nodded.

"Him don't like this movie," said Maria.

"I tell him he is working for you," said Madelaine.

"Uh-huh," said Maria.

"I am thinking the Eye of the Needle," said Du Pré.

"We are thinking we got holes, the pirogues," said Maria.

Ben sighed.

Du Pré looked at Maria and then at Ben.

"Last night someone set fires in all four of the boats," said Ben.

Du Pré laughed.

"That wood too wet to burn," he said.

"By itself," said Ben, "but whoever set these fires used propane torches. Set them so they burned against the sides of the boats and set paraffin blocks around the flames. So they all are ruined."

Du Pré looked at Maria.

"How bad?" he said.

"All four got big holes, one side," said Maria.

Du Pré nodded.

"We fix them," he said.

Ben Burke looked at him.

"Lewis and Clark, they don't got that epoxy," said Du Pré.

CHAPTER 13

"They must have come in by the river," said Kit Van Der Meer. "I expect that they put in up at Little Clay Creek and floated down all quiet and then got out at the bridge. So there was at least two of them."

Du Pré nodded.

The crew was fitting patches of cottonwood into the deep notches sawn out of the boats, where the fire had charred through.

"Six of the fellers here are local," said Kit. "I can't figure why this got done."

Trey Binder was standing off a ways, looking at the far shore. A mule deer buck was running up the hill, stopping every hundred feet to look back.

"We had some fences cut, couple times the last few years," said Kit. "It don't take much of that to piss folks off."

"Mr. Van Der Meer," said Binder, "what should I do? I want to make this movie. It may be important, and it may not. I mean no harm."

"I know you don't," said Kit, "Thing is we been alone out here such a long time we want to keep it that way."

Binder sighed.

"Yeah," Kit said, "there's a reason this is the only section of the river looks like it did two hundred years ago."

"Our budget won't take hiring twenty-four-hour security," said Binder. "Is there anyone who could be a night watchman?"

Kit spat. He nodded.

"Old Harry maybe," he said.

Binder walked over.

"Used to be a deputy," said Kit. "Tough old bastard."

"Where can I find him?" asked Binder.

"Roadhouse," said Kit.

A Land Rover roared down the dirt track that led to the cottonwood grove. It was bright red, and the lights were on.

Binder whooped.

Du Pré and Van Der Meer looked over at him.

"It's Sam Smythe," said Binder, "the producer."

The red Land Rover hit a hole hidden in the thick weeds and bounced high in the air. The driver jammed on the brakes and the big red truck bounced on its shocks for a moment, and when all motion stopped the driver ground forward very carefully.

The driver's door opened and a woman got out, rubbing her head.

"Fuck!" she said. "Damn!"

Du Pré laughed.

Binder was running toward her.

She turned, and Du Pré saw a trickle of blood on her forehead.

Trey Binder mopped at her forehead with his handkerchief.

She nodded and smiled. They walked back to Du Pré and Van Der Meer.

"Sorry," said the woman, holding out her hand. "Sam Smythe. I should have known better than to drive that fast. Mr. Van Der Meer? Mr. Du Pré? Delighted." She held out her hand.

She was small and wiry, about forty, deeply tanned, with gray-blond hair cut short.

"We got troubles," she said, looking over at the boats.

"They fix OK," said Du Pré.

"Hard to blame whoever set them on fire," said Sam. "It is very quiet out here."

Du Pré nodded and looked at Van Der Meer, whose face was blank.

Boat motors roared downriver.

"This section of the river's closed," said Van Der Meer, "less it's someone from BLM."

"It isn't," said Sam.

Binder and Du Pré looked at her.

"It's Wally Williams," said Sam.

"Shit," said Binder.

The boat motors screamed. Du Pré looked down the river. A small sportfishing boat was wallowing on the water.

One of the engines quit.

The boat made for the shore where the current was slow.

"Mr. Van Der Meer," said Binder, "I'd appreciate it if you'd run that bastard off. He's a self-proclaimed expert on the Lewis and Clark Expedition, and he's been quite a pest. Wanted to write the script."

"Sure," said Van Der Meer. "He can come up as far as the high-water mark. That's the law."

"Let *me* handle this," said Sam.

Van Der Meer and Binder and Du Pré looked at her.

"*I've* been the one that little peckerhead has been bothering," she said.

"Sure, Sam," said Binder.

"Fucking turkey," said Sam. She started marching down to the water's edge.

"We should go along," said Binder. "It will be a lot of fun."

They walked fifty feet behind Sam Smythe, who stopped on a high bank and stood there, fists on hips.

The boat came up, the engine was throttled back, and a young man jumped out and grabbed the painter and braced and let the boat ground.

A bald man in his fifties looked over the cabin.

"Sam!" he said.

Sam Smythe said nothing.

"Disgraceful what is being done to this poor river," said the man. "Cattle tearing down the banks. We got stuck down below. God, those damned land maggots sure mess things up."

Sam Smythe said nothing.

"Well, I'm here," said the man.

"How'd you feel if they were buffalo?" said Sam.

"Buffalo?" said the man.

"You little prick," said Sam Smythe, "how many ways do I have to tell you to fuck off?"

"Come on, Sam," said the man, "you need me. You really do."

"Uh-uh," said Sam, "no way."

"This film needs to be a statement," said the man. "Get the cattle off the public lands. The Jaws that ate the West."

Du Pré walked down to the bank, downstream from the boat.

A stream of gasoline was running from one of the engines, making a rainbowed streak on the water.

"You got a permit for this damned boat," said Van Der Meer.

"Permit?" said the man.

"River's closed to motorboats," said Van Der Meer, "for *environmental* reasons."

"We need some gasoline," said the man.

"You can drift back down to the bridge," said Van Der Meer.

"The guy with the trailer is up above," said the man.

"River's closed, mister," said Van Der Meer.

"We leased this ranch," said Sam Smythe, "and you are not coming on it. At all. Just fuck off and head back down."

"No," said the man. "I won't."

Du Pré rolled a cigarette and lit it. He looked upstream at Sam and Binder and Van Der Meer.

"I hear you got John Thomas Tipton to play Lewis," said the man. "Layla Dalton for Sacajawea. You know how to properly pronounce that? Soc-gaw-go-ga-wah, you know."

"Go away," said Sam.

"I just *won't*," said the man.

The water behind the boat burst into flames, and the leaking engine caught. The fire grabbed rapidly.

"Jesus!" screamed the man.

The young man holding the painter turned his face away from the heat.

Wally Williams dived over the side and ran through the shallow water to the mud shore.

The young man holding the painter let go. The boat turned and the flames grew. The current began to pull it downstream.

"Jesus! Jesus!" said Wally Williams. "Christ, do something!"

No one moved.

He began to scrabble up the bank.

Kit Van Der Meer walked over to him.

"Nope," he said.

Williams ignored him. He crawled up and got to his feet.

The boat was burning quickly.

The young man came up the bank, shock on his face.

"Jesus," said Williams, looking at Du Pré, "you set it on fire."

Du Pré looked at him.

Williams started to walk past Van Der Meer toward Sam Smythe.

Van Der Meer put out a hand and grabbed Williams by the throat.

"You can walk back down to the bridge," he said, "but don't get above the high-water mark."

Williams's eyes were very large.

Another boat came down the river.

Van Der Meer let go of Williams.

He waved to the man in the boat, who waved back and turned toward the shore.

"Sam?" said Williams. "Jesus."

Sam Smythe was laughing.

"Give me a ride?" said Williams.

"You got your ride, you little shit," said Van Der Meer.

The man in the boat had on a tan twill uniform and a badge and a gun in a holster.

The man grounded the boat, slid out, and walked up to Van Der Meer.

"Williams," said the BLM ranger, "you were told the river is closed. And is that your stinkboat burning out there? A hazard."

Van Der Meer grinned.

"Afternoon, Bill," he said.

"Kit," said the ranger.

"He's trespassing after warning," said Van Der Meer.

"Oh," said the ranger. "Well, that's no good."

CHAPTER
14

"T J's what they call me," said the woman behind the bar at the roadhouse, "so what'll you have?"

"Whiskey ditch," said Sam Smythe.

Du Pré looked at her. So did T J.

Du Pré looked at T J.

They both laughed.

"OK," said T J. She scooped ice into a highball glass and added whiskey and water and she set it in front of Sam.

Sam drank down half of it. She sighed happily.

"Well," she said, "here I am."

Maria and Ben and Trey Binder were sitting on the nearby stools. The rest were taken up by the movie crew and the ranch folk. The tables were still empty.

It was about four in the afternoon.

"That pain in the ass was in here got arrested, I hear," said T J.

"Wally Williams?" said Sam. "*That* pain in the ass?"

"Dunno his name," said T J. "He come in here bitching at the top of his lungs about there weren't enough places to put his boat in or take it out. 'Course the river's closed to motorboats. He bitched and he whined, and I got tired of it. Told him we raised cattle round here, not goddamned tourists, and get the hell out of my bar."

"And he went?" asked Sam.

"Buck Keifer was in here and when that loudmouth started in. Buck sorta picked him up by the scruff of his neck and hauled him outside. I dunno what Buck said, but the loudmouth left," said T J.

Sam Smythe laughed.

"I don't suppose there is anyone around here who would just shoot him, do you?" she said.

T J shook her head.

"That fool ain't even a good varmint," she said, "nobody'd waste a shell. No doubt he's one of those real good environmentalists."

"Oh, yes," said Sam Smythe. "Lies awake nights worrying about the rain forest and the harp seals."

"His first book was pretty good," said T J.

"Yes it was," said Sam.

"What happened?" said T J.

"He made a lot of money," said Sam.

"That'll do it," said Sam, "just about every time."

"Uh-huh," said T J. She looked up and down the bar and went off where the empty glasses lay.

"Play some music here, Papa," said Maria. She smiled, the smile she had used when she was a little girl to get whatever it was that she wanted.

Du Pré snorted.

"These people would like that," said Maria.

"I am by myself," said Du Pré. "I got no sound system, no Bass-man, no Tally, nobody."

Maria nodded.

Du Pré got up and went off to the john to piss. He washed his hands and he looked at himself in the mirror.

My face looks like the prairie, Du Pré thought, soon I be under it and asleep.

He walked back out, down through the narrow hallway.

Bassman was wheeling amplifiers in the door. Tally was moving his accordion case on its rollers, his crutches on each side of the big black box.

"Ah," said Du Pré. He went to Maria and kissed her.

"Your guys want anything to drink?" said T J.

"Beer and shot, Bassman," said Du Pré. "I don't know what Tally will want."

T J pushed the beer and the whiskey across the bar.

Du Pré took them to Bassman.

"Pret' good this," said Du Pré.

"Yeah," said Bassman, "haven't played awhile."

"Where is your blonde?" said Du Pré.

"I mislaid her," said Bassman, and he grinned. Bassman had, usually, a burlap blonde, one so like another Du Pré had to write the names down.

"You want a drink?" said Du Pré to Tally.

"Beer," said Tally. "Big beer they got it."

Du Pré went off. He got Tally his beer, then he went to his old cruiser and got his fiddle out of the trunk.

Bart wheeled into the parking lot with Madeline in the passenger seat of his green Land Rover.

Du Pré waited for his woman.

Madelaine was laughing when she walked up to Du Pré.

"Very boring no music," she said.

"Whose idea, this," said Du Pré.

"Some people," said Madelaine. "Toussaint is coming, lot of them anyway."

"Toussaint is driving, hundred some miles, hear Du Pré," said Du Pré.

"They got no taste," said Bart.

Du Pré nodded.

A long line of pickups and big cars was coming down the road. Du Pré recognized all of them.

"I call this T J," said Madelaine. "She say she is not doing food, it is the summer no one much comes. She got hamburgers, steaks, so we work something out."

"At least there will be food," said Bart.

"Bart," said Madelaine, "you are picking on Du Pré. You go on, do that, it is good for him, I cannot do it enough."

The cars and trucks pulled in and people began hauling out big coolers and Susan Klein and Benny were carrying a huge metal hot box.

"OK," said Du Pré.

Benny Klein was wearing his sheriff's uniform.

"People steal stuff, you are gone," said Du Pré.

"Yeah," said Benny, "but the thieves will all be here listening to your music so it is out of my jurisdiction."

Du Pré nodded.

He took Madelaine's arm, and they walked inside. Madelaine went behind the bar and she and T J grinned at each other and they hugged. People trooped into the back, carrying heavy loads.

Madelaine tended the bar while T J went back to the kitchen.

Du Pré went over to Tally and Bassman, who had everything plugged in and were fiddling the knobs on the board. He took his fiddle out and tuned it.

"Some good country this," said Bassman.

"Look just like North Dakota, yah," said Du Pré.

Tally unsnapped the leather keepers on his accordion's bellows and let it out. He touched a few keys.

The tones were sweet and a little bent. Tally was careful with the reeds.

Bassman plucked a string, and Du Pré nodded.

Du Pré turned and drew his bow over the strings, a long straight lamenting note. He turned and nodded and he began "Boiling

Cabbage," and after a few minutes of that he went to "The Red
Bateau."

> . . . *pull them paddle, push them pole, haul along that Red*
> *Bateau*
> . . . *cry for me Evangeline for I am far away.* . . .

Du Pré and Tally and Bassman played straight for fifteen minutes without a pause, and lots of people came into the bar in that
time.

They finally stopped and people cheered and hooted and
stamped their boots on the floor.

Trey Binder and Sam Smythe were jumping up and down and
talking to each other.

Oh, good, me, I do music, the movie, Du Pré thought.

There were a lot of people Du Pré didn't know, local people.
He saw Kit and Lou Van Der Meer and their two sons. The girl
wasn't with them.

"Oh," said Bassman, "we do the movie, huh?"

"Yah," said Du Pré, "we do 'Baptiste's Lament' first though."

Du Pré began.

They played for another half hour and then took a break. Bassman wandered off looking for a blonde. Tally sat wearily down on
the edge of the little stage. Du Pré bent.

"You want something?" he said.

Tally smiled, blazingly.

"A beer be good," he said.

Du Pré nodded. Maria came with two huge schooners, and she
gave one to Tally and set the other on top of an amplifier.

"Thank you," said Tally.

Maria kissed him on the forehead.

"You play good," she said.

Du Pré went to the bar, where Madelaine had a tall whiskey
ditch waiting for him.

Du Pré rolled a smoke and lit it.

Binder and Sam Smythe were standing behind him.

"Du Pré," said Binder, "we'd like you . . ."

"Yah," said Du Pré, "we do it. You talk to our agent there, though."

"Who?" said Binder.

Du Pré looked around the room.

"That guy there," said Du Pré, pointing at Bart.

"Him?" said Trey Binder.

"Him," said Du Pré.

CHAPTER
15

People ate great slabs of prime ribs and baked potatoes and coleslaw. They drank a lot. In time, they danced, though the little floor in front of the stage could hold only a dozen or so couples.

The roadhouse was hot from all the people in it.

Du Pré and Tally and Bassman finished the second set.

Bart came to the microphone and he took off his tractor-driver's hat and held it up.

"Give generously," he said. He handed the hat to the nearest man who took a bill from the clip in his pocket and put the bill in the hat and he passed it on.

Du Pré was hot, and he walked outside. The night was cool and clear. Bullbats flew around the mercury lamp on the tall pole, grabbing moths out of the air.

Du Pré rolled a cigarette and he lit it and he walked around the rutted parking lot. There were a good eighty cars and trucks there; few of them carried one person when they came.

A motor home slowed on the blacktop road and lumbered down into the parking lot and stopped, blocking several of the other vehicles. The lights were shut off.

Du Pré walked over to the huge thing. The door opened and a young man got out, dressed in what New York thought was outdoor clothing. His jacket had pockets all over it. He wore big clumsy boots.

He did not see Du Pré.

"You better move that," said Du Pré, "them people they can't get out."

The young man jumped at the sound of Du Pré's voice.

"Move it where?" he said.

Du Pré sighed. He waved toward the other end of the parking lot, empty but for a Dumpster.

The young man got back in the motor home and started it up and backed and turned, and the motor home lurched off and came to a stop by the Dumpster.

Du Pré walked back to the front door.

The young man stopped twenty feet from Du Pré.

"Samantha Smythe?" he said. "I am here, in the parking lot, at least I think I am." He was talking to a cell phone.

Du Pré laughed.

Sam Smythe and Trey Binder came out and they went to the young man and everybody hugged.

"Du Pré," said Sam, "this is the famous John Thomas Tipton, who will play William Clark."

Du Pré nodded.

"Say," said Tipton, "Is there music going on here tonight?"

"Yah," said Du Pré.

"Could I do a guest set?" said Tipton.

Samantha Symthe's eyes turned to Du Pré, begging.

Du Pré shrugged.

"Yah," he said.

Tipton ran to the motor home and he went inside and he came back out with a guitar case.

Oh, God, Du Pré thought, not one of *them*.

Maria had had a collection of records of whining long-haired idiots who all played mournful guitars badly.

She had had a poster of one of them on the wall of her bedroom.

Du Pré didn't know where the poster was. Maria had asked him.

They all went in and Du Pré walked over to Bassman and Tally and told them.

Bassman glanced over at Tipton.

"Him clear this place out quick as a drunk Sioux with a chain saw," he said.

"Yah," said Du Pré. Bart brought the hat. It was crammed with bills.

"We got the money," said Tally. "So what?"

"Him do what I think," said Bassman, "this crowd, they beat the shit out of us and take it back."

"We go count it," said Du Pré.

Several young girls in the crowd were pulling on parents' sleeves and pointing at Tipton, who strapped on his guitar and stood waiting for a reverent silence.

The place did get quiet.

Tipton launched into a song, playing lush chords on his guitar.

He sang something about the pain of having your true love as gone as the buffalo.

Du Pré and Bassman and Tally sneaked back to the kitchen to count the money and hear the nice sounds of dishes being washed.

"There is a back door here yes?" said Bassman.

"There," said T J, pointing at a big rack full of stainless-steel pots. "Behind that."

They had made a couple hundred apiece. Bassman and Tally went out the back door to find a quiet place to smoke some weed.

Du Pré sighed.

He went back out to the bar. He found Maria and Ben and Sam and Binder standing at the end of the long bartop and he went past and got behind them, where Madelaine was sitting on a stool.

The crowd was polite.

Tipton concluded a song, and he modestly said he was going to quit, but he stood there expecting to be applauded wildly. The polite patter trailed off. He looked nonplussed. Then he went to the guitar case and put his instrument in it. He shut the thing and then he put on his jacket and went out the door.

People relaxed and talked happily.

"Oh, God," said Sam Smythe. She started to put on her coat.

"Sam," said Binder, "he'll be OK."

"Maybe," said Sam. "I didn't want him and neither did you and we got him so he's my problem, and so I had better go and see."

She went off.

Du Pré looked at Binder.

"Getting money for this documentary was tough," he said. "Some of the people wanted something for their backing."

Du Pré laughed.

He took his fiddle and he tuned it and began and Tally and Bassman came in the front door and they made their way to the stage and Du Pré launched into "Lewis Captain and Cruzatte." Shoot him in the ass for an elk, lots of Métis scouts got eyesight that bad. . . .

The crowd began to whistle and shout and stamp.

Madelaine came to the dance floor, and she began to do the old dances, the ones done on the buffalo hide pegged out on the prairie, step dances, her hands on her hips. She tossed her long black hair, some streaked with silver.

Maria joined her, and they danced back to back. Bootheels tapping on the floor, heads shaking to the time.

Du Pré stopped and so did Madelaine and Maria and the people in the roadhouse clapped and cheered.

Maria and Madelaine walked back toward the bar and Du Pré and Bassman and Tally played a waltz and then some slow music, so that people could dance closely.

It was getting very late. Du Pré and Tally and Bassman bowed and the crowd clapped, but everyone was tired now, and people began to file out the door. It was early in the season and there would be much to do at sunup tomorrow.

Du Pré went out to cool off.

The motor home and Sam Smythe's Rover were both gone.

So she had led Tipton off toward the ranch and the river.

"Shit," said Trey Binder, behind Du Pré.

Du Pré turned.

"That politically correct little asshole is going to be a lot of grief," said Binder, "and I don't even know Layla Dalton. She's nineteen."

Du Pré snorted.

"And?" said Binder.

"What is this politically correct?" said Du Pré.

"There are only certain opinions which may be held by good folks," said Bart, from the porch.

"Yeah," said Binder.

"Oh," said Du Pré.

"Funny time we live in," said Trey Binder.

"They are all funny," said Du Pré.

"There he is," said Bart, pointing at an old battered pickup that had just turned into the parking lot.

"Who?" said Binder.

"Harry, I think," said Bart, "you know, the old deputy that Van Der Meer thought would be a good guard for you."

The truck rolled up to the porch, and it stopped.

Engine is nicely tuned, Du Pré thought.

The door of the truck opened and the cab light came on. A small bent old man wearing a stained and battered narrow-brimmed Stetson peered out, and then he slid off the seat and to the ground. He moved slowly. He wore old patched bib overalls and high-laced black shoes.

"Evenin'," said the old man, "I am looking for a Mister Trey Binder."

"That's me," said Trey, "and you must be Harry . . ."

"Harry," said Harry. He offered no last name.

"Would you be able to guard our film site?" said Binder.

"I suppose," said Harry.

"When can you start?" said Binder.

"Now," said Harry.

"Oh," said Binder.

"Lefty, come here," said Harry.

A huge black dog got out of the cab of the truck.

"This is Lefty," said Harry, "and this is Mr. Binder."

The dog sat and looked at Binder.

CHAPTER
16

Du Pré kissed Madelaine good-bye and she got in her car and headed north toward Toussaint. It was after two in the morning, and everyone else had gone, even TJ. Only old Harry was still parked in the lot.

"Good time," said Du Pré, "I be home tomorrow night maybe, night after, couple days."

"Nice woman," said Harry. "Lefty, you fat bastard, that is one big damn bone."

Lefty had a big beef rib bone in his mouth. He looked very happy.

"Knew your pa," said Harry.

Du Pré nodded. Knew Catfoot. Maybe I hear some of the rest of the story tonight, maybe later on.

"We was in the same platoon, Normandy," said Harry. "Used to scout together. Wouldn't go with no one else."

Du Pré nodded.

Harry was at the funeral, Papa and Mama, they are killed, the train. I don't know him we don't talk. I am some sad then.

"These little peckerwoods makin' the movie here," said Harry. "Better they did it down to Hollywood."

"Yah," said Du Pré.

"How'd Catfoot's boy come to this sorry end?" said Harry. "I'd love to know."

"I was drunk," said Du Pré.

"Sure," said Harry, "and when you sobered up you was in the moving picture business."

"My daughter Maria's boyfriend he is the assistant director," said Du Pré.

"Not too damn long till that Bye-Centeeal," said Harry. "There's too damned many people on the river now. Used to be it was quiet here."

"Yah," said Du Pré.

"So your boats got burned," said Harry. "You find who did it?"

Du Pré shrugged.

"You know where this is goin'," said Harry. "Somebody's gonna get killed, is where."

Du Pré nodded.

"I was a deputy forty-six years," said Harry, "and I don't hold with folks killin' each other. But they do it. Usually they do it drunk and mad. Against the law."

Du Pré rolled a smoke.

"You're camped with them people out to Van Der Meer's?" asked Harry.

Du Pré nodded.

"Keep an eye out, you're around there?" said Harry.

Du Pré looked at him.

"Come on," said Harry. "Might's well be the night watchman now."

Du Pré went to his cruiser and he got in and started it and he turned round and followed Harry out on the blacktop to the dirt road that led off southwest toward the Carbonado. Harry drove fast; his old truck had had some work done on it.

They went through the huge gate, two massive tree trunks and a crossbar with the ranch brand hanging from it. The tires thrummed on the cattle guards.

Harry barely slowed.

They went along the hills above the river, on the dirt track, and then down toward the camp. There were four big motor homes there and two big tents. The lights were on in two of the motor homes.

Harry went past the camp and on for several miles, to a place where the Missouri fetched close to the bank, the river chewing away, the main current showing driftwood black in the moonsilver on the water.

Harry stopped and got out. Lefty came, too, and he raced off, gone in the dark. Then he began to bark.

Harry turned on a five-cell flashlight. He waited for Du Pré to come up and then he started to walk down a path that led down the face of the hill to a brushy flat place. There were a few dead cottonwood trees on the flat, with ghostly white trunks and broken branches.

Harry went toward Lefty's barks.

He shone the light on a long mess of driftwood piled up in a curve of the river. There would be a long spur of rock there.

Du Pré squinted.

There was something white in the piled wood.

Then the wind changed and he smelled the rotting flesh of humans.

"Few days ago," said Harry, "canoe fetched up downriver. Nothing in it said who it belonged to. Nobody's called, see if anyone's been found. Hard to tell when these folks landed here. I see two, yes?"

"Yah," said Du Pré.

Lefty went on barking.

"Lefty finds bodies," said Harry.

"He found these," said Du Pré.

"Way the river is," said Harry, "dead cow'll float to here and get stuck. See, there's an underground channel there, a hole through the rock, so the wood hangs up here and don't get washed away. Cows hang up here. People hang up here."

"You out here earlier?" said Du Pré.

"Nope," said Harry, "but there was the canoe and nobody missing, at least nobody calling. Next place up the river does this, catches things, is up there twenty-four miles. Not that everything comes here, you know, but, it usually does. So I thought we'd maybe come down here and see what Lefty thought of all this."

"Jesus," said Du Pré, "what happened those people?"

"They ended up dead," said Harry.

"Why the canoe don't get stuck here?" said Du Pré.

"Without the people in it it'd float high and the water'd carry it on," said Harry. "Good canoe, had a lot of foam in it so it'd float. Had gear lashed in good. So it bumped along awhile and then it went on. Swamped on a bridge piling, and went on some more. The foam. Finally fetched up on a sandbar. River rises and falls all the time."

Du Pré rolled a cigarette and lit it.

"Canoe fetched up on a side channel sandbar, sorta outta sight," said Harry. "Ranch hand saw it, told his boss, who says 'Wal, we got work to do other'n helpin' goddamned tourists catch canoes done got away from 'em.' Took their own sweet time, finally sheriff's office sends out a flyer on Rupe and Lee and this canoe, red it was, and the ranch hand calls it in."

"When you look at this canoe," said Du Pré.

"This afternoon," said Harry. "Had something on it puzzled me."

Du Pré drew in smoke and then blew it out.

"Groove on top of the gunwale," said Harry, "little thing, no more'n an inch long. Now them canoes usually got the two paddlers, one in the front, one in the back. You put one of them lead pencils in the groove it points two ways. One down in the river, one maybe up on the bank. So if somebody was to shoot the paddler in front with a rifle, go through soft tissue there, it just might groove that gunwale 'fore it went on into the water. Course it coulda been something else did it, too, some accident or other. . . ."

"You think that sooner," said Du Pré, "maybe it help."

"Didn't see the canoe till today," said Harry, "was having my gallbladder cut out. Got outta the hospital yesterday."

Why this old bastard is doing this I do not know, thought Du Pré.

"Catfoot was a good man," said Harry. "I expect you are, too. Now, we got to go on back up to my old truck where I got a radio and call this in. Then we got to wait. . . ."

Harry whistled, two notes, and Lefty came.

The big black dog was wet, and he smelled.

Du Pré waited while Harry spoke into the mike.

The dispatcher said to get some rest and they'd be out at first light.

"We get some sleep then," said Harry. "You do anyway. Where you bunked?"

"I got a bedroll back there," said Du Pré. He hated tents and campers. His bedroll was off in a little dell away from everyone.

Harry pulled his bedroll from the back of the truck and looked round and picked a spot, one with thick grass and no rocks and he took the bedroll over and dropped it.

"I expect I'll sleep here," he said. "See you tomorrow."

"You need me, come here?" said Du Pré.

"Damn right," said Harry. "The State boys will be here, too, and it ain't gonna be our job dig them corpses out of the driftwood there. But you know damn well what this means, Du Pré."

Du Pré nodded.

"We can identify them people then we maybe know a little more," said Harry. "But I expect we know what happened."

Du Pré nodded.

"This's good country, good people," said Harry, "but they ain't fond of them 'vironmentalists, and this here Bicenteenal means a lotta them are gonna be relivin' history floating down the river. A lot of them think this oughta be some goddamn theme park, and the folks ranching here oughta up and leave. They ain't gonna."

"Yah," said Du Pré.

"I's born here," said Harry, "long time ago, and I remember real hard times in the twenties. We come here, tried to homestead, but there weren't enough rain to farm. My pa and ma worked theirselves to death. I was an orphan at ten. Ranch family took me in. They'd homesteaded earlier, gone over to cattle. Country gets deep in some people, and I don't like nowhere else."

Du Pré nodded.

"So you go and get some sleep," said Harry, "and I'll see you in the mornin'."

Du Pré drove off toward the camp.

It was a clear night with many brilliant stars burning down low.

Du Pré drove as close to his bedroll as he could get.

He got out and he pissed and he had some whiskey and a smoke and then he turned in.

One mosquito whined.

Du Pré waited until he felt the prick of the mosquito's bite and then he crushed it.

It is that Bill Rupe's son Jack down there, his friend the writer, thought Du Pré, like we all thought.

But I wait to call Rupe till they are sure.

Du Pré tried to sleep.

"Shit," he said.

He got up and pulled on his shirt and pants and boots and he drove to the place where the motor homes were camped.

He pounded on the door of Trey Binder's mammoth contraption.

Binder finally came to the door, half-pissed.

He looked at Du Pré.

"Got that veracity," said Du Pré, "and I need a telephone."

"Damn damn damn," said Harvey.

"Yah," said Du Pré. "It is them for sure, one body maybe it is somebody else, not two."

"Two of them. Down in the logjam," said Harvey.

"Close together," said Du Pré.

"It could happen," said Harvey.

"Old Harry, this old deputy, says it is where bodies end up, next trap is twenty-four miles upriver," said Du Pré. "Him know the country, know the river."

"I have a nasty and suspicious nature," said Harvey, "so who the fuck is Old Harry."

"Old guy," said Du Pré. "Old fart."

"What's his *last* name," said Harvey.

"Dunno," said Du Pré. "He's got a dog named Lefty."

"Well?" said Harvey.

"I don't know," said Du Pré.

"Probably," said Harvey, "most of the people in the country are in on this one way and another."

"Yah," said Du Pré.

"Shit," said Harvey. "I guess I best call Bill Rupe."

CHAPTER 17

The men wore white moon suits. They slid ropes around the bloated bodies and slid them carefully onto stretchers and then they slid the stretchers onto a flatbottomed dory. They climbed in and got black body bags around the stinking corpses.

"Awful," said Maria. She stood near Du Pré, the flesh around her eyes white.

Du Pré nodded.

A helicopter flew past, low, a camera trained on the dory.

Old Harry chewed his tobacco and spat at the grass.

A motorboat with a huge engine roared down from up the river, journalists peering over the windshield. The boat's engine throttled down and the heavy craft swung in the brown water and then grounded on mud. The newsmen came over the side. One had on waders, the other did not.

"Tell you what, Missy," said Harry, "I'll give ya an ex-clusive."

Du Pré snorted.

The reporters were squelching near the shore. They got out and they looked up at Du Pré and Maria and Old Harry and they looked at each other and then at the bank, searching for a way up.

"Come on," said Du Pré. "We let them dance with Old Harry here."

"I don't dance," said Harry.

Du Pré and Maria went to his old cruiser and they got in and drove off before the journalists got up the bank.

There were clouds to the west, and it would rain late in the day.

Du Pré lurched the cruiser up the track and the land flattened and the old car quit jumping on its springs.

"Some damn mess, Papa," said Maria.

"Yah."

"What happened?" she said, looking over.

Du Pré shrugged.

"You are always like this, Papa," said Maria, "don't talk, these things. You talk to me, yes?"

"Harry think they were shot," said Du Pré.

"Were they?" asked Maria.

"Probably," said Du Pré.

"I took this class," said Maria, "couple of years ago, guy teaching it called himself a *deep ecologist*. He wanted all the people on the Great Plains taken off. Put back the buffalo, put back the wolves."

Du Pré nodded and spat out the window.

"So I say to him, you are wrong. There are people living out there, been there a long time," said Maria.

Du Pré nodded.

"He say they need to move, I say maybe they don't want to, he say they have to, I say why?" said Maria.

Du Pré turned off the potholed track and drove on the flat ground beside it.

"He say that is the right thing for them to do. I ask why is it right?"

Du Pré waited.

"He get really mad," said Maria, "so I just tell him he is sounding a lot like Adolf Hitler and then I leave. Drop the course."

Du Pré laughed.

He pulled up next to the motor homes.

Trey Binder and Sam Smythe and John Thomas Tipton were sitting in folding captain's chairs, drinking coffee.

Du Pré and Maria got out.

Tipton was walking off toward his motor home.

"Morning," said Trey Binder, "Coffee?"

He got up and went to a small table with a gas stove on it and he turned on the flame under the pot.

"Pretty bad, huh?" said Sam Smythe.

The helicopter racketed past.

"Wanted to start some filming," said Trey, "but I guess not. How long will this go on?"

"Today maybe," said Du Pré, "but I don't know."

"Well, it's good that Van Der Meer closed the ranch off," said Trey. "At least they have to come by the water. Or they can drive over on the other side of the river and swim across."

The water had been hot and it boiled and Binder poured it into a French press and he waited a moment and then he put down the plunger.

He poured coffee into blue enamel cups.

I hate them things, Du Pré thought, metal get so hot you can't drink your coffee till it is cold.

"Where is Ben?" said Maria.

"Down at the boats," said Binder. "We thought we'd best cover them up. It's supposed to rain."

"You don't want TV pictures of them," said Maria.

"That, too," said Binder.

"We start filming in a couple of days," said Binder. "Layla will be here today, I think."

Du Pré looked over at the west.

Couple of days it is pissing rain here, yes, he thought.

That Lewis and Clark they go through the rain, too.

Veracity.

Sam Smythe's cell phone chirred.

"Shit," she said, "it's too early for it to start."

She took the thing out and opened it and listened.

"What?" she said, "calm down. CALM DOWN!"

She listened, her face screwed up.

"I'll be right there, John Thomas, hold on, good buddy," she said.

Everyone was looking at her.

"I'll tell ya," she said, "but you can't laugh. *Do not laugh.* No fucking noise."

Everyone nodded.

"There is wildlife in John Thomas's Winnebago."

Everyone looked at everyone else.

"A chipmunk is in there. John Thomas is sure it has personally singled him out, to give him hantavirus."

Everyone grinned.

"No fucking noise," said Sam Smythe. "I must go and get that beast out of there. I am, after all, the producer."

Maria had her hand across her mouth, and she was gagging.

Sam Smythe sprinted off toward John Thomas Tipton's motor home.

"Oh, God," said Trey Binder.

"Veracity," said Du Pré.

"Maybe the goddamned thing *does* carry hantavirus," said Binder.

Tipton was screaming. He was angry and scared.

"No . . . fucking . . . noise," said Maria.

Tipton came flying out of the door of his Winnebago, and he backed away from the motor home.

Sam Smythe appeared in the doorway, with a broom.

Tipton screamed and pointed, and Sam got down and looked.

She stood with him.

Finally, he went back inside.

Sam walked back over to Du Pré and Maria and Binder.

She was rubbing her eyes.

"Good on ya," she said. "I was half-expecting hysterics over here. Which would have caused hysterics over *there*."

"They charge sometimes," said Du Pré. "Me, I have spent time, up in a tree, chipmunks dancing around down there."

"Right," said Sam.

"Thank you," said Binder. "I don't think I could have done it nearly as smoothly and well."

"My female nurturing instincts," said Sam. "I wish to Christ that asshole would break a leg or something."

"Now, Sam," said Binder.

"We'd get someone worse," said Sam.

Du Pré laughed.

"I read every word of Lewis and Clark's journals," said Binder, "and they didn't mention being charged by a chipmunk."

"It was too traumatic," said Sam. "They couldn't face their fears and write about those awful chipmunk charges."

"Are we gonna get through all of this?" said Binder.

"We will," said Sam, "like we did the last time."

"Is our bet still good?" asked Binder.

"Yup," said Sam.

Binder looked at Du Pré and Maria.

"We got a running bet," said Binder, "about when we are going to get a leading actor who has table manners."

"So far," said Sam, "none have."

"Mind you," said Binder, "we work with obscure actors, which is all we can afford."

"I am here to tell you," said Sam Smythe, "that the expensive ones don't have table manners either."

Du Pré shook his head.

"It is maybe going to rain today, next few days," he said.

Binder looked up at the blue sky.

"Huh?" he said.

"Maybe not," said Du Pré. "You going to film this, the rain?"

"No," said Binder. "Real rain doesn't look like rain on film. It just washes everything out. Movie rain has to be made with a rain-making machine, big fat drops."

"How long will it rain?" asked Sam.

"Three four days," said Du Pré.

"OK," said Sam, "I bite, frontiersman, how can you tell?"

Du Pré stood up and he motioned to Sam to come.

He pointed to the west.

"That gray, there," he said, "it is rain, moving slow. Black is thunderstorms moving fast, but that is rain, moving slow."

The wind had changed round to the west, and smelled of rain.

CHAPTER
18

The rain began about three in the afternoon. A gray mass of cloud slid over the sky, and a fine steady drizzle came down.

Everyone went to the roadhouse.

T J was knitting when Du Pré and Maria and Ben and Sam Smythe got there. She had her faced screwed tight and her lips pursed.

"Damn it," she said, "Left the instructions at home."

"May I?" said Sam Smythe. She went back of the bar to help T J puzzle it out.

"You bartend a minute, Maria?" said T J.

"I never see men tending bar here in Montana," said Ben. "Why is that?"

"Not so many fights," said T J. "Guys don't listen to guys but they usually listen to girls."

Ben nodded.

"Who is this Layla, anyway?" said Maria, mixing a tall ditch for Du Pré.

"She was a model," said Sam. "They all want to act. She looks sort of Indian."

"Oh," said Maria.

"There aren't any speaking parts in this film," said Sam. "The actors just sort of . . . provide a tableau. We'll cut back and forth to historians and other interesting people, and use the film footage to spread the short interviews."

"What you do there is a chipmunk stampede?" said Du Pré.

"Shut," said Sam, staring at the knit. "Up."

"Chipmunk?" said T J.

"Death," said Sam.

"To hell with the sweater," said T J. "I wanna know about the chipmunk."

"All *right*," said Sam. "John Thomas Tipton went to his Winnebago and there was a chipmunk in it and he freaked out."

"Oh," said T J.

"And this son of a bitch," said Sam, glaring at Du Pré, "was supposed to keep his goddamned mouth shut."

"Who saved him from the chipmunk?" said T J.

"She did," said Du Pré, "that is what movie producers do, it is that *veracity*."

"This," said Sam, rubbing her eyes, "stinks of doom."

"Chipmunk in his Winnebago," said T J, "the pore li'l thing."

"Christ," said Sam.

"I got to pee," said T J, dropping the knitting.

"Du Pré," said Sam, "I ought to hang you."

She put the knitting down and made herself a drink and she came round the bar and sat down.

T J was gone for five minutes. She looked very happy when she came back.

Trey Binder came in and some of the crew members. They were

all laughing. The local workers went to the pool table and racked out the balls and began to play eight ball.

A harried-looking young man came in, and he looked around and saw Trey Binder and ran to him and talked earnestly.

"Bring her on in," said Trey.

The young man ran back out.

"Layla is here," said Trey.

"How does she feel about chipmunks?" said T J.

"Please," said Trey Binder. "Oh, God."

The door opened and an impossibly beautiful young woman came in. She was followed by several people, all of whom carried things.

The young woman looked round the room.

The cowboys stared.

She looked at the floor and walked over to the bar.

"Miss Dalton would like a glass of . . ." said the harried young man.

"White wine," said Layla Dalton.

T J fished a jug of screwtop out of the beer cooler and poured a glass. It fizzed like beer.

She set it in front of Layla.

Layla, her assistants, and Binder stared at the glass in horror.

"I simply cannot do this," said Layla Dalton. "Take me back to the airport."

She swept out, her assistants behind her.

Sam Smythe ran after them.

T J drank the offending glass of wine.

"I don't think," said Du Pré, "she was the sort of woman, like them chipmunks."

"My movie here is going to be done in by a goddamn chipmunk," said Trey Binder. He went on out the front door.

"A chipmunk is just another squirrel," said T J. "You know all them stories about actors and actresses . . . I bet they all are true."

Maria went over to the little window and peered past the beer sign. She stared. Then she turned away.

"She left I think," said Maria.

Sam Smythe and Trey Binder came back in, looking sober.

"She quit," said Sam.

"She the only one there is?" said T J.

Sam shrugged.

"We'll find someone else," she said.

The cowboys at the pool table were back playing eight ball.

"We'd better talk," said Sam to Trey Binder. They went off to one of the small tables in the front corner of the room, away from the pool table.

"It was OK wine," said T J, pouring herself another glass. "We got some bottles of California white in the cooler. They must be good. They got corks and all."

Du Pré heard a big truck outside, an eighteen-wheeler. The truck slowed and stopped and the engine kept popping.

He went to the door and looked out. Bad time of year for shipping stock.

A man in a tan jumpsuit got down from the truck and walked toward the front door of the roadhouse. Du Pré opened it for him.

"Obliged," said the man, nodding as he passed. He stopped and he looked round and he saw Sam and Trey at the table.

"We're here," he said.

"Good enough," said Trey. "I'll guide you out there."

"No," said Sam, "I will. My job, man."

"Mobile studio'll be here first thing in the morning," said the man in the jumpsuit. "Got a couple of motor homes coming, slowly. You know how they drive."

"Cameras and crews," said Sam as she passed Du Pré.

Du Pré shrugged.

In the rain.

"Is Van Der Meer expecting us?" said the man in the jumpsuit.

"Yeah," said Sam, "but I'll go with you."

"There's no rush, Sam," said the man in the jumpsuit, "it's supposed to rain the next four or five days."

"This is supposed to be the goddamned Great American Desert," said Sam.

"Ma'am," said the man in the jumpsuit, "I'd like a beer and a shot."

"Bar whiskey?" said T J.

"Sure," said the man. He came over to the bar and he put a bill down and he waited.

"Might as well wait here for the rest of the crew, Sam," he said.

"This is Gordon," said Sam. "That lady behind the bar is T J and this is Du Pré and Maria—his daughter—and Ben Burke the AD."

"Gordon Ketter," said the man in the jumpsuit.

"Gordo and his merry crew are one entire film studio on wheels," said Sam.

Trey Binder cleared his throat.

"In view of it all I suggest we might get really drunk," he said.

Gordon Ketter laughed.

"Expensive weather," he said.

Trey Binder nodded.

"Layla quit. She left anyway."

Gordon shrugged.

"Happens," he said.

"Play pool?" said Trey.

"Sure do," said Gordon. The cowboys had left the table. They went off.

"Why is Trey so upset?" said Maria, looking at Ben.

"Oh," said Ben, "it costs a lot of money per day to lease the equipment, and every day has to be paid for whether you can film or not. So four or five days of rain could be . . . a hell of a lot of money."

"I maybe go on, Toussaint then," said Du Pré, "come back when it is not raining."

"There'll be a lot of technical questions," said Sam. "We need you."

Du Pré sighed.

"We need music, too," said Sam. "It's tough being stuck out here with no work for everybody."

Du Pré went off to the pay phone.

"You know anything about those bodies out to the Carbonado?" said T J, looking at Maria.

"Just saw them being pulled out of the driftwood," said Maria.

T J nodded, and she walked down the bar.

Du Pré came back.

"I call Bassman," he said. "They will be here."

"Hooray!" said Sam Smythe.

She and Trey Binder were staring at Maria, who was shaking her head.

"Papa!" said Maria, "they want me to play Sacajawea! I am no actress!"

"I am no *consultant*," said Du Pré, rolling himself a smoke.

He grinned at Maria.

"I am doing this," he said. "You can do it, too."

Maria threw up her hands.

CHAPTER
19

Du Pré woke, and he saw stars above. He sat up, stretched and yawned and pulled on his clothes and boots, a little damp. Dew glistened on grass blades.

He rolled a smoke, lit it, and looked around. He walked to a bush and pissed.

Coyote's breakfast, a piss and a look-around. Some fine day today.

"Coffee's ready," said Old Harry. He had drifted in behind Du Pré.

Du Pré nodded and followed Harry to Harry's little camp. A fancy gas stove sat on the tailgate of Harry's old pickup. A battered blue enamel coffeepot steamed. Harry poured Du Pré a big cup, blue metal like the pot.

Du Pré looked at the gas stove.

"Any damn fool can be uncomfortable," said Harry. "You want to make a fire outta buffalo chips, I'll take the coffee back."

Du Pré laughed.

"Croissants," said Du Pré. "should have them, yes?"

Harry set a small aluminum box on another burner. An oven. It was already hot.

"Had some chokecherry jam it'd about do," said Harry, "but I don't."

"I do," said Du Pré. He walked to his old cruiser and got a jar of Madelaine's jam out of the grub box. He walked back.

They ate croissants and jam and drank coffee while the sun came up.

"You bake these croissants?" said Du Pré.

Harry shook his head.

"General store gets 'em," he said, "three times a week. Pretty good. I got to likin' em when I was in France."

Du Pré looked at him.

"Third Army," said Harry, "them damn French, they'd fire up the ovens soon as the Krauts left and bake. Hell, I got some fresh croissants not five minutes after shooting a Tiger tank all to hell."

Lefty stirred and came out of the cab of the truck, looking off toward the river. He looked at Harry.

"Someone's comin'," said Harry, "early riser like us."

Lefty trotted off toward the willows. He sat and waited by a deer path, and a young man came out of the hole in the trees, his head down, his crumpled hat shining with water.

"Good morning," said the man. He was in his early twenties and very handsome. He was talking to the dog. He reached out and patted Lefty's head. Lefty sat in his dignity.

The young man looked up then, and saw Du Pré and Harry.

"Oh," he said, "excuse me. I didn't mean to intrude." He turned to go back into the willows.

"Oh, hell, intrude," said Harry, "intrude on some of this here fine coffee."

The young man turned back.

"If you've enough," he said, "I'd surely like some."

"We are gonna make more," said Harry, "and ain't you Jason Parks?"

"Yes," said the young man.

Du Pré looked at Harry.

"Big movie star," said Harry, "My granddaughters get all moony at his name. He's gonna play Lewis."

Parks came to them. Harry filled another cup.

"You're most kind," said Parks. His accent was British, his face open.

Parks sat on a log. He was wearing cloth chaps of dark green, and beads of water ran down them. His boots were rubber Wellingtons.

"Jason Parks, I think," said Old Harry, "I'm Old Harry. This here's Doo Pray, famous for his fiddling and a few other things, I guess."

"Delighted," said Parks, rising and offering his hand, "Jason Parks, and . . . have you a last name, sir? I should call you Mr. . . . ?"

"Yer manners is excellent, young feller," said Old Harry, "but I ask you to call me Old Harry, as I get confused easy. Doo Pray's first name is Gab-ree-ell, but I never heard nobody call him nothin' but Doo Pray."

Du Pré laughed.

"Jason, please," said Parks, "and the coffee is excellent."

"Take hair off a damn badger," said Harry, "but it helps the mornin'. What the hell are you doin?"

"I got here last night," said Parks, "and got directions from a nice lady at the bar, T J, she insisted I call her. I came down here, and I slept in my truck."

"You got that little rice rocket with the shell on it?" said Harry. "Big movie star like you I'd a thought you'd have an a-partment on wheels."

Parks grinned.

"One is coming," he said, "but I thought I'd get here a few days early. I rather like sleeping in the back of my truck and living on bologna and beer."

Du Pré looked at Harry.

Harry glanced slyly at him.

"Ol' Du Pré here was snorin' like a fat ol' dog when you drove in last night," said Harry. "I seen ya but you coulda parked top of Gabe and he'd a gone on sleepin'."

Du Pré laughed.

So did Parks. He lifted his cup, a salute to Harry.

"Want a couple of cross-ants," said Harry.

"My," said Parks, "that would be lovely."

Harry served them up and Parks wolfed them down.

"You want to hide out till you got to be here?" said Harry.

Parks nodded.

Harry looked at Du Pré.

Du Pré shrugged.

"Pull yer rig over there," said Harry, pointing, "and we'll keep you covered. I expect you got a false nose and some moustaches in yer truck."

"Matter of fact," said Parks, "I do." His voice was now coated with a Western accent, Northern Rockies.

Parks walked off and in a few minutes he drove back, in a small black pickup with a low shell on the back. The license plates were from Connecticut.

There was music spilling from the windows of the pickup. Du Pré's music, a tape he had made years ago.

Du Pré laughed.

Jason Parks stopped and turned the music down, but not off.

He got out.

"Where you get that?" asked Du Pré.

"Ben and Maria," said Parks. "Ben and I grew up together."

Du Pré nodded.

"They know I am coming," said Parks, "and I should tell them so they can tell Samantha Smythe, but if it went no farther I'd appreciate it. I . . . fame has its viler aspects."

"You play Lewis," said Du Pré, "because Ben is your friend?"

Parks nodded.

"My agency pitched a terrible fit," said Parks. "They thought I could make a lot more money doing another movie. That's true, but I don't need more money."

Jason Parks got up and he stretched and he yawned and he looked over the river to the low hills beyond.

"The eleventh of June," he said, "1805. Lewis and Clark and most of their party passed by here. Shields and three men were hunting ahead. They left deer carcasses hanging from the trees. There were no buffalo, they had gone somewhere."

Du Pré looked at the actor.

"Damn," said Parks, "I would have liked to have been there, as an ordinary soldier, crossing the country for the first time. But then there were the Rockies . . . they got maps from Métis living with the Blackfeet, didn't they?"

Parks looked at Du Pré.

"Yah," said Du Pré, "they don't believe them so they go on and over Lemhi Pass, down to the Snake River. Have to turn back . . ."

"Pierre Cruzatte fiddled in the camp each night," said Parks, "and they swatted mosquitoes."

The air was warming, and a gray mist of the bloodsucking insects rose from the brush.

Old Harry held out a bottle of bug dope. Du Pré put some on his face and his neck. So did Parks.

The mosquitoes danced, whining, but they did not land and bite.

"Nearly two hundred years ago," said Parks.

"Long time gone," said Du Pré.

"Our great national epic," said Parks.

"Bein' bugbit," said Old Harry.

"It could be a good movie," said Parks.

"I wouldn't know about that," said Old Harry.

Jason Parks nodded, and he held out his cup for more coffee.

CHAPTER
20

Du Pré and Maria and Ben and Jason Parks and Sam Smythe were sitting at the bar. T J was smoking, and looking at the front door.

Buck Keifer came in, laughing.

"Damn it, Buck," said T J. "You know there's no fighting in here."

"It wasn't," said Buck slowly, "exactly a fight."

"You bust his camera?" said T J.

"Stomped the sucker," said Buck.

"There's gonna be a stink," said T J.

"Buy a fan," said Buck.

Du Pré laughed, and then so did the others.

"It's my fault," said Jason Parks. "I shouldn't have come here without a disguise."

"No," said T J, "it ain't your fault. That ill-mannered son of a bitch who wouldn't leave you the hell alone is whose fault it was. They act like this all the time?"

Parks nodded wearily.

"They sell the photographs to those newspapers one sees in grocery stores," said Parks, "the ones with the articles on three-headed babies and serial sex murders in the Vatican."

Hamburgers sizzled on the grill. T J served them up, and she pointed a finger up and down the bar. No one wanted another drink.

"Old Harry gone to town?" said T J.

"Yah," said Du Pré, "see about those people we find in the river."

"I hope," said T J, "that you can do your movie without anyone getting killed."

"That ain't the only movie, I hear," said Buck.

"What?" said Sam Smythe.

"Neighbor of mine, got land on the river, said he got a call about renting his place, a lot of money. Some outfit wanted to make a Lewis and Clark movie."

"Did he say which outfit?" asked Sam.

Buck shrugged.

"Damn," said Sam Smythe, "I don't like this."

"There were several films planned, Sam," said Ben, "and we can't stop them."

The telephone rang. T J went to answer it. She spoke for a moment, then she laughed and turned.

"Du Pré," she said, "it's Madelaine."

Du Pré got up and went to the phone and took the receiver.

"Yah," he said. I hate this thing.

"Du Pré," said Madelaine, "there is some crazy man wants you to do music for another movie, says you will get hundreds of thousands of dollars for it. He is . . . he call me looking for you, someplace in California."

"No," said Du Pré.

"I tell him that you probably don't want to," said Madelaine, "still it is a lot of money."

Du Pré stood for a moment.

"You want to be the first Métis, own a yacht, sail it on Cooper's Creek there?" said Du Pré. Cooper's Creek was six feet wide.

"No," said Madelaine, "but maybe you want to run off, California, have groupies, wear a shirt open to your crotch."

Du Pré laughed.

"Canada," he said. "Maybe we go there till Lewis and Clark are not so much."

"People making money from this," said Madelaine, "that is what is wrong."

"So I call him?" said Du Pré.

Madelaine gave him a telephone number.

Du Pré read the phone number back.

"Tell you what," he said. "You tell them that Bart, he is my agent."

"That is mean, Du Pré," said Madelaine.

"Bart he needs this," said Du Pré.

"OK," said Madelaine, "but someday you are going push him too far, and then you will be one sorry Métis."

Du Pré snorted.

"See you Friday there," said Madelaine. "Kiss that Maria for me." She hung up.

Everyone was looking at Du Pré.

"I will quit your movie," said Du Pré, "more money, they are sending a limousine from the airport, bigger movie. I will be famous, get rich."

"Bullshit, Papa," said Maria, "what is this?"

"More movies," said Du Pré.

"We are supposed to start shooting in three days," said Ben Burke. "The river is cleared."

Du Pré spread his hands.

"This is such fun, campers," said Sam Smythe.

There were sounds of engines outside, and one by one they shut off.

T J frowned.

Feet on the boardwalk and the door opened and T J relaxed. Just local ranchers, in for a beer on a hot day.

Du Pré and Ben and Maria and Sam and Jason left then, going out to their trucks and cars.

Du Pré looked off across the rolling plains.

Country for not many people, tough country, and this is no good, he thought, this movie is no good. This Lewis and Clark Bicentennial is no good.

Damn, they should stay home.

"Papa," said Maria, "you come now. We are going to the river, see about the pirogues."

Du Pré nodded. Maria and Ben had ridden with him. They got in his old cruiser and Du Pré drove off toward the Carbonado Land and Cattle Company.

Du Pré rolled a smoke.

"Always something," said Ben, "always some damn thing. Making a movie is like nothing else. One star is afraid of chipmunks. There are extras who have never been off asphalt. The river is there, and it is big and mean. God, what must it have been like for those people. Walking month on end, towing heavy boats, crossing the Rockies, living on the coast of Oregon for the winter, going home?"

Du Pré speeded up.

Jason Parks's little pickup was right behind him.

The light was fierce, and the prairie glowed yellow at the edges.

Du Pré glanced at the rearview mirror. The little black pickup was a hundred feet back.

Du Pré slowed to turn into the ranch, and he went over the cattle guard and down the hill.

They went past the fork that led to the main ranch and down toward the river and the boats and the motor homes.

There was a police cruiser parked near Old Harry's pickup, and Harry and a cop in a suit were sitting on the tailgate of Harry's truck, their heads close together. Lefty sat on the ground, looking at Du Pré approaching.

Du Pré pulled up and he stopped and they got out.

"We see you later, Papa," said Maria, glancing at Harry and the cop.

Du Pré nodded.

Jason Parks drove past, on his way to the camp farther down by the river.

"Du Pré," said Old Harry, "this here young feller is Detective Pruitt. Has news of them bodies."

The cop got up and he smiled.

"Pleased," he said, "Gabriel Du Pré. Heard a lot of stories about you."

Du Pré shook his hand.

"Them two was doing some sort of article," said Harry, "writer and a photographer. They wasn't missed because they didn't call Rupe's father. Rupe and Lee their names was."

Du Pré nodded.

"Put in way the hell up," said Harry. "Damn near to Great Falls they was, well, Fort Benton anyway, and just set off, paid someone to drive their rig to Malta, was going to call on one of them little phones."

Du Pré nodded.

"They must have camped two or three nights," said the cop, "maybe more. But we don't know where exactly, and there wasn't anything in the canoe that told us anything. Techs went over it with care."

"I was tellin' him they was killed 'tween here and that elbow up the river bout twenty-four miles," said Old Harry.

"We flew over it," said the cop. "Only places that are good to camp are on the south side."

"Wondered maybe we could go and take a look," said Harry. "You know how to run a canoe?"

"Nobody saw anything," said Pruitt.

"River might tell us," said Old Harry. "Take us a day."

Du Pré looked off, toward the brown water.

He nodded.

CHAPTER
21

Old Harry looked out over the river. The brown water flowed steady, stately, toward the sea.

"Good old river," said Buck Keifer. He had driven them up in his pickup. A battered fiberglass canoe stuck out of the back of the bed.

"Canoe much?" said Old Harry. He looked at Du Pré.

Du Pré shook his head.

Don't work so good in dust, that sagebrush. I got ver' little Swampy Cree in me.

Du Pré looked up at the white hills, old clay from the huge lake that had been there when the ice held the river. Some Herefords grazed on the grasses sprouting in clumps in the hard soil.

"Got to canoe on the river 'less you want to use a stinkboat," said Harry. "An' you use a stinkboat, you don't see much. God-damn things anyway, hell of a way to get around."

"Horses don't swim fast enough, Harry," said Buck.

"Ask me," said Old Harry, "the in-vention of the autymobile was not a good day fer mankind."

Du Pré laughed. Buck began to take off the bungee cords that held the canoe in the truck. The canoe wiggled as the tension lessened.

Du Pré took off the cords on his side, and they let the canoe down gently. The paddles and life vests and a soft cooler were strapped inside.

Harry looked off to the west. The sky was a brilliant blue.

"Rain about four," he said, "but we should be off the river then. If we don't dick around on the banks too much."

"I got work to do," said Buck, nodding at Du Pré and Harry. He got in his pickup and drove back up the track that led to the country road.

"Well," said Harry, "I guess we can't back out now. Get the other side of this old bastard." They carried the canoe and the gear down to the river. A sandbar touched the bank, and there was deeper water just below it.

"You want one of these?" asked Harry, pointing to the vests.

Du Pré shook his head.

"Wal," said Old Harry, "take the front. Holler if you see the Loch Ness monster or anything."

They pushed off and Du Pré dipped his paddle in. He pulled, and the canoe moved swiftly out to the main current. The land flowed by in silence. A cougar lapped water in a dell. Beaver chewed willows on the sides of sloughs. A bald eagle sat in a dead cottonwood, waiting.

"Need to pull over t' the other side some," said Old Harry.

Du Pré dug his paddle in the water and the canoe slid across the current and Old Harry jammed his paddle in the water and swung the prow downstream. Du Pré looked over. There was an odd boil on the water, as though it was flowing over a big rock.

Then a huge rootball filled with stones broke the surface, like a giant fist. It hung for a moment, then sank beneath the water.

"One a them," said Old Harry, "sure would spoil your day."

"Yah them sawyers," said Du Pré.

"Used to was that there was government boats sent all along the river pull them out," said Old Harry. "Called 'em Uncle Sam's tooth pullers. But they quit in the twenties, when the steamboats quit, too."

"The twenties?" said Du Pré.

"Yup," said Old Harry. "Still run cattle downriver in 'em, grain and such, some of these ranches. Too far from the railroad, and it cost less to ship on the river than it did to haul it to the railhead. Then they put in that Fort Peck Dam and that was the end of the river. Used to be a quarter million acres of the best cropland in Montana by the river there, but it's all underwater."

They drifted on, silently. Mule deer fed unconcerned on the banks, a black bear dug at a stump. A red fox darted from its hole under a fallen log. An osprey stooped and grasped a fish and flew off. The bald eagle left its tree to mug the osprey.

"I don't think Jack Rupe and Davis Lee woulda stopped anywhere along here," said Old Harry. "Seems they mighta done so few miles down maybe."

"Whose ranches are there?" said Du Pré.

"South bank's all the Carbonado," said Old Harry. "North bank's not much, BLM land all of it, and it's pretty damn bleak. There's water back of the river so them cows seldom come down to the Missouri. So no one comes lookin' for them."

Du Pré tried to guess their speed. Seven or ten miles an hour, something like that, fast as a man could trot.

Four hours if they just floated along, less if they paddled and added speed.

Old Harry looked up to the north bank. Twisted junipers rooted in clefts in the soft rock. An ancient riverbed cut through the cliffs, dry now and had been for several thousand years.

Du Pré looked downriver. The south bank was green, so there was a pan or a floodplain there. Fence posts. Signs.

"Seems to me," said Old Harry, "fellers take off in the morning some upriver from where we put in, and along about noon or so they'd be here."

Harry stabbed his paddle in the water and swung the prow of the canoe to the south shore. Du Pré pulled a few strokes.

A bank undercut by the river collapsed and gouts of brown water shot up.

"Best not to hug them cutbanks too close," said Old Harry.

More of the bank sloughed off.

They went past the roiling muddy water and into slack and they pulled the canoe toward some cattails. There was a slough there, and probably a place to beach the canoe.

Harry steered the canoe into a hole in the cattails and Du Pré went over the side and pulled the canoe up onto the shore. Old Harry got out of his crouch, very stiffly.

"Don't get old," he said, "It don't *pay.*"

Du Pré looked round the meadow, grazed flat but with a lot of new growth coming up.

Water table must be at the bottom of the roots, he thought.

Man gets out of a canoe he wants to walk, get his legs loose again. A muscle in Du Pré's thigh quivered, about to cramp. Du Pré walked toward the cottonwoods and rubbed the twitching muscle.

A fallen tree had gone to silver wood, and by it there was a dead fire and a small rick of wood, driftwood sawn neatly into lengths.

Du Pré walked round the fire. Week old, maybe a little more. Footprints, men, good-sized. Wafflestomper boot soles. Winston cigarettes.

Du Pré found a place a bit smoother than the rest of the ground.

Set up a tent here, one of those that pop up.

"Camped here you think?" said Old Harry.

Du Pré nodded.

"Me, too," said Old Harry. "You know who them dead folks was? A couple of them en-vironmentalists, wrote articles with pictures.

121

Ol' Pruitt was scratchin' his head. Wonderin' what the hell they wanted with this part of the river."

Du Pré nodded.

"Talked to their editor he did," said Old Harry. "They was canoeing in the path of Lewis and Clark. They coulda put in sixty miles the day before I guess, which would about have them at Knife Creek. Roadhouse there right near the river, there is, Pruitt was gonna check, see if Rupe and Lee was there."

Du Pré looked at him.

"Which they was," said Old Harry, "had a few drinks, a hamburger, asked a bunch of questions."

Du Pré nodded.

"Pissant questions," said Old Harry, "like what-do-you-think-of-the-buffalo-commons? Ranchers don't think highly of bein' thrown off their land so a bunch of flatlanders can have theirselves a nice zoo."

"Somebody make a telephone call," said Du Pré.

"Spect so," said Old Harry. "Knew the river they did, said Rupe and Lee would camp about here. There ain't any good place for fifteen miles upriver there and they'd have passed that, maybe one o'clock."

"They were killed here," said Du Pré.

"Yup," said Old Harry. "About four hundred yards through the trees there the river got a high south bank. They'd a put the canoe in and they'd a been fifty yards from shore at most, and a hell of a lot less if they was being lazy."

Old Harry walked to a clump of trees. He kicked something. An empty Jack Daniel's whiskey bottle rolled out on the sand.

"I expect they was feelin' lazy," said Old Harry.

Du Pré nodded.

"Well," said Old Harry, " 'spect we could look at the place that the bushwhacker stood in when he shot 'em."

CHAPTER
22

Du Pré looked at the ground. The heavy rains had been caught by the trees and their leaves, and though a lot of water had softened the marks, they were still clear.

The killer had stood there, leaning against a tree trunk, and had shot the men as they went by, and then the current had carried the canoe on. The men would have fallen to the far side of the canoe and it would have gone over.

Over in three seconds. Five if it was a bolt-action rifle.

Du Pré walked a little to his right. There were tracks in the high grass. The shooter had bent, looking for the expended brass shell.

"Pretty good, don't ya think," said Old Harry. "Picked up the brass there. High-powered rifle, the slugs went on through those fellers and into the river there. So we ain't gonna even know what the gun was."

Du Pré looked over the river. A canyon, very narrow, cut through the land and down to the brown water.

They walked back to the canoe and launched it out into the river and they began to paddle hard. The pace picked up and the land swept past.

In an hour they saw the long benchland and the thick stands of cottonwoods where the pirogues lay and the movie company was camped.

Old Harry steered them into an odd rectangular slot in the bank, much like the hole dug for the foundation of a house, but it had been cut out long ago.

"Steamboat landing," said Old Harry, "them little sternweelers woulda put in here. Funny, even with the floods you can still see where they docked . . . more'n a hundred years ago."

Woodhawks settled by the rivers back then, lone men who cut wood for the boilers of the little steamboats. The captains left money if they took any wood. Cottonwood burned quickly but gave little heat. It took a lot of cottonwood to run the steamboats.

Du Pré stepped out on the bank and held the canoe while Old Harry got onto the shore, then they lifted the canoe and slid it up on the flat. They climbed up after it.

Maria came running to them, her long dark hair flying in the wind. She was dressed in a long suede dress, one that was elaborately beaded and fringed.

She had tall Pima moccasins on her feet.

"Pret' good thing walk across America in," she said. "I wonder what Sacajawea really wore."

Greasy buckskins, thought Du Pré, maybe some bright cloth. She had liked bright things, as a bird does.

"Lookin' might nice there, Missy," said Old Harry.

Maria bowed her head to the compliment.

"It's a movie," she said. "I feel silly."

Du Pré snorted.

"They are painting the canoe with fat and ocher," said Maria. "I think they will be sorry. It will get on everybody's clothes."

Du Pré laughed.

"I tell them to use paint," he said. "Use that fat we will have all the flies in Montana, here."

"You talk to them," said Maria. "I don't think paint will stick to the pirogues any more."

Du Pré shook his head.

He was hungry.

"Papa," said Maria, "the caterer is here, you can get good food at the big green tent, you are on their list."

"Beans," said Old Harry, "are a good thing."

They walked to the tent and when Du Pré could see into it he started.

There were a dozen young men wearing rough clothes, the leather uniform of the voyageurs. Unfringed buckskins, smeared black in places.

The Hudson's Bay Company, the Here Before Christ Company, who gave two of these suits to their employees each year.

A young woman with a clipboard came to them.

"Names?" she asked.

"Harry," said Old Harry.

"Your last name please?"

"McPartland," said Old Harry.

The young woman ran down her list.

"You aren't on here sir," she said.

"He is with me," said Du Pré.

"Your name?" she asked.

"Gabriel Du Pré," said Du Pré.

"Oh, yes, Mr. Du Pré," said the young woman, "you and your guest may just go through the line."

Harry and Du Pré got trays and they went down the short counter. The food was ordinary fare, meat loaf and mashed potatoes and green beans.

"Thought these damned Californians et roots and bark," said Old Harry, putting his tray down on a table. Du Pré set his down and he went and got glasses of iced tea for them.

Samantha Smythe came in, looking harried, and she saw Du Pré and hustled over to him.

"They are having trouble with the pirogues," she said. "I told them I would ask you if I saw you."

Du Pré nodded. He sighed and he got up and he went out rolling a smoke as he walked. A passing crewman glared at him.

No smoking area, keep off the grass, thought Du Pré.

Du Pré found some crew members at the river, trying to drag the red pirogue upstream from the bank.

The lines to the log boat were run through a ring on the prow.

"Du Pré," said Trey Binder, "what are we doing wrong?"

Du Pré laughed.

"You got to get in the water," he said, "you got to wade."

The crew members looked at each other.

"Shit," said one young man.

Yah, they say that about every other word from Saint Louis to the Pacific. Not so much on the way back, they are floating down with the current. Say shit a whole lot, the trip up.

"Thanks," Trey Binder whispered to Du Pré. "I knew that but I thought it was better that they hear it from you."

"Let's walk through it," said Binder to the crew. He stood on the bank.

The crew members waded out into the river, holding the lines in their hands.

"Put the ropes over your right shoulders," said Trey Binder, "and walk upstream."

The heavy pirogue wallowed in the current, tugging at the ends of the lines.

One of the crew members suddenly sank out of sight.

His head bobbed back up.

"What is that," said Trey Binder, "a hole?"

Du Pré shook his head.

"Quicksand," he said. "Got a spring coming up under the river there."

"Quicksand?" said Binder, looking horrified.

126

Du Pré nodded.

"Lewis and Clark they have quicksand a lot," said Du Pré.

The crew was stopped dead.

"What do they do?" said Binder.

"Go out farther in the current," said Du Pré. "No quicksand out there."

"Go out farther!" Binder shouted.

The crewmen in the water looked at him.

"Shit, Trey," said one, "we'll be up to our *necks*."

"No help for it," said Trey Binder.

The crewmen looked at each other.

They moved farther out into the river, and their bodies appeared.

The water was shallow there.

"I'll be damned," said Binder

"See that line on the water there?" asked Du Pré, pointing.

Binder squinted.

"That is where they want to walk," said Du Pré

"I think that I see it," said Binder.

One of the crew members screamed.

He pushed at something in the water.

"Christ," the man said, "it was a sunken log."

"You all right?" Binder asked.

"Yeah."

The crew began to pull the pirogue upstream. The big log boat waffled back and forth.

"This is going to be hard with a load of people in it," said one of the crewmen.

"Sure," said another, "but we won't be pulling it then."

"Har de har har," said a voice behind Du Pré and Binder.

One of the actors dressed in the buckskins stood there.

Du Pré grinned at him.

The actor looked up to heaven and rolled his eyes.

CHAPTER
23

"Kit was up the river there lookin' for a horse," said Old Harry, "Found a feller trespassin' and the feller says he knows you. Kit ain't sure, but 'fore he calls the sheriff you might drive on over see about it."

Du Pré nodded.

He got in his cruiser and drove on the track that led up to the crest of the old river edge. The Missouri had cut down through the country a lot in ten thousand years.

He went about four miles, and then he saw Kit's big red four-wheel pickup down by the water. There was a man standing near the shore, white-haired and leaning on a cane.

Du Pré sighed and wallowed down a steep set of ruts and across the pasture, cropped short by the horse herd.

Bill Rupe waved once as Du Pré pulled up.

Kit was leaning against the grille of his pickup.

"You know him?" he said.

Du Pré nodded.

"He is the father, one of the men we found," said Du Pré.

Kit looked sharply at Du Pré.

"Jack Rupe was his son," said Du Pré.

Kit looked at the old man.

"Why the hell didn't you say so, mister?" he said.

Rupe shrugged.

"I'm sure sorry, sir," said Kit. He threw up his hands and he got in his pickup and he backed and turned and drove off.

"I just wanted to see where my son was when he died," said Rupe. "I didn't mean to cause trouble."

Du Pré shrugged.

Sometimes I go, look at the railroad crossing where Papa and Mama die, he thought, I get this feeling, want to go and see it. Right after there was lots of broken glass. Not so much now.

"What you come down in?" said Du Pré.

"Canoe," said Rupe. He pointed with his cane.

Du Pré looked and couldn't see it for a moment. It was so carefully painted with dull marsh colors it blended with the plants.

Du Pré heard horse hooves, and he turned and saw two riders. One was Kelly Van Der Meer, the other Maria.

A third rider lagged way behind the women.

Poor Ben Burke, trying to keep up with horsefolk who had been in the saddle before they could walk.

Maria waved, and they swerved and came down the hill flat out, and they slowed and stopped only at the last moment.

Kelly and Maria were laughing.

Ben, he look like he is fucking a hummock, thought Du Pré. He looked at Maria and grinned.

"You gonna kill your boyfriend there?" he said.

"Got to cull them, Papa," said Maria. "You know, the fit survive."

Du Pré laughed.

Kelly Van Der Meer got down from her big stud horse and began to walk him round a little.

129

She was smiling. Du Pré had never seen any expression on her face.

"My daughter Maria," said Du Pre to Rupe.

"Bill Rupe," said Rupe. He took off his worn old hat.

Maria nodded.

"That is my friend Kelly," she said.

Kelly Van Der Meer looked coolly at Rupe.

"Canoe yours?" she said.

"Yes," said Rupe.

Kelly nodded, and she mounted and rode off without looking back.

"She don't like strangers," said Maria.

"I wouldn't think so," said Rupe.

"It was his son we found," said Du Pré. "He came to see where Jack died."

Maria's face softened and she shook her head.

"I am so sorry," she said.

"Thank you," said Rupe.

"How you are riding with her?" said Du Pré.

"Hah!" said Maria. "She is good, but no rider never gets thrown. That stud toss her when she is near us, and I caught him and took him back to her. She thanked me, and I said I would like to ride."

Du Pré laughed.

Maria turned. Kelly was riding toward poor Ben, who was having trouble with his horse.

"She is awful angry, Papa," she said. "She is mad, especially at her father, thinks he could have held on awhile longer, didn't have to sell out."

"Bart pretty good guy to sell to," said Du Pré.

"You been a princess, Papa," said Maria, "hard to find yourself a servant. She feels like that."

"You talk with her more maybe?" said Du Pré.

Maria nodded.

"I am very sorry for your son," said Maria.

"A word?" said Rupe, looking at Maria.

Maria raised her eyebrows.

"Sure," she said.

"Jack and Davis were doing a long book on the Missouri," said Rupe. "They thought the ranchers here were getting a raw deal. The propaganda campaign the enviros have waged against the ranchers was terrible. Jack and Davis wanted to do something about that. They respected these people."

Maria nodded.

"Wrong people got killed," she said.

"Yes," said Rupe, "they did."

Maria smiled once and turned her horse and rode away, toward Kelly and Ben, up on the high banks.

"What do you think, Mr. Du Pré?" said Rupe.

Du Pré shrugged.

"I don't know anything yet, Mr. Rupe," said Du Pré.

"Jack quit working for the Audubon people, for ethical reasons, he said," said Rupe.

Du Pré nodded.

"I am sorry," Rupe said. "I want whoever did this to know. That is all I want. I don't care if they are tried and convicted. I just want them to know what they have done."

Du Pré rolled a smoke.

"Could you help me shove off?" said Rupe. "My leg . . ."

Rupe began to walk down a path that led to the brown water.

He had to turn round and back down a drop of a couple of feet, and then he went on, toward the patched old canoe drawn up on the mudbank. The mud was old and solid, and Du Pré could see deer tracks in it, just a couple of inches deep.

Rupe clambered into the canoe and stretched his stiff leg out in front.

Du Pré looked at the gear, the faded boat bags with the stencils, the worn dry-bag that would have the sleeping bag in it, the small cooler, the big water jug.

The stuff a man who had spent thousands of nights sleeping under the stars would own.

"Please remember that," said Rupe. "I don't want revenge. I want my son back and that cannot be. I don't care about the damn law."

Du Pré nodded.

"Here," said Rupe. "Please take this, and if you find who did it, please give it to them."

He tossed a plastic bag at Du Pré.

There was a tiny cassette in it.

Du Pré put it in his shirt pocket.

"Thanks, Du Pré," said Bill Rupe.

"You could get out here," said Du Pré. "I strap your canoe, my car, drive you where you want to go."

Rupe laughed.

"Many thanks," he said, "but a shuttle service will have my Rover for me, downstream in four days, at Beck's Landing. I want to be here. It is a fine old river, Mr. Du Pré, and will be here, a living creature, long after we have long been forgotten. So I find comfort in that."

Du Pré nodded.

Rupe pulled his paddle in.

Du Pré grabbed the bow and he lifted and shoved hard and the canoe went out in the water.

Rupe turned it deftly and then he dug his paddle in and pulled the canoe out into the current.

When he was where he wished to be he turned and waved at Du Pré.

Du Pré waved back.

Over seventy, crippled, brave man Du Pré thought.

Rupe went out of sight behind a stand of cottonwoods.

Du Pré turned.

Maria and Ben were riding toward him.

Kelly had gone.

CHAPTER
24

Maria and John Thomas Tipton and Jason Parks walked through the meadow, men in buckskins filing along behind. Maria carried a bundle that held a swathed doll.

Cameras ran along tracks, ahead of the actors.

"Cut!" yelled Trey Binder. Some one clapped a small blackboard and the gaggle of people stopped and relaxed.

Some of the expedition took out packages of cigarettes and lit them.

"Very good, people," said Binder, but we need to try this one more time."

Du Pré shook his head.

That makes fifteen times they do this, he thought, for maybe twenty seconds of the movie. Maybe they be done by the time Maria is a hundred.

Du Pré walked away, back down toward the camp he shared with Old Harry and Jason Parks, who had gracefully thanked Sam

Smythe for the elaborate motor home and then used it only to take showers. Du Pré had a key so he could bathe there, too.

Old Harry was asleep in the shade, lying atop his bedroll. Lefty was curled up under Old Harry's pickup, snoring loudly. He woke when Du Pré got near, looked at him for a moment, farted, and went back to sleep.

"Got a smoke fer an old feller," said Harry, not opening his eyes.

Du Pré pulled out his tobacco and papers and he made two and he lit them and he handed one to Harry, who had sat up.

Harry yawned.

"How's the movie goin'?" he said.

"Over and over," said Du Pré, "they do this scene and that scene some from the beginning of the story some from the end, it is funny."

"Funny?" said Harry.

"You see a movie it is a story," said Du Pré, "made up out of bits. It is pret' hard work."

"Nah," said Harry, blowing out blue smoke, "it just takes a lot of time."

Du Pré had left in the morning before Harry had gotten back from wherever it was he had been last night.

"That other crew is supposed to be upriver tomorrow," said Harry. "A mob the size of this one. County's about doubled in population. They're on state land up there, and I don't envy 'em. That's a funny piece of country."

Du Pré crouched on his haunches and looked at Harry.

"Bad water," said Harry. "Lots of it. I expect they will get sick some of them. That little bastard Wally Will-yums is there, I hear, pissing about everybody off."

Du Pré laughed.

"Claims that you set his boat on fire," said Old Harry. "Shame on you, and kin I shake your hand?"

Du Pré stood up. He went to a tree and sat against it, in the shade.

"They's throwin' a lot of money around," said Old Harry, "awful lot of money. Compared to what Binder can offer. Big Hollywood outfit I guess. Moving in a whole tent city, I'm told, even a water plant on wheels."

Du Pré looked off through the cottonwoods. Fluff danced in the little winds, and a blue jay flew past, screeching.

"Think maybe somebody's tryin' to bust this up," said Harry.

Du Pré looked at him.

"Sheriff said they got a call complainin' about *pollution* this bunch is doin'. Said that some state pollution inspectors was coming to look things over. And they tried to buy the bar from T J. Offered her about five times what that little old shack is worth. Liquor license and all."

Du Pré looked at Harry.

"Seems they want to be the only movie or somethin'," said Old Harry.

Du Pré waited.

"Got enough money you can about do anything I guess," said Harry.

Du Pré nodded.

"What about that Bart feller, if you don't mind tellin' me. He's rich I hear. Digs holes in the ground, which is an odd habit for a rich man."

Du Pré laughed.

"Bart he is rich, good man," he said, "good friend. He did not have a happy life, does the best he can."

Old Harry nodded. He stood up.

"Got a few errands to run," he said. "Be back about sundown. Now, the river's closed for these movies to get made which ain't the same thing as them not havin' boats on 'em."

Du Pré looked at Harry, who was looking down at Lefty, who was looking off upriver.

They waited a few minutes and then Du Pré heard the sound of boat motors, high and yapping.

"Well," said Harry, "I expect you can find out what the hell that is. I got to go."

Lefty went to the pickup, jumped through the window on the passenger side, and took up his spot, riding shotgun.

Old Harry drove off.

Du Pré wandered down to the river. A few branches floated by. It was raining in the mountains. The water was higher than it had been yesterday.

A boat came down the river, in the center channel.

Du Pré looked hard.

Wally Williams was standing at the helm of the sportfishing boat. He saw Du Pré, and he cut the engines back and moved toward the shore.

Du Pré waited.

Wally Williams nosed the boat into the shallow water, and when it began to ground he jumped out, caught a line, carried it to the shore, and tied it to a tree.

"Just stopped by to see how they were doing," he said, moving past Du Pré.

Du Pré shot out a hand and grabbed Williams's shoulder.

"No," he said, "you go on now."

"I have to talk to Trey Binder," said Williams. He was smirking.

Du Pré just looked at him.

"I'm trying to *help*," said Williams.

Du Pré shook his head.

"They are ver' busy," said Du Pré. "Now, this river it is closed. You go on, get out of it."

"I have special permission," said Williams.

Du Pré looked at the boat. It still had some fire damage visible on it, but the new work had been done well, and quickly.

Du Pré heard a pickup behind him, grinding slowly over the rough ground hidden by the tall grass.

Kit Van Der Meer and Kelly.

They drove up to Du Pré and Williams.

Van Der Meer got out and walked slowly over.

"What," he said, "is this pompous little bastard doing here?"

"He is leaving," said Du Pré.

136

"Mister," said Van Der Meer, looking hard at Williams, "the damn river is closed, and you will stay off my land."

"I don't believe it is yours anymore," said Williams. "I need to see the movie director Trey Binder."

Kelly had gotten out of the pickup and was leaning on the side. She looked much like her mother, very pretty, with hard blue eyes.

"It's important," said Williams.

"If you aren't off this property in two minutes I will arrest you and dump you in the back of my truck and deliver you to the sheriff," said Van Der Meer, "and it's a bumpy ride."

Williams looked at Du Pré and at Van Der Meer.

He shrugged and returned to his boat. He waded out and climbed in and he started the motors and backed off. When he had swung the boat around he goosed the engines and roared off upriver.

"What a little prick," said Van Der Meer.

Du Pré nodded.

"I am gonna call the BLM," said Kit. "That little shit shouldn't be on the damn river in that thing."

Van Der Meer and Kelly got back in the pickup and drove away.

Kelly looked back once, and then they were gone.

Du Pré walked down to the bank. Williams was just going out of sight up the river.

Some geese flew down from the sky and splashed into the river, honking and flaring their wings.

Du Pré rolled a smoke.

Kelly Van Der Meer, Du Pré thought. Ver' angry young woman.

Her land, in her heart.

Old Harry says there is nothing much on the north side of the river.

She looks toward those trees, once.

A little too long.

CHAPTER 25

After lunch Trey Binder moved the cameras and crew five miles up the riverbank, saying that the actors should follow about 4 P.M. They would try for some river footage and walking footage in the afternoon light.

Maria was exhausted. The leather clothes she was wearing were heavy and hot, and the endless repetitions broken only by standing around in the sun had gone on for eight hours.

She went off with Ben to bathe and rest for a time.

Du Pré went with the crew to look at the new site. There were stakes on the ground by the river, and tendrils of red surveyor's tape fluttering from their tops. People with clipboards ran back and forth.

Du Pré walked to the riverbank and looked down at the Missouri. A bleach bottle floated past, and a glob of yellow goop. Some Styrofoam cups. A boat cushion.

A small plane droned down from the sky and passed close overhead.

Du Pré stared at the riverbank. There was a path up from a long shelf of yellow rock, a well-worn one, with footholds dug in a band of rock three feet thick.

Good spot to get out. The water off the bank was deep downstream from the shelf of rock, which plunged into the river.

Du Pré rolled a cigarette and smoked.

They come up here lining that pirogue, maybe camp here.

Du Pré wandered off toward a line of green alders and willows, the tops of the trees sticking up through the prairie grass.

A deep cut down through the earth opened beneath Du Pré, and water glinted at the bottom. Du Pré walked up it, toward a round hill that had a ledge of earth, shaped like the toe of a boot, sticking out toward the river.

The little cut had been carved by a large spring that flowed out of a fracture in the mother rock. There was a good flow, and over time it had worn away the rock, worn away the earth below. It was far from the slackwater and the sloughs so mosquitoes would not be so bad there.

Good place to camp, good clean water, wood near, breeze carry away the bugs.

Du Pré heard boat engines, and he looked downstream. Some of the crew were towing the red and the white pirogues upstream, on lines. The heavy wooden boats wallowed in the current, their prows swinging from side to side. The little motorboats were struggling to haul the pirogues, and then the current slackened and they picked up speed.

Du Pré found a piece of shade by a rock and some grassy earth to lie on and he lay down and fell asleep.

He woke up with a start.

Maria was standing there, dressed in her beaded and fringed buckskins. She bent over.

"Papa," she said. "Papa, it is here." She was whispering.

Du Pré squinted and shook his head. He glanced at the sun. He had slept for two hours.

"What?" he said. He sat up, scratched his neck, and then he got to his feet.

"The sweat lodge, when I sang with Benetsee," said Maria. "I saw that little hill there, saw that piece of earth in front. We got to dig there."

Du Pré looked where she was pointing.

The grass grew right down the gently sloping front of the ledge.

"Oh," said Du Pré.

"Benetsee said I have to dig right away," said Maria, "or it will disappear."

"Mean I dig," said Du Pré.

"I got to make a movie," said Maria.

"People!" Trey Binder yelled. "Places!"

Du Pré sighed. He went to his cruiser and he got a shovel out of the trunk and he walked back to the little ledge of earth, very like a coffer dam.

Du Pré squatted and stared at the front face of the grassy boot toe.

He looked round.

Good place. Drains good, gets just enough water keep the grass growing, not so much it will flood.

What the hell they leave here?

Du Pré took the shovel and jammed it into the earth. The grass roots were tight and tough, and it took a moment to wedge out a clod of earth.

Du Pré cut a line across the front of the odd mound. He kept it about three feet up, gouging a furrow, then cutting down both sides. Then he made three vertical cuts and began to peel away the sod. Down about six inches the roots thinned enough so he could cut them easily with jabs of the shovel.

The sod peeled away.

Du Pré put the shovel in the earth, then he went back to the cruiser, got the lug wrench, and used the chisel end to probe in the soil.

140

There was nothing in the middle or on the left side, but when he poked it into the right the soil got softer.

Du Pré dug two feet into the wall.

The earth was bright orange, and he could see hairs in the dirt.

"Son of a bitch," said Du Pré.

Cover the front of the cache with a buffalo robe, put the soil over that, put the cut turf back. Cut it in a circle like a bathtub plug.

Du Pré shoveled, and suddenly he saw air, a blank, nothing.

He pulled shovelfuls of earth away.

He went to the cruiser and he got a flashlight and looked in.

A smell of rot and soil wafted out of the cache.

Du Pré cut more earth away. He shined the light inside. There was a small barrel-shaped object and some rotted boxes of rawhide.

Du Pré reached in and pulled at the little barrel, about the size of a three-pound coffee can. It popped away from the earth and rolled to him; it was surprisingly heavy. He wiped dirt away from it. It was crusted with yellow soil.

Du Pré took his knife and scraped.

Dull metal gleamed. The knife had cut it.

Lead.

They had gunpowder in lead cans, cut the tops away, take out the powder, melt the lead down for rifle balls.

Du Pré glanced back at the movie crew. They were hard at work a quarter mile away.

He reached in and grabbed at one of the rotted rawhide boxes, which crumbled. Old oilskins wrapping something.

Du Pré used the hook end of the lug wrench to pull things to him. When he got something out he carried it to the trunk of his cruiser. The barrel weighed perhaps seventy pounds. The other items were dirty and crusted, knives and hatchets, trade goods probably.

The last thing Du Pré could see was a flat packet that stubbornly clung to the earth until he reached the shovel in and pried it up. It was light, and the oilskins, though rotted, had been wrapped many times around whatever it had in it.

Du Pré looked carefully in the hole, then put the sod back. It slumped some, but in a few seasons it would heal the cuts in the earth.

Du Pré scraped dirt away from the flat oilskin packet.

Somebody leave this here, Du Pré thought, somebody cache this, probably trappers. Country has thousands of caches never got found again.

Us Métis we got a song about that, too.

Du Pré carefully cut the old oilskins away, and he found the lower layers were in pretty good shape. A white centipede crawled out of a fold and writhed off. Du Pré shook it out on the ground.

Du Pré cut away the last layer of rotted oilskin, and he found another thick with wax, still reddish.

The package was perhaps a foot long and a bit less than that wide.

Du Pré scraped away the wax, and found parchment.

He carefully cut the reddish crumbly wax away, lifted the corner of the parchment with his knife point, and then peeled it off.

More wax, but a thinner coat.

A book. The leather it had been bound with was still flexible, but it cracked when Du Pré bent it.

Du Pré carefully opened the book. The first page was stuck to the cover, but not the second. The script was strange and much whorled and elaborated.

". . . musketors terrible last 3 days . . ."

Son of a bitch, thought Du Pré.

Trappers don't leave a book bitching about the mosquitoes. Most can't read or write, them people. Why they need to?

Benetsee say this was here.

It is.

Lewis and Clark they leave this here and they never come back. Never find it again. Maybe float past it in the night, don't recognize this place, coming back down.

Du Pré went to the river to wash his hands.

CHAPTER
28

"Oh God," said Bart.

Du Pré grinned, and he lifted his whiskey and water.

"No shit," said T J. She looked at Du Pré. "Right down by the river."

"I maybe think so," said Du Pré. "Somebody maybe put it there for a joke, you know."

"A hoax?" said Bart.

Du Pré nodded. Bullshit a hoax, Maria see that in the sweat lodge with Benetsee, so it is not a joke.

"There is going to be a fearful great stink," said Bart.

Du Pré shrugged.

"We could have it authenticated," said Bart.

Du Pré nodded.

"Am I supposed to keep this a secret, Du Pré?" asked T J.

Du Pré shrugged.

"Naw," said Bart. "If Du Pré wanted it a secret, he wouldn't have told anybody. The son of a bitch is gonna set up Wally Williams with this is what he is gonna do."

"Him?" said T J. "I hate watching you pick on that dwarf. I would a lot rather watch you kill him. Christ what a pompous moron."

"Yah," said Du Pré.

"I'll call Foote," said Bart. He went out to his cruiser, where he kept the cell phone he hated but had to use from time to time anyway.

"I suppose he would own it," said T J, "since I hear he owns the Carbonado."

Du Pré shook his head.

"It is Maria's," he said, "she knew where it was."

"How?" said T J.

Du Pré shrugged.

"I expect that this will bring a lot of folks here," said T J. "I better add a couple of wings and a second story." She looked around the worn comfortable roadhouse.

"They go away," said Du Pré. "This country don't like too many people in it, you know."

"Used to was," said T J. "A lot of things used to was."

Du Pré rolled a cigarette and lit it. T J took his glass and she held it up and he nodded.

"Mighty fine music you play there, Du Pré," said T J. "I don't suppose that after all this hootin' and hollerin' dies down you'd come back and play for us, now would you?"

"Sure," said Du Pré. "You like my ugly band, too?"

"A lot. You know that bass player? My son wants to be a rock and roll bass player, and every time he's around Bassman looks my kid up and shows him things, tells him to study this or that."

Du Pré nodded. Bassman, he blow a lot of dope, he do this, and sometimes that, but he is a good guy. Get in trouble, you find out how good he is.

I know that.

144

Bart came back in, laughing.

Du Pré looked at him.

"He said," said Bart, "to shoot you and bury you and this stuff in the same hole. That was his best legal advice."

Du Pré nodded.

"But he will call back. He thinks it is important to keep the whereabouts of these artifacts unknown, and not to tell anyone where they are. He said you would know what he meant."

Du Pré nodded.

"As soon as he can get someone here, they will take a look," said Bart. "Down to the crossroads at midnight, as it were."

Du Pré nodded.

It was coming on dark outside, and the movie crew was still at it somewhere. The door opened and Buck Keifer came in, along with the smell of coming rain.

"Heard you found the only lost cache of Lewis and Clark stuff, Du Pré," said Buck.

Du Pré nodded.

"Where'd you hear that?" said T J, looking shocked.

"Ya called my wife not fifteen minutes ago, T J," said Buck. "Now would you get me a beer and quit battin' your baby blues so much. It makes me sneeze."

"Buck," said T J, "people will think I am a gossip."

"They're gonna think yer a murderer you don't get me my damn beer," said Buck, "as it is hot out there I tell ya and I am near dead of thirst."

T J popped open a can of Bud and slid it over to him.

"So it really looks like they left it there?" said Buck, looking at Du Pré.

Du Pré nodded.

"How can you be sure?" said Buck.

"Things that are in it, are not from trappers," said Du Pré. "They would leave pelts and maybe some pemmican, the trip back home. Not lead and powder though."

Keifer nodded.

"Should raise some dust," he said.

Bart's cell phone chirred. Bart looked at the thing with loathing, and then he opened it and spoke and he walked back outside.

"That should about do it," said Buck. He was looking down into his beer can.

The door opened and a few of the movie crew members came in, all laughing. A long day's work over, and now it was time to relax.

Du Pré finished his drink and he went outside and he saw Maria and Ben drive in. Maria was in jeans and a soft white shirt, and her gold skin and black hair were bright.

Du Pré waited while they got out.

"Papa!" said Maria. "What is it you found?"

Du Pré grinned. He led them to his old cruiser, lifted the trunk lid, and pointed at the things, still crusted with yellow-gray earth. He tapped the little lead barrel.

"They have their gunpowder in this," he said, "seal it up and then they can melt the can down for bullets, them."

Maria touched it. Du Pré lifted up the book. Maria took it gently and she opened it and stared a long time at the page.

". . . Cruzatte fiddled in the camp and we had joy of the music . . . days long and hot . . . still no mountains . . ." she said. "This is hard to read, ver' hard."

Ben Burke looked stunned.

"These were our people with them," said Maria.

"LaBiche, LePage, Cruzatte, Charbonneau," said Du Pré, "all of them in your blood."

"Charbonneau?" said Ben. "The interpreter, the husband of Sacajawea?"

Du Pré nodded.

"His little son, Clark call him Pomp, he live a long time, dies maybe 1870. My father, Catfoot, he take me to Canada, I meet a very old woman who knew that Jean-Baptiste Charbonneau, when he was ver' old."

Long time gone.

Ben smiled.

"Wonderful," he said.

Maria was still staring at the page.

"Papa," she said, "I think this says that . . ." and she tugged at the page that was stuck to the cover. It came free, rather easily.

A list. A bill of lading.

Maria read it, slowly.

"Keg of powder, knives, hatchets, astrolabe," said Maria. "Also some of the flutes Cruzatte made."

Du Pré looked at her.

"They rot away," he said.

"Maybe not."

Other people from the movie crew were arriving. Du Pré put the book back in the trunk of the cruiser and shut the lid.

"Long time gone," he said. "Now there will be many people who will all want these things, but they are yours, Maria."

Maria nodded.

"Yah," she said.

"Scholars will want these," said Ben, looking troubled.

"Maybe they get to look at them," said Maria, "maybe not, depends."

Du Pré laughed.

"It won't be long before this gets out," said Ben.

Du Pré nodded.

"The government will probably sue," said Ben. "After all it was an expedition financed by them."

Du Pré shrugged.

"Maria sees it, in her vision," said Du Pré, "so it is hers."

He looked out at the road.

There were a lot of cars coming.

CHAPTER
27

"Meriwether Lewis," said the man with the mask. "If you had sent me a photocopy of the page I could have told you."

Du Pré and Bart and the masked man were standing near a gravel pile on a back road. The book Du Pré had dug out of the ground lay on the hood of his cruiser.

"I'm sorry," said Bart, "it's a long way to bring you for a few minutes' work."

"Oh, no, no," said the man in the mask, "I am delighted. Delighted. I hope to be able to examine this all in detail someday. I would love to. So would about four thousand other scholars, any one of whom would instantly be of note if they got their hands on this stuff. If I had a gun, I would shoot you both and be gone. I do not have a gun. Matter of fact, your lawyer had the pilot search me and my luggage before I got on the plane. That fellow Foote thinks of everything."

"Almost," said Bart.

"Do you have any idea of the value of what you have here?" said the man in the mask. "After Lewis and Clark and their men returned there was some hoopla, but it died, and in time the specimens they had gathered were dumped at sea. The journals survived. Lewis committed suicide not long after their return. Clark went on from strength to strength. But what you have here is priceless. The artifacts were with the expedition, though since you haven't got a doctorate and you haven't got a tenured professorship, there will be quarrels unto the end of time in the matter of their authenticity."

Du Pré laughed.

"Laugh, Mr. Du Pré," said the man in the mask. "I am wearing this ridiculous garb because I wish to be able to deny ever having been here or ever having seen this stuff. Word got out I did this my dear colleagues would rend me into dog kibble and piss on the pile. They would nail my hide to several walls several miles apart."

"What they mad at?" said Du Pré.

"You have to understand," said the man in the mask, "that we college professors are a bitter and vicious lot. We are failures, or we would be doing something other than pitiably attempting to install learning in the tiny brains of teenyboppers. We practically faint if we are able to get published in a learned journal. We spend our lives deep in the study of matters which no one else gives a shit about. We squabble over nothing whatever. If I had any balls, I would go deal dope or do *something* interesting."

Du Pré and Bart laughed.

"Get this stuff someplace that no one knows about," said the man in the mask, "because you are going to have slavering scholars all over you and some of them will be backed by a great deal of money. For one thing, I would expect that one or another of these terrifying infants who were smart enough to drop out of college and now are worth several billion dollars, due to some mysterious company which does something on the Internet, which I do not understand and neither do you and we are about as useless as any other extinct species—one of those little bastards will hire goons to obtain this journal. It is the only one. Then the little prick can build a museum around it and carve his or her name in stone, like any other robber baron."

Bart grinned.

"I am not kidding," said the man in the mask. "And now if you do not mind I would like to be flown home forthwith so that I may, as the late unlamented Richard Nixon was fond of saying, *maintain deniability*. If anyone asks, I was at the bedside of my beloved great-aunt, who croaked."

"Thanks," said Bart.

"Thank *you*, Mr. Fascelli," said the man in the mask, "and your friend Mr. Du Pré. I have seen the Grail and that will be enough. I hope to make it to my pension and doddering old farthood, and if anyone should find out I was here, I will not. My fellow faculty members will turn on me like so many rabid wolves, and they will all *chew*."

"That bad?" said Du Pré.

"Worse, Mr. Du Pré," said the man in the mask, "than you can imagine. America could shoot us all and be better off, and we know it."

Du Pré roared.

Bart and the man in the mask got into Bart's cruiser and they left.

Du Pré waved. The man in the mask looked back once and waved, too.

Du Pré looked at the sun. He got in his car and started it and he turned around and roared off toward the north as soon as he came to pavement and then he settled down and had a pull from his flask and a smoke.

The speedometer said 120.

So this stuff was set there by Lewis or Clark. Probably to pick it up on the way back down the river. But they missed the place. Big country some looks like everywhere else.

We got a song about caches, too. Most of them are lost, like hearts. *Let me in, Helene . . .*

150

Du Pré passed three or four cars on the asphalt, and then he saw the Wolf Mountains rising to the north and east. He turned on the east–west highway and roared on, passing a couple ranch trucks and one huge motor home wallowing along in the winds.

Du Pré turned off on the back road that led toward the bench-lands and to Benetsee's. He turned up the rutted track and bumped along to the cabin.

The old man and Pelon were sitting out in back, smoking and drinking screwtop wine.

Benetsee looked up when Du Pré came near. He grinned, his old brown stubs of teeth showing.

"You find him," said Benetsee, "now you try to keep him."

Du Pré nodded.

Benetsee and Pelon got up and followed Du Pré to his cruiser, where Du Pré opened the trunk and they all looked in. The old crusted packages sat there, mysteries in the earth.

"Long time gone," said Benetsee. "Them Lewis, Clark, they come through here, long time gone. Hee. Plenty people want this stuff."

Du Pré nodded.

Benetsee reached in and he grabbed a bundle and hefted it and he grabbed another. Pelon got the little lead barrel, and Du Pré the book and the last two bundles. They walked back behind the cabin. Benetsee looked around. He nodded, then went back in the grove of cottonwoods that hugged the stream. One had blown down long ago and gone to silver wood, the bark had sloughed off and it was rotting in from the ends, chalky chips of reddish rot sat in a pile on the grass. Some mushrooms grew at the sides of the heap.

Benetsee set down the bundles and he took his knife from its sheath and walked along the log, whistling, and then he stabbed the blade into the trunk and he twisted it and the side of the log broke away. Benetsee lifted the piece, six feet or so long and a couple wide, and he set it to the side.

The log was hollow. It had rotted while standing and left this cache hole in its center.

They piled the goods and the book in the dry hole and Benet-see put the piece of wood back. He slapped it with his hand.

It looked like an old log.

"Maybe people come search for that," said Du Pré.

Benetsee grinned.

"They don't find it," he said. "It belongs to that Maria, yes?"

Du Pré nodded.

"Grandfathers and grandmothers want her to have it," said Benetsee, "so we see that she does."

"If that stuff is real," said Pelon, "we will have lawyers in packs howling around here."

Pelon had had another life before Benetsee had plucked him away.

"Who are they?" said Benetsee. "They talk better than the old ones?"

Du Pré and Benetsee and Pelon laughed.

"You go," said Benetsee, "you go back, they are waiting for you there."

Du Pré nodded.

"This stuff," said Benetsee, "it will not be here long but Maria can find it anytime that she wants to."

Du Pré nodded.

"You find that good man Rupe's son," said Benetsee. "Yes?"

"Both of them," said Du Pré. "Both shot dead."

Benetsee looked away to the south.

"Ver' sad," he said. He walked away, shaking his head.

Pelon looked at Du Pré.

"You are going?" said Du Pré.

Pelon nodded.

Du Pré took some tobacco and money from his pocket. He handed it to Pelon, who put it in his.

Du Pré left, and he drove back south.

CHAPTER
28

"Christ," said Old Harry. "Ya happy now? Kick up a stink worse'n a skunk at a christening. Sheriff's phone lines just melted down. All sorts of people screaming. Keep yer eye on the horizon, there, all five hundred TV channels and half the newspapers in America will be comin' over it in about ten minutes."

Du Pré shrugged.

"Ya coulda *left* it there," said Old Harry, "gone back to . . . North Dakota, buried it there. I hear they are real lonely in North Dakota and would like more people to come there. That's what I hear anyway. Lewis and Clark done went through North Dakota, and we don't got to be so selfish, now do we?"

Du Pré shrugged.

"You son of a bitch," said Old Harry. "It's bad enough we got all these idiots movin' here with their golf clubs and fly rods without you got to give more of 'em an excuse."

"They go to the mountains," said Du Pré. "How close is the nearest golf course, huh?"

"Great Falls," said Old Harry. "I hear that anyway."

Old Harry was at their camp, pacing around his pickup truck and looking out on the Missouri River.

The film crew was working upriver, getting shots of Maria and Jason Parks and John Thomas Tipton standing nobly in the front of the big red pirogue, which put the bow down and spoiled the line against the water. Trey Binder had the crew load the back end with stones to straighten things up. Du Pré had got tired of watching it.

"Maybe it not be that bad," said Du Pré.

"It's gonna be hell," said Old Harry. "My right knee aches, which tells me the weather's changing."

A helicopter came over the bluffs to the west, dipped down toward the river, and went out of sight behind the trees on the banks.

"Here they are," said Old Harry. "Dan Rather is probably in that there helicopter."

Whock whack whock whack whock.

The helicopter rose up again and flew straight toward Du Pré and Old Harry.

Another helicopter came from the south. The side door was open and a man sat in the doorway pointing a camera.

"North Dakota," said Old Harry, "coulda used this."

Du Pré shrugged. He got into his old cruiser and backed around and he drove off up the hill and over the flat to the ranch gate. He saw a couple of cars parked there, ones with dish antennae on their trunks.

Du Pré drove past them and watched in his rearview mirror as they turned round and came after him.

Du Pré punched the accelerator and the old cruiser screamed as it got up speed.

By the time that he got to the roadhouse his pursuers were so far back in the dust he couldn't see them anymore.

There were several brand-new cars in front of the roadhouse. Some SUVs.

Du Pré went in, walked up to the bar, and sat down. Several groups of people were at one or another table, all drinking and laughing.

"If they knew you was here," hissed Buck Keifer, "they'd be on ya like stink on shit."

Du Pré nodded.

T J pushed a tall whiskey and water over the bartop. Du Pré put down a bill and T J went off to take another order.

Du Pré looked at the newspeople. They were young and dressed like city folks do when they go to the outdoors. One young woman took a cell phone from her pocket and she opened it and listened a moment and then she went to the front door and looked out and she turned and looked at Du Pré. She said something into the phone and shut it and then she marched over.

"You found the stuff?" she said. "You left my buddies in the dirt, there, actually the ditch. Meredith Paul, ABC News."

Du Pré just looked at her. He sipped his drink.

"We don't even know your name yet," she said, "but we will soon enough."

Du Pré looked at her. He rolled a smoke and lit it.

"What's his name?" said Meredith to Buck Keifer.

Buck shrugged.

"Ma'am," said Meredith to T J, "is there a way to get these guys to talk? What am I doin' wrong here?"

"You got any little brothers?" said T J to the newswoman.

Meredith nodded.

T J leaned over the bar so her head was between Du Pré and Buck Keifer.

"That" said T J, nodding to Gabriel Du Pré, "is Gabriel Du Pré who dug up the cache," and T J nodded at Buck Keifer, "and that is Buck Keifer, who wishes it had been him. Fer Chrissakes, Du Pré, the lady asked you a question, answer it. You didn't want to talk, you'd be lost out in the country."

Du Pré and Keifer laughed.

The rest of the newspeople had seen something going on and crowded around Du Pré.

"I find some things from Lewis and Clark," said Du Pré. "I find them on the Carbonado, on private land. They are not here. They are some long ways away now."

People began to shout questions, but Du Pré shook his head.

"Outside," said Du Pré. "I talk to you there. T J, she is running her business here."

Du Pré got up and walked out the front door. The helicopters were setting down in a field across the road.

Du Pré stood next to his old cruiser.

"I find some things from the expedition," he said, "one of them is a journal."

The journalists were scribbling or speaking into little tape recorders.

"They were found on private land, they are not here now, and I will not say any more."

People began to shout questions.

Du Pré ignored them. He went back into the bar.

The newspeople followed.

Du Pré got a fresh drink and sat with his back to the room.

"It ain't gonna be as simple as that," said Buck Keifer.

Du Pré shrugged.

Du Pré turned around.

Wally Williams came in the door, red-faced from running.

He looked at the newspeople, and they looked at him.

Williams saw Du Pré.

"You!" he screamed. "You bastard, I had almost found that cache! I want that stuff, goddamn you!"

He rushed across the floor toward Du Pré.

"You," he said, stopping, "you burned my boat."

Du Pré looked at him.

"How much do you want?" said Wally Williams.

Du Pré looked at him.

"How much?" he screamed.

Du Pré turned around and had some more of his drink.

"I wouldn't do that I was you," said Buck Keifer, sitting sideways on his stool.

Du Pré didn't bother to turn around.

"I'll sue you," said Wally Williams. "I almost had it."

He backed away. Du Pré watched him go out the front door, a few of the newspeople following.

"Friend a yours?" said Buck.

Du Pré shook his head.

"Who would own that stuff?" said Buck. "Fascelli owns the ranch, but who would own it? I suppose it amounts to abandoned government property."

"Them lawyers fight about that," said Du Pré. "Probably fight a long time."

"This was some nice quiet country once," said Buck. "I kinda miss it."

Du Pré laughed.

"How's the movie goin'?" Buck asked.

"I don't know," said Du Pré, "it is ver' strange work."

"No shit," said Buck.

Wally Williams was yelling outside.

A couple of ranchers came in, looking amused.

"Ya add strippers or somethin', T J?" said one.

T J shook her head.

"Next week," she said.

"I hear they found some of Lewis and Clark's stuff," said the other rancher.

"Maybe I should open a hot dog stand," said the rancher.

"You want a beer, Mert?" she said.

CHAPTER
29

"Backwoodsman finds Lewis and Clark treasure," said Harvey Wallace.

"Oh," said Du Pré "I know what I am now."

"I shit you not," said Harvey. "Front page of the *Washington Post*. By-line Verdammt, Montana. There goes somebody's head."

"I don't know no Ver-damped," said Du Pré.

"I think it means 'goddamn' in German," said Harvey. "All you know it could be the name of the place. Think of some poor fat Kraut coming to the land of milk and honey, and ending there. Christ, you have to walk ten miles to come up to lonesome."

Little towns had sprung from the prairie and sunk back into it. Half of the places on a 1900 map of Montana weren't there anymore.

"So when I see you?" said Du Pré.

"You don't see *me*, Du Pré," said Harvey Wallace. "It seems that there is a flag in our computer program here, and when your name is fed into it instructions pop up. "Do not approach that half-breed son of a bitch. Call Harvey Wallace and spoil his day. Don't even talk to the prick. Call Harvey Wallace. If possible, send Harvey Wallace away from his wife and kids to the sagebrush. Harvey hates the sagebrush but it builds his character," said Harvey.

"I don't do nothing wrong," said Du Pré.

"Du Pré," said Harvey, "what you found there is a priceless relic of the good old days, red, white, and blue American history. Why, if Lewis and Clark had not lumbered through the country it might have been years before the whites came to slaughter all the Indians. Fuck-ups. They didn't, and look at us now."

Du Pré laughed.

"You Blackfeet don't fight much, Harvey," said Du Pré.

"Smallpox," said Harvey. "We all died from smallpox. Actually, I think I am an Eskimo."

"Yeah," said Du Pré. "Now what is it they are bitching about back there, threatening to arrest me?"

"Election year," said Harvey. "The thieves we elected the last time desperately need to convince us they are not thieves. Therefore, they will point fingers, and you are just standing there."

Du Pré was sitting on the hood of his cruiser, talking to Harvey on Bart's cell phone.

"You done ripped off our priceless national heritage," said Harvey, "right there in Montana. Just dug it up and carried it off. Senator Grunt and Congressman Snort will save it for America. You bet."

"What are they going to *do?*" said Du Pré.

"Nothing," said Harvey. "Congress does not do anything. Thank God. But they call us and scream. Congressman Snort actually called me this very morning. I asked him if the pizza was satisfactory, then I hung up. What the fuck do they want me to do? Arrest you, that's what."

Du Pré laughed.

"You oughta go and get it and turn it over," said Harvey, "You can make a million or two with a book."

"I don't write a book," said Du Pré.

"Of course you could," said Harvey, "and when you do, confess all the felonies in the first chapter. I hate reading books by friends anyway."

"Right," said Du Pré, "I do that."

"Suuuuure you will," said Harvey, "Say, is there anything in the air over to the southeast there?"

Du Pré looked.

"No," he said.

"I don't think that anyone knows what the law is here," said Harvey, "but I can tell you that they will find a law that says you can't keep it and if you do and hide it and all you will be thrown in jail for contempt—that's when you tell judges to fuck off, they don't take it well at all—as in defying a court order to 'fess up."

"I don't know where it is," said Du Pré.

"I believe you," said Harvey. "I also believe that you know who does know where it is by now, and they will ask you who and if you do not tell them they will and etc. etc. etc."

"I don't know," said Du Pré. "What is so hard about that?"

"Du Pré," said Harvey, "this country cares about money and damned little else. What you found is worth a great deal of money. You are worth a great deal of money. How are you for talk shows?"

Du Pré laughed.

"Where is the lovely Madelaine?" said Harvey.

"In the bar," said Du Pré. "She is dancing alone in front of the jukebox."

"That," said Harvey, "is very sad. It almost makes me want to come to Montana. Some people like Montana, but I do not. I like things that Montana does not have, like oysters, softshell crabs, and rain. They have lovely soft rain here. Things grow. When I was a kid I raised a cactus with my spare piss, which was not needed for the family garden. It was a good and faithful pet. Here, however,

160

we have water, so my kids may have gerbils, hamsters, cats, dogs, and snakes."

"Snakes," said Du Pré.

"Yup," said Harvey, "my youngest boy likes snakes. Has a boa constrictor twelve feet long. He took it to school in his backpack a few years back, when it was only nine feet long, and it caused comment. Yessir, it was a subject of much talk. I actually got a call from the principal. Private school, of course. Feller screamed at me. He did. It seemed he was afeared of snakes. Imagine that."

Du Pré laughed.

"Course," said Harvey, "consider the poor man, arriving to work, leaving his offices to see the little heathens his life is dedicated to file obediently into their classrooms, sit just so, eager for learning and knowledge. Beam a little at the children, those conniving monsters, and then go back to his office and pull open his file drawer and there is Emily, all coiled and hissing as she hates small dark places."

Du Pré roared.

"Young Charles was in bad odor after that, though he did recover the snake and tuck her back in his backpack. The principal was trying to keep his dignity. I dunno why. That little fucker put Emily in my gym bag once and there's nothing quite like reaching in your bag for your squash racket and finding Emily there, let me tell you."

"Sounds like a good kid," said Du Pré.

"He is," said Harvey. "Or was. Glands, you know. He is now thirteen, and I hate talking to glands. There's no use in it."

"Send him out here," said Du Pré. "I put him in with Jacqueline's herd there."

Du Pré looked off to the southeast. A small plane glinted on the horizon.

"Now," said Harvey, "I hope I did not answer any of your questions."

"Yah," said Du Pré.

"Congressman Snort will be calling me again soon, and I can barely contain my excitement."

"Him can fuck off, too," said Du Pré.

"Gabriel," said Harvey, "just go and get the stuff, willya? We can lock it in a nice vault at the Smithsonian and we can all get some sleep."

"No," said Du Pré.

"I tried to help," said Harvey. "I really did."

"What can they do?" said Du Pré. "Just talk about it."

"How many newshounds you got there?" said Harvey.

Du Pré made a quick count.

"Forty maybe," he said.

"They are there until they get the story, Du Pré," said Harvey, "and you have it."

"We run them off the ranch, get an order keep them from flying over the place, mess up the movie," said Du Pré.

"Just a minute," said Harvey, "I got another call, just a sec."

The line went dead.

Harvey was gone for two minutes.

"Sorry," said Harvey.

"Well, I go now," said Du Pré.

"Just a minute," said Harvey, "You see a plane yet?"

"You son of a bitch," said Du Pré.

The plane was quite close.

Somebody jumped out of it and began to fall.

A wide parachute opened, and the jumper swung from the lines.

"Nice talkin' to you, Du Pré," said Harvey.

"Fuck you I leave now," said Du Pré.

"Be nice," said Harvey. "Special Agent Van Dusen was saying just last night how much he missed you all. *Missed.* His very word."

The parachute was the sort the jumper could guide. It was making straight for the field across the road.

"You prick," said Du Pré.

"You got to give it up, Du Pré," said Harvey.

162

"No," said Du Pré.

"Say hi to Ripper, there," said Harvey.

"Christ," said Du Pré.

"Gabriel," said Harvey, "Bill Rupe is overdue. Never got to his Rover, parked down by Fort Peck."

"God*damn*," said Du Pré.

"Time to be an archangel," said Harvey.

"Shit," said Du Pré.

CHAPTER
30

Ripper glided smoothly in and he landed and rolled once and then he jumped up and bagged his chute. He stuffed his nylon jumpsuit in the bag, and the helmet and the goggles, and he lifted the parachute and the duffel bag he had carried down and ambled over to Du Pré.

"No," said Du Pré.

"Yes," said Ripper.

"No."

"Du Pré," said Ripper, "Auntie Harvey's tummy is all upset. He has elected representatives calling him and having trash like that on your case is dreary and produces excess stomach acid and in Harvey's case fearful great throbbing hemorrhoids. Harvey is in *pain*."

"Him want that Lewis and Clark stuff," said Du Pré.

"Lawyers are even as we speak assembling gibberish which will assure you a nice cell," said Ripper, "Come, let us reason together, and I need a fucking beer."

"OK," said Du Pré.

They walked across the road and past the news trucks and some of the people.

T J looked up when Du Pré came in. She looked at Ripper.

"Who," she said, "the hell is that?"

"Charles Van Dusen," said Ripper, "but please call me Ripper."

"Right," said T J.

"Him FBI," said Du Pré.

"Friends from all over," said T J.

"A beer, please," said Ripper, "and a bottle and a funnel for my friend here." Ripper put a twenty on the bartop.

"Du Pré," said Ripper, "couldn't you just maybe turn the stuff over like a nice guy and then I can go home?"

"No," said Du Pré.

"Why *not?*" said Ripper. "That stuff is the property of the United States government."

"Yah," said Du Pré.

"So what's the problem?" said Ripper.

Du Pré pulled out a folded sheet of paper. He opened it up and he handed it to Ripper.

Ripper studied the paper. He began to shake. He began to laugh. He howled. He gasped. He drank some of his beer.

"Oh, yes," he said. "Oh, please, I must call Auntie and let him know. He will want to know so he can inform the elected representatives who devil his days, of just what is *happening.* Oh, yes."

Du Pré had some of his drink. Ripper opened his cell phone and punched in numbers.

"Hi,'tis me," said Ripper.

Ripper listened for a moment. He lifted the paper.

"Not," he said. "No. Well, perhaps you should . . . shut the fuck up, Harvey. Du Pré's about to bust the national balls."

Ripper nodded as Harvey yelled.

"Francois LaBiche, Baptiste LePage, Pierre Cruzatte, Toussaint Charbonneau," said Ripper. "I will give you a hint. All Métis. Sorta like Du Pré here. Well, all of them were supposed to get—you'll love this, Harvey, you'll absolutely love this—for their services, in the matter of going all the way to the Pacific and back with Lewis and Clark, eight hundred dollars in pay, and twelve hundred acres of land, each, first dibs in the Lousiana Purchase. Which they did not get either. Du Pré here . . . points out that his daughter Maria is descended from all four of these cruelly wronged Métis, and . . . why you do get the picture, now, don't you, Harvey."

Ripper put his hand over the phone.

"Harvey is having an attack of mirth," said Ripper. "I hope his wife is there with his digitalis."

"No, Harvey," said Ripper, "it seems that Du Pré had expert advice, and what with compound interest and all, the thirty-two hundred in 1806 has grown a bit, a mere matter of eighteen million dollars, but it is the land that is truly interesting, for in this document 'first dibs' means Maria should be able to choose what forty-eight hundred acres she would like to have and it seems the place of choice is downtown Denver, Colorado, which is probably worth a bit more than it was in 1806, too. I think Du Pré is pointing out that Uncle Sam is a chiseler and a weasel and Du Pré feels like hanging on to the goodies until the back bills are all paid up. Yeah, they'll be shitting pickles."

Ripper held the telephone away from his ear. Harvey was howling some Blackfeet war chant into it.

"He wishes to talk to you," said Ripper. He handed the phone to Du Pré.

"Very nice," said Harvey, his voice hoarse from laughing, "and though I have a law degree and I do not know all of the fine print, this will not get tangled up in aboriginal title argument. Pretty straight stuff. Overdue bill."

"I think that I go and tell them newsmen now," said Du Pré.

"Do that," said Harvey. "And if you don't mind get Ripper in the picture, so I can point to the evening news and say, see, we're *on the case!*"

"Sure," said Du Pré.

"Who put you up to this?" said Harvey.

"Most Métis aren't even citizens till 1957," said Du Pré. "That put me up to this, yes."

"Right," said Harvey.

Du Pré handed the telephone back to Ripper, who put it away. They touched glasses and drank.

"What the hell is going on?" said T J.

"I give them news now," said Du Pré.

"Well, do it outside," said T J.

"That won't help," said Ripper. "Kind of news Du Pré has, well, ma'am, it will probably cause a riot and the fall of the government."

"The government'd fall over," said T J, "that'd be nice."

Ripper sighed.

"I work for the government," he said, "I am the family imbecile and couldn't do anything else."

"That's no excuse," said T J. "Young feller like you could make something of himself he had a mind to."

Ripper grinned at T J. T J grinned at Ripper.

"What's this crap gonna make the government keel over and sink?" said T J.

"A bill," said Ripper.

"A bill. The government owes ol' Du Pré some money?" said T J. "I don't see how . . ."

"It's complicated," said Ripper.

"Use them small words," said T J, "and speak slow."

Well," said Ripper, looking at Du Pré, who nodded, "it seems that some of Du Pré's ancestors guided Lewis and Clark faithfully and well, but they never got paid for their work."

"You *need* another beer there, son," said T J.

"So," said Ripper, "it seems Du Pré found some priceless artifacts of the Journey of the Corps of Discovery, and he proposes to do a l'il dickering with the government, 'bout their having screwed his ancestors."

"You are completely full of shit," said T J.

"Yes, ma'am," said Ripper.

"I ain't nothing but a barkeep in the ass end of Montana," said T J, "and my people borrowed all they could to raise wheat for that same government, 1918. Crop came in, war's over, so that same government says, you can keep it. Lost the farm on that one, like they say. Now you are tellin' me Du Pré here will make those bastards behave?"

"Well," said Ripper, "I doubt it truth to tell, but this could be really embarrassing for them, there in that government."

"Yer tellin' me that after the likes of Richard Nixon and Bill Clinton the government can actually get embarrassed?"

"I see your point," said Ripper.

"I could mention a few other things," said T J.

"I am trying to explain," said Ripper.

"You can't," said T J. "Here's your beer."

Du Pré was laughing.

T J walked to the front door of the roadhouse and opened it.

"Get in here, you sorry sons of bitches," she yelled. "Du Pré has got some news for you."

Ripper leaned close to Du Pré.

"Jack Rupe was a friend of mine," he said, "and Bill is one of the world's gents."

"Du Pré nodded.

"Officially, unofficially, whatever," said Ripper, "I want those bastards."

Du Pré nodded.

Feet sounded on the board porch.

CHAPTER
31

"Papa," said Maria, "what in the hell you are doin'?"

Du Pré looked at her.

"I point something out," he said. "That is all."

"We live out here a long time," said Maria. "Nobody knows us, what we do, who we are. Now we got TV cameras all the time. Big stuff."

"It will go way in a few days," said Ben Burke. "It really will."

"Du Pré is having his joke here," said Madelaine.

Du Pré nodded. He went to the lamb on the spit and he turned it and he wedged the end of the spit with a chip of wood stuck in the collar. The fire was very hot and the lamb smelled delicious, garlic slivers thrust into it, basted with its own juices and pepper and rosemary.

They were sitting at a trestle table. A bright red-and-white cloth covered it, and there were covered bowls of cold salads and loaves of Madelaine's good bread.

Old Harry and Booger Tom were walking around down by the river, talking. Once in a while one or another of the old monsters would laugh, very loudly.

"What I do," said Du Pré, "is just say something, maybe make people thinks some. That Black Jack Pershing he shove eight hundred Métis on boxcars, send them off to North Dakota, it is winter and dozens of them die, the cold. We do all right, we have to. But no one remembers that. Long time gone."

Ben Burke looked sad.

"My God," he said, "I didn't know."

"Nobody knows," said Du Pré. "So when this happens, here, this stuff Lewis and Clark left, then they are listening. About the only time anyone hear at all."

"Quite right," said Ben.

"Goddamn brilliant is what it is," said Ripper, "though just what you want out of this is unclear, at least to me."

Du Pré shrugged.

"Well," said Ben, "we certainly thank you. All of our money worries have evaporated. We have people *begging* to help with the costs of the movie."

Du Pré turned the lamb again and stuffed the chip in the collar. He pulled his hands away quickly.

"God that smells great," said Ben.

It was about one in the afternoon. Sunday.

Jason Parks drove in in his old black pickup and got out with a huge grin on his face. He went to the back of his truck, opened the shell, and took out two cardboard boxes. He piled one on the other and walked over to the table. The boxes had stencils on the sides, faded and in French. Jason took out his pocketknife, slit the cardboard tape, and lifted out a wooden case.

"My my," said Ripper. "Yquem. Very nice. What's in the other case?"

"More," said Jason. He pried up one of the thin boards on the top and fished out a bottle, shreds of excelsior hanging from it.

He handed the bottle to Ripper. Ripper put it on the table, then he got down on his knees and genuflected several times.

Jason opened the bottle and took a small taster's glass from his jacket pocket. He poured a tiny amount of wine into the glass and handed it to Maria.

Maria dumped the wine in her mouth. She swished it round, and she swallowed.

"Oh, my," she said, "what good wine."

Jason carefully gave a small taste to everyone.

"Good with lamb," said Jason.

"That," said Ripper, "would be good with cat food."

"I needed this," said Ben Burke. "We aren't quite on schedule, but Trey was good enough to give everyone a day off. This is the place in making a movie when no one thinks it can be done."

"It will get done," said Maria, patting his shoulder.

"I am trying to have faith," said Ben.

"How long?" said Ripper.

"Just another week," said Ben, "if all goes well, which it won't, but it is still possible that we could be done."

"Good," said Du Pré. "You don't need me anyway, now."

"Yes we do, Papa," said Maria. "You are not going to stir all this up and then go off, the Wolf Mountains, while we are here with everybody yelling."

"Du Pré," said Madelaine, "no fucking way. You stay here. You got ever'body looking here, you use that."

Du Pré nodded.

Booger Tom and Old Harry had wandered back. They had pretty well done with the pint of whiskey Tom had had when he came.

Madelaine looked at them.

"We go back a ways," said Booger Tom. "Seems Old Harry here once about put me in the hoosegow."

"Would've" said Old Harry, "but his pal shot one of my tires flat."

"What are you doing shooting at Harry's tires?" said Madelaine.

"It's a long story," said Booger Tom.

"You and your long stories," said Madelaine. "What are you stealing Harry is after you."

"A horse," said Booger Tom.

"You are being a *horse thief*?" said Madelaine, shocked.

"It was a horse got stole once already," said Booger Tom.

"Very famous horse," said Old Harry, "made a lot of money at the races."

"Races?" said Ripper. "What was it, a thoroughbred?"

"Nah," said Booger Tom. "Quarter horse. You know, the *American* horse. Been all over brush racin'."

"Brush racin?" said Ripper.

Old Harry looked at Ripper with a pitying gaze.

"Not one of them fancy-pants derby things," he said. "There used to be races out here, lot of money on 'em, too. This here horse won about a half million dollars, but then he pulled a tendon and that was that. Stud horse he was. But feller down here stole him to breed him. Booger Tom and some other thieves come to steal him back. They did, too. Left me there on the road, with my dead tire."

"Couldn't you radio somebody?" said Ripper.

Booger Tom and Old Harry looked disdainfully at Ripper.

"Wouldn't have been sportin'," said Old Harry, "use a *radio*. They didn't have no *radio* to use."

"They were breaking the law," said Ripper.

"No excuse fer me not to act a gentleman," said Old Harry. "I expect you do things different back East, but here we try bein' fair and square."

"I am being lied to," said Ripper.

"Of course!" said Booger Tom and Old Harry, in perfect unison.

"I never learn," said Ripper.

"Yer young yet," said Old Harry. "Ya got lots of time."

"Maybe he don't," said Booger Tom. "He's awful slow."

"Don't pick on him," said Old Harry. "Altitude has frothed his brains all up."

"Give me more wine, please," said Ripper, turning his back on the old farts.

Du Pré turned the lamb a bit more.

"John Thomas isn't coming," said Jason. "He had somewhere else to go, it seems."

Du Pré laughed.

Some of the people from the crew began to arrive, and then Sam Smythe and Trey Binder came, in Sam's big red SUV.

They had a half barrel of beer in the back, and Ben and Jason set the tap up, putting the aluminum keg in a tub full of ice.

People laughed and talked and Du Pré kept turning the lamb, and Madelaine unfolded the grill Du Pré carried in his old cruiser and began to build a charcoal fire under it. The charcoal caught fire quickly, and Madelaine put pieces of chicken on to grill, for those who didn't like lamb.

One of the crew members had brought a salad of wild greens and another had somehow managed to bake some flat cakes. The vendors who ran the food tent had the day off, and so did everyone else.

Du Pré looked up toward the road on the benchland. Cars were parked there, and once in a while a camera lens glinted as some photographer tried to get a shot with a telescopic lense.

Du Pré yawned.

Maria brought him a whiskey and water. Du Pré kissed her on the forehead.

"You know what you are doing, Papa," said Maria. "I know that. Ben said that the publicity means we might even get to show this movie in real movie theaters, not just on television."

Du Pré shrugged. He walked back over to the trestle table.

Du Pré rolled a cigarette.

Someone came to the table, and Du Pré looked up to see Trey Binder, who put a hand out to the top of the table and then he turned and sat down. He had a puzzled expression on his face.

"My arm hurts," he said, rubbing his left arm with his right hand.

He sat there for a moment.

Then he got halfway up to his feet and fell, making a strangling noise as he hit the ground.

CHAPTER
32

Kit Van Der Meer lifted the barrel of oats onto the back of his pickup truck. He set it against one side and ran a bungee cord around it and he hooked it on an eyebolt.

"Well," he said, "now the lawyers can have their fun. Too bad Binder just died like that."

"Unforeseen circumstances," said Bart, "like blood in the water."

"So what happens now?" said Kit.

"They get another director," said Bart, "and in a damned big hurry I would think. But finding one to come in on a project that is half-done, and for a small amount of money, is difficult."

"Contract's the same," said Kit, "and they've been damned good so far. After what happened to Buck Keifer, I was worried."

Du Pré looked off toward the river, out of sight behind low hills.

"We'll hope for the best," said Bart. "And in the meantime, we will ask Old Harry to keep an eye out."

"Somethin's worryin' you," said Kit.

Bart shook his head.

"Something like this is worrisome," he said.

Du Pré rolled a smoke.

"Well," said Bart, "we have to go. Hearing is in three hours."

Kit laughed, and he looked at Du Pré.

"Got 'em stirred up, ain't ya?" he said.

Du Pré nodded.

"I think it will only get worse," said Bart. "Come on, god-dammit."

Du Pré got into Bart's cruiser, and they drove off to the little airstrip that served the ranch. A blue-and-white Piper Cherokee sat there, prop idling.

Bart and Du Pré got in, and the pilot let out the brakes and they sped down the dirt runway and into the air. The day was clear and the wind soft.

The river rolled brown toward the east, cutting through the rocky country, bluffs along its course.

The pilot turned south and left the river and they began to cross the Big Dry, endless rolling hills yellow with grass, cedars in the breaks, and damn little water.

"Du Pré," said Bart, "whatever you do, don't sass the judge. This is a federal judge."

"Why I do that?" said Du Pré.

Bart nodded.

"Uh-huh," he said.

Du Pré dozed and in little time they were descending to the airport in Billings, the long runways up on the Rims above the city. A haze of dust and auto exhaust clouded the air, and the Yellowstone rolled clear through the town.

The pilot circled the airport once and set the plane down. They taxied to the small aircraft pads, and Du Pré and Bart got out and began to walk to the terminal.

Bart got keys to a rental car and they found it in the lot and drove down to the federal building. The hulking gray courthouse looked blankly out on the traffic.

They parked and got out and went in and an attorney waiting in the lobby got up from a bench and he came to them.

"Mr. Fascelli?" he said. "Thank God. I thought you might be late. Never a good idea."

"Sorry," said Bart. "This is Gabriel Du Pré, and this is Prentice Murphy, I believe."

"Sorry," said Murphy, "my manners are defective."

Du Pré shrugged.

"This is just a hearing," said Murphy. "The Department of the Interior is making a motion, demanding that you turn over the things which you found and which you claim are material left by the Lewis and Clark Expedition."

Du Pré nodded.

Murphy was dressed well, suit and tie and vest and polished wing-tip brogans.

He led them upstairs and down a corridor and to a courtroom, empty but for another attorney at a table in the front.

The judge appeared suddenly, and the attorney stood.

The judge sat and nodded at the two attorneys, and then at Du Pré and Bart.

The attorney who had been there first rose and talked for some time, looking at a sheaf of papers in his hand.

Du Pré sat and waited.

The judge seemed to be sleeping, up there on his bench.

The attorney for the Department of the Interior thanked the judge for his patience. The judge nodded, once.

"All right," he said. "Mr. Murphy?"

"My client," said Murphy, "Mr. Gabriel Du Pré of Cooper County, Montana, claims possession, Your Honor, and I have here several motions . . ."

"Which I may read at my leisure," said the judge. "Now, your client found these things, allegedly from the Lewis and Clark

177

Expedition. The government of the United States claims that they own them. Now, Mr. Du Pré, are you claiming that you own them?"

Du Pré stood, and he walked down the aisle to the front of the courtroom.

"I don't claim that," said Du Pré. "I think it will take much time in court, decide who owns them."

The judge raised his eyebrows, and he nodded.

"The government—I am going to use that word rather than the Department of the Interior—says it worries about the safety of said items. Do they know what these items *are*, exactly, counselor?" said the judge, looking at the other attorney.

Who shook his head.

"Where are they, Mr. Du Pré?" said the judge.

"I gave them to a medicine person," said Du Pré.

The judge was trying to keep his face straight.

"You want to mess with them pickles, counselor?" said the judge, looking at the government attorney.

"This is hardly a tribal matter," said the attorney.

"I think," said the judge, "the government's case is not. Further, I look forward to many years of instructive litigation, right here in my courtroom."

"We ask that in the meantime," said the attorney, "that these items be surrendered for safekeeping."

"Nice try," said the judge. "But for all we know some Boy Scouts built a cache in 1955, put things in it, and forgot about it, so we aren't quite sure just what it is we want, there, right?"

The government attorney shook his head.

"I'll let you know what I think," said the judge. "In good time, and court is adjourned."

Du Pré got up from his seat.

The judge stood, too.

"Mr. Du Pré," he said, "I have some questions, mere curiosity. If you and Mr. . . . ."

"Fascelli," said Bart.

"Come to my chambers, if you would," said the judge.

He motioned them to a door in the side of the room. They left the two attorneys standing there.

By the time Du Pré and Bart got into the hall the judge had his robe off and he was carrying it over his arm. He was younger than Du Pré.

"Do you think this really is from the Expedition?" he said.

Du Pré nodded.

"We flew in an expert who authenticated it," said Bart.

The judge nodded.

"In writing?" he said.

Bart shook his head.

"Smart guy," said the judge. "Marvelous. After all this time. What was in it?"

"Lead barrel," said Du Pré. "The gunpowder was in those. Some knives and hatchets, maybe, some other things, haven't opened the old oilcloth yet."

"A fiddle," said the judge. "Was there a fiddle in there, Mr. Du Pré?"

Du Pré shook his head.

"Pierre Cruzatte played the fiddle, all the way to the Western Sea and back," said the judge. "As you do, sir, and very well I might say."

Du Pré grinned.

"Take good care of those things, please," said the judge, "because, well, they . . . belong to all of us."

"Yah," said Du Pré.

"Thank you," said the judge.

CHAPTER
33

Du Pré sat at the bar in the Toussaint Saloon, rolling a smoke while Madelaine beaded a tobacco pouch. She lifted the needle up to see the point against the light. She squinted.

"I am young," said Madelaine, "I read a newspaper, twenty feet away. Then one day I am not feeling older but my eyes are. Just like that. Go to bed, they are fine, wake up, they are old."

Du Pré nodded.

"Your eyes they are still good," said Madelaine. "So maybe you help me here, Du Pré." She put some beads on a saucer and handed Du Pré the needle.

Du Pré had some of his drink. He burped.

"Du Pré," said Madelaine, "I think you maybe got eyes like a hawk, see things far away, up close you got eyes like a pocket gopher."

Du Pré grunted.

"Put a bead on that fucking needle," said Madelaine.

Du Pré picked up a bead, poked the needle at it, and missed.

Madelaine laughed.

"I see you read," she said. "Now, you hold that book out there, like this."

Madelaine held her arms out rigidly, and she squinted and moved the imaginary book around.

"OK, Du Pré," said Madelaine. "You try these on, yes."

Madelaine lifted a paper bag from beneath the counter. She handed it to Du Pré. He opened it and looked inside.

Glasses. Lots of glasses. Still had the little tags on the frames.

"Got numbers on them," said Madelaine. "Smaller numbers mean that they don't magnify so much. Start with them, I don't want, you hurt your own feelings, Du Pré."

Du Pré looked through the glasses, settling on one that said "1.50."

He put them on. He looked at Madelaine.

"It is you!" he said. "I have not been sure, some time now."

"Uh-huh," said Madelaine. "Who you think you been sticking your dick in anyway, Du Pré, long as we are talking?"

Du Pré put the glasses on the bar top.

"Rosie La Touche," said Du Pré.

"Put those glasses back on," said Madelaine, "so I can break them, your nose, too."

"I see better," said Du Pré blinking.

Madelaine looked at her beadwork, a splash of stars in a dark blue sky, a coyote dancing upright, with a fiddle in his paws.

She handed it to Du Pré.

"Rosie La Touche," said Madelaine. "Yah, right. When are you going back, that movie?"

Du Pré shrugged.

"They said they call me," said Du Pré.

"Too bad about that Binder," said Madelaine. "He was an OK guy, I thought."

Du Pré nodded. Binder, sitting down, looking puzzled, dying then.

"While you are in Billings," said Madelaine, "some asshole was here, offered ten thousand dollars to anyone tell him where the stuff you found is."

"You take it?" said Du Pré.

Madelaine looked at her beads.

"Ten thousand dollars is not so much anymore," said Madelaine. "I wait, because there will be a better price."

"Who is he?" said Du Pré.

Madelaine shrugged. She went to the cash register, fished out a business card, and handed it to Du Pré.

LAWTON MORTON PRIVATE INQUIRIES and a telephone number.

Du Pré handed it back.

"Somebody figure out you give them to Benetsee," said Madelaine. "It is not so far to think, you know."

Du Pré nodded.

"Yah," he said. "Benetsee, he will take ten thousand dollars, drink it up that awful wine him like."

"You buy him all he wants," said Madelaine. "What he need ten thousand dollars for? Any fool goes there, tries to find that stuff, Benetsee have a lot of fun with them. Him, he tell Maria where they are, don't he, in the lodge?"

Du Pré nodded.

"You are right," said Madelaine. "Him take Maria to them, them old ones, you know."

Long time gone.

"She is liking that movie stuff," said Madelaine.

"No," said Du Pré.

"She is now," said Madelaine. "Maria likes it now, she will not like it soon enough."

Du Pré laughed.

"She love that Ben," said Madelaine, "and he is a nice man, good man, too, maybe."

Du Pré nodded. Better be a tough man, too, my Maria eat him, spit out the bones.

Bart came in, covered with mud, wearing his coveralls and heavy rubber boots.

Madelaine looked up.

"Out, earthmover," she said, "you got some shoes, your car. Maybe you leave your work someplace else, this floor I got to keep clean."

"Oh," said Bart. He backed out the door. He was back in three minutes, in a shirt and jeans and running shoes.

He sat at the bar.

"Sorry," he said, "I was thinking about something else."

"Me, I am thinking about the floor," said Madelaine. "Du Pré, he is wearing glasses now."

Bart nodded.

"Put them on, Du Pré," said Madelaine. "You have not seen Bart up close for years."

Du Pré sighed and put on the glasses. He ripped them away from his face.

"Him ugly," said Du Pré. "These don't help."

Bart laughed, and so did Madelaine.

"Somebody offer Madelaine ten thousand dollars, tell where the stuff is," said Du Pré.

"Lots of folks looking," said Bart. "Lots of them."

Ripper banged through the door, his cell phone stuck to his mouth.

"I went there, Harvey, and the old goat is gone, so, we done crossed them i's and dotted them t's. I have been a good and faithful investigator, and I cannot find them."

Ripper listened.

"Of course," said Ripper. "I'm sure he'd love to."

Ripper handed the phone to Du Pré.

"Very nice," said Harvey. "Nice bit with the judge. They weren't all that serious, you know. It will get serious. You gave the stuff to that old bastard?"

Du Pré didn't say anything.

"Hello?" said Harvey.

"They got things pick these words out, the air?" said Du Pré.

"Yes," said Harvey.

"So shut up," said Du Pré.

"They'll find the old man soon enough," said Harvey.

Du Pré sighed.

"Who?" said Du Pré.

"It's a lot of money, Du Pré," said Harvey. "The things are worth a lot of money, and the story is worth a lot of money."

"What they do to Benetsee?" said Du Pré.

"Hard to tell," said Harvey. "But there will be folks searching around out there. They will bother the old man, you know, try to find a way to bribe him."

"They don't got anything Benetsee want," said Du Pré.

"Probably not," said Harvey. "Have you talked with him lately?"

"No," said Du Pré.

"Give him my best when you do," said Harvey, "and could you do me a huge favor? I'd love you forever."

"What?" said Du Pré.

"Shoot Ripper," said Harvey, "you'd have the thanks of a grateful nation."

Du Pré laughed.

"Harvey says he wants me, shoot you," said Du Pré to Ripper.

Ripper grinned happily.

"Oh," he said. "He really cares! Thank you for sharing!"

"Too bad about the movie director," said Harvey.

"Yah," said Du Pré.

"Go and see Benetsee," said Harvey. "Please . . ."

"Yah," said Du Pré.

CHAPTER
34

Ripper and Du Pré walked round the back of Benetsee's old cabin. There was no one around, and the sweat lodge was open, the flap set on the top.

Du Pré looked at the ground.

Wafflestompers. Perfectly useless in this country, too heavy and stiff.

Du Pré wandered back and forth. He went up on the back porch. The door was a little ajar. Du Pré pushed it open.

Someone had rifled through everything in Benetsee's cabin. There wasn't much, and nothing had been damaged. The old rug had been pushed away, by someone looking for a trapdoor. There wasn't one.

Du Pré set the boxes Benetsee kept his things in one atop the other as they usually were. He closed the curtains that shut the pantry off.

Everything that had been under the old man's bed had been pulled out. Du Pré pushed them back in with his toe.

"Sons of bitches," said Ripper.

Du Pré nodded.

Ripper had a little black box in his hand, and he went round the room. He stared at a dial on the top of it.

"Oh ho," said Ripper. He pointed the box toward a crack in the logs. He stuck a finger in and pulled out a little dingus.

"Ain't this some shit," said Ripper. "Bugging the old man's home. Modern times, what fun."

Du Pré looked at the thing.

"I don't think the fool who set this was the fool who tossed the place," said Ripper. "Imagine. Wish the old goat was here."

Du Pré nodded.

Ripper dropped the dingus on the floor and crushed it with the heel of his boot. He pitched it into the woodstove.

"Pricks," he said.

Du Pré went back outside.

"Used to be was," said Ripper, "that only your friendly government could afford that shit, and now you can get it at Wal-Mart."

Du Pré laughed.

"Parents bug their children's bedrooms," said Ripper, "and that is not smart. No parent *wants* to know everything."

Du Pré shrugged.

"Rupe and Lee," said Ripper. "You want to know what they were doing? They were doing a photo essay on the Missouri and the ranchers, both of them had long since had it with the econinnies. Fucking little Nazis. You know their writings are identical to Nazi writings on the environment in the twenties and thirties? Not similar. Fucking *identical*. So here they are, and they get whacked. Jack Rupe was one fine feller. So was Lee. I want the shooters."

Du Pré shrugged.

"Rupe and Lee," said Ripper.

Du Pré looked at him.

"Yah?" said Du Pré.

"That's what I am really after," said Ripper. "See, they worked for this magazine and that magazine is all in a crank because they don't think these rubes out here—meaning you—are thinking enough about who shot them."

Du Pré shrugged.

"So," said Ripper, "either you and that old goat Harry find the murderer, or I will have to, and if it's all the same to you, you do it."

Du Pré looked at him.

"Man, Pruitt," said Du Pré, "was here, the state police, he said they would, look at this."

"Pruitt doesn't know I am here," said Ripper, "and he ought to go on not knowing that. I don't want this, Gabriel, at all. I am on leave, but, well, you have the badge you aren't ever on leave, but at least I haven't got a ree-port to write. But, well, you want about forty of our best assholes here, just dick around."

"I am not a cop," said Du Pré.

"True," said Ripper. "But if anyone here knows who did it, it's you. You may not know yet. But when you do it would be good if you goosed old Harry there, since he ought to arrest the bastard."

Du Pré shrugged.

"I need to go back to unlovely Washington, D.C.," said Ripper, "and consult with Aunt Harvey. Which is a nice way of saying find the fucker in a week or I'll be back with the troops."

"I maybe not do this," said Du Pré.

Ripper sighed.

"Goddamn it, Du Pré," he said. "About all we need right now is for all my fellow jackbooted government thugs to go tramping over the country and anyone in our path. How fucking dumb do you think I am? These people out here have had it, basically, with the twentieth century, and who can blame them? But potting passing canoe paddlers is, and I must make this perfectly clear, like the late Tricky Dick, not going to be the protest of choice. It's illegal. It's also wrong."

Du Pré nodded.

"OK," said Du Pré.

"What a guy," said Ripper.

Ripper yelped and he jumped three feet in the air and he turned and he looked at the thick willows. He yelped again.

Yellow jackets. Something had stirred them up. Du Pré could see more coming out of the trees, and he began to run toward his cruiser. Ripper was right behind him. They dived in and rolled up the windows and a dozen of the yellow-and-black insects banged against the glass for a while, and then they went away.

"Son of a *bitch*," said Ripper, regarding a swelling left hand. His right eye was almost shut.

Du Pré started to back out of the rutted track that led to the cabin.

Benetsee and Pelon were standing up by the road.

Du Pré stopped, and he rolled down the window.

"Him," said Benetsee. "Get out."

Ripper opened his door warily, looking for vicious insects.

Benetsee spat a wad of green stuff into his hand, and he put the paste on Ripper's stings.

"Them others," said Benetsee. "They leave in a hurry, too."

Du Pré sighed. Of course.

"We find a thing in your house," said Du Pré, "microphone, somebody wanted to know what you are saying there."

Pelon was whistling.

"Yah," said Benetsee. "You find them digging, the shit pile out back of the saloon."

Du Pré laughed.

"Idiots," said Pelon.

Benetsee jerked his head toward the road, and Du Pré followed him.

"One more thing to find," said Benetsee.

Du Pré waited.

Benetsee held up his old brown hand. There was a scar on the flesh between the finger and thumb, and it ran clear to the wrist.

"See a tree looks like this," said Benetsee, "cut it down, cut the fork apart, there . . ." and he pointed to his hand.

Du Pré nodded.

"You see it you know," said Benetsee.

"What is in there?" said Du Pré.

"Something," said Benetsee. "You know it when you see it."

Du Pré sighed.

"You be here?" said Du Pré. "Maybe I need you, I have to find a bad person."

"Don't need me," said Benetsee. "You pret' good at that now."

Du Pré shrugged.

"Bear," said Benetsee, "I see one of those big white bears used to live, the river bottoms."

Pale grizzlies, Du Pré thought, them damn river bears. Lewis and Clark kill some of them, hard to do.

"OK," said Du Pré.

"Where is that Harvey?" said Benetsee.

"Not here," said Du Pré.

"Him be here soon," said Benetsee. "You got some wine?"

Du Pré laughed and went to the trunk of his car and he got out a jug of screwtop wine and handed it to Benetsee.

The old man grinned, his eyes twinkling.

"Good," he said.

"I come sweat maybe," said Du Pré.

"We got to go," said Benetsee. "Use the lodge. Them bugs don't bother you, I talk to them."

Du Pré nodded.

Benetsee began to walk back toward his cabin.

Pelon followed him.

Du Pré got back in his cruiser. Ripper was sitting there.

"Those stings are about gone," he said.

CHAPTER
35

"You are FBI man?" said Pallas. She was sitting next to Ripper at the long trestle table in Jacqueline's kitchen. The table could seat twenty people and often did.

"Yup," said Ripper.

"Why you here?" said Pallas.

"I was sent here," said Ripper.

"Why that Harvey Weasel Fat send you here?" said Pallas. "I am a kid. No reason to bullshit me."

Ripper looked down at the little girl.

"You're Pallas?" said Ripper. "I'm Ripper. Nice to meet you."

"Crap," said Pallas, "Why you here?"

"Your grandfather is being a pain in the ass," said Ripper, "is why I'm here."

" 'Bout the Lewis and Clark things?" said Pallas. "He find them. What is the business, the government has with that?"

"The government *paid* for the expedition," said Ripper. "So they think they own anything Lewis and Clark may have left."

"They don't pay manygrandpapa LaBiche, manygrandpapa LePage, or Cruzatte or Charbonneau," said Pallas, "So why those cheap sons of bitches bothering my grandpapa for things they screw out of the Métis?"

"How old are you?" said Ripper.

"Seven," said Pallas.

"Jesus," said Ripper.

"Scary, huh," said Pallas, "when we own that Denver, Colorado, I see they pay their rent on time. Big rent."

"Right," said Ripper. He passed a big bowl of mashed potatoes when it appeared in front of him.

"You are going, arrest my grandpapa?" said Pallas.

"If you piss me off I am," said Ripper.

Pallas thought about that for a moment.

"That's dumb," she said, finally.

Ripper sighed. He looked down the table at Du Pré, past many little heads rising like steps toward their parents and grandfather.

"Help," said Ripper, looking pleadingly at Du Pré.

Du Pré shook his head.

"You ever wake up," said Du Pré, "there is a rattlesnake on your chest, looking at you? Rattling?"

"No," said Ripper, "but I have read about it."

"This is good practice, that," said Du Pré. "You want more meat?"

"Sure," said Ripper, "raw if you have it, so I can toss it to the monster here."

"I don't eat raw meat," said Pallas, " 'cept on special occasions."

"I can well imagine," said Ripper.

"You don't arrest my grandpapa," said Pallas. "I am warning you."

"Threatening a federal officer is a crime," said Ripper.

"Right," said Pallas. "You are going, drag me in a court, point to me, say to the judge, this little shit, she threaten me. Judge like that, you bet."

Ripper took a venison chop from the platter. He slathered it with bing cherry mustard and ate.

"Utterly wonderful," said Ripper, smacking his lips. He dabbed at them with a paper towel. He looked at the family around the table.

"May I be excused?" he said.

"Sure," Jacqueline said, laughing. "Run fast."

Ripper got up and went down the hall to the front door.

Pallas looked after him, and she smiled.

Ripper came back. He went to Pallas.

"Where . . . is . . . my . . . gun?" he asked.

"Probably where, your badge is, that plastic thing anyway," said Pallas.

Ripper sighed.

"Kid," he said, "this is a federal offense."

"I want a lawyer," said Pallas.

"You aren't under arrest," said Ripper, patiently.

"Damn right," said Pallas. "You got no badge how the hell we know you are a FBI man?"

"Argh," said Ripper.

"Leaving dangerous weapon around where some innocent child might find it," said Pallas. Ripper nodded at Pallas, showing a lot of his teeth.

"Kid could get hurt," said Pallas.

"No shit," said Ripper.

"Go off, leave your gun like that," said Pallas.

Ripper looked at her.

He threw his hands up. He put them to his face. He was laughing.

A cell phone chirred. Pallas lifted it from the floor beside her chair.

"Hi," she said, "Uncle Harvey."

"Jesus *Christ*!" said Ripper. "Give me that!"

Pallas dived under the table.

"Well, Unca Harvey, you send this guy, arrest my grandpapa, he is so dumb he lose his badge, his gun, and his telephone I am talking to you on. That is right. Yes."

Du Pré was roaring, and so were Jacqueline and Madelaine

"Unca Harvey," said Pallas, "you don't be mad with Ripper, hi, he is just not very smart."

Ripper pulled his chair out and he sat, looking at the floor.

"You promise?" said Pallas. "I was going, give him back his stuff anyway. He was going, arrest *me* . . ."

Pallas shuffled down the length of the table on the floor, and Ripper's cell phone appeared in front of Du Pré.

"Harvey wants to talk, you," said Pallas.

Du Pré took the phone.

"Yah," he said.

"Nice kid," said Harvey, "good extortionist."

"Yah," said Du Pré.

"Rupe and Lee," said Harvey. "If we could have the killer, I think Ripper could go away."

"Pallas would be sad," said Du Pré. "He is more fun than TV cartoons. She is at, stage of *development*."

"Right," said Harvey. "Ripper is one of my smartest agents. I am always reminded of that, by Ripper. Ripper *is* very smart."

"Pallas like him," said Du Pré.

"Good," said Harvey. "I hate explaining line of duty deaths to the parents of my agents."

"Those guys from the magazine," said Harvey. "Now the magazine says they were tipped off about the Lewis and Clark stuff."

"No," said Du Pré.

"I know that," said Harvey, "but it is a clever way to make us look for those things, dragging them into a murder investigation."

"Why you anyway?" said Du Pré.

"Because we are here," said Harvey. "And because somebody leaned on the governor there, who leaned on the cops, who then said, well, we can't figure this one out. Also some bullshit about it happened on the Missouri and the Coast Guard is responsible and so the feds and so forth. All bullshit but all plausible."

"OK," said Du Pré.

"You still got your newsmen?" said Harvey.

"Yah," said Du Pré.

Harvey sighed.

"How's Ripper doing there," he said.

"Sitting, head in his hands," said Du Pré.

"And his dick in his ear," said Harvey. "I *love* this. If I send you twenty bucks will you buy ice cream for Pallas?"

"Yah," said Du Pré.

Harvey sighed.

"I may have to come out there," he said.

"Madelaine like that," said Du Pré. "Dance some."

"Right," said Harvey.

Pallas's little hand reached up and tugged the telephone away from Du Pré's hand.

"When you be here, Uncle Harvey?" she said. "I wait, give that Ripper his gun and badge and phone you get here."

Silence while Pallas listened.

"OK," she said, "but I want one, these little computer things."

Silence while Pallas listened.

"Not good enough," said Pallas. "Think it over, call me back."

She crawled out from under the table.

Ripper put out his hand. Pallas gave him the cell phone. He put it in his pocket.

Madelaine laughed.

The telephone rang and Jacqueline answered it. She listened for a moment.

"I tell him," she said. She hung up.

Jacqueline came back to the table.

"They got a new director," she said. "They want Du Pré back there now."

CHAPTER
36

"I have seen the Beast and I have lived," said Ripper. "Can't you drive this fucking thing a little faster?"

Du Pré had just shot off the top of a hill, and his old cruiser had been airborne for a few seconds.

"Beast?" said Du Pré.

"That monstrous child," said Ripper. "No offense to proud grandpapas."

"Yah," said Du Pré, "she is way too smart. She likes you though."

"Good," said Ripper. "I am very glad of that."

"She told me, that Ripper, he is a pret' good sport," said Du Pré. "Lots of people, they break down, Pallas having fun with them."

"Her teachers must be scared to death of her," said Ripper.

Du Pré shook his head.

"Nah," he said. "They like her, stick her in front, the computer, leave her alone."

The cruiser shot along the narrow blacktop. There was no one in sight anywhere, not on the road, not on the land around.

"Lonely country," said Ripper.

Du Pré rolled a cigarette. He lit it.

"So the movie is up and running," said Ripper. "Too bad about . . . Binder, Trey Binder, that's right."

"Yah," said Du Pré. "Them heart attack, once, it is over."

Du Pré slowed to take the road east. They turned and he punched the accelerator and they were soon back up to ninety, a hundred miles an hour.

The Carbonado came into view, and Du Pré turned off and he went through the uprights, with the huge log across them.

Du Pré followed the graded track down to the movie camp. A big yellow machine had smoothed the dirt, and would again soon; the traffic was heavy.

Du Pré stopped the old cruiser near the big green tent that held the tables and the kitchen. People were standing around outside, and some were sitting in the shade.

Ben Burke came trotting out of the tent, and he made for Du Pré and Ripper.

"Good," said Ben. "Hirsch wants to speak to everyone in half an hour."

"But not me," said Ripper, "so I will hie myself to the roadhouse and have a nice beer and a burger with T J. Say, Ben, have you ever met that little horror Pallas?"

"Her," said Ben. "Yes, well . . ."

"That little shit swiped my gun, my badge, and my cell phone," said Ripper, "and then she waited for my boss to call to tell him all about it. Harvey loved it. Just loved it. I will never hear the end of this."

"Sorry," said Ben. "All she did to me was tell me she would cut my balls off if I wasn't nice to Maria."

"See ya," said Ripper. He got into Du Pré's cruiser.

"No," said Du Pré. "You take that thing you have."

Ripper made a face. He got out.

"I don't want to drive that nice new piece of shit," he said.

He walked to the tan government sedan, got in, and drove off.

"What is this new director?" said Du Pré.

"Lew Hirsch," said Ben. "He's directed some movies, actually I wonder why he's doing this. Public television doesn't pay that much, compared to Hollywood salaries."

Du Pré nodded.

He looked up the newly graded road. A green SUV was coming down it, bouncing from the driver braking and accelerating.

The SUV got to the bottom of the hill and it roared and swerved and slid into the movie camp.

Both doors opened. The driver was a middle-aged man dressed entirely in black leather, with huge black sunglasses on his face.

The other was Wally Williams, the man whose boat had caught fire one day on the river.

"Oh, no," said Ben.

The man in the black leather stalked toward the big green tent, and he paused outside and he preened for a moment. Wally Williams tagged along, like a small yappy dog.

"AWRIGHT!" said the man in the black leather. "I'M LEW HIRSCH AND WE HAVE WORK TO DO."

Hirsch went in the tent, yelling.

They were behind everyone had to work double hard . . . no slack . . . shooting first thing in the morning . . . you don't like it leave now . . . have to get this project done . . .

"Where the hell is the AD?" bawled Hirsch.

"Oh boy," said Ben Burke. He stood and he walked into the tent and up to Hirsch.

"We have a script conference," said Hirsch. "Director's motor home. Which is?"

Ben led Hirsch and a smirking Wally Williams off toward what had been Trey Binder's motor home.

Some of the crew members came out of the tent.

"Shit," said one. "I worked with that son of a bitch once. He's a tyrant. Last place I would ever have thought to see him again is here."

"We signed the contract," said another.

Maria came out of the tent, holding a can of Coke. She nodded to Du Pré, and she walked over.

"This don't look good, Papa," she said. "I don't like that man."

Du Pré nodded.

"Take me, the roadhouse," said Maria.

They walked to the cruiser and got in and Du Pré drove off, bouncing up the hill and then along the dirt road to the narrow blacktop. It wasn't far to the roadhouse.

T J looked up when they came in.

"That loudmouth in the motorcycle suit find you?" she said.

"Yah," said Du Pré.

"I think," said T J, "I may eighty-six him."

She pushed a whiskey and water over to Du Pré.

"Whatcha want, Missy?" said T J.

"Whiskey and water," said Maria.

T J made another and made change from the bill Du Pré slid onto the bar.

Some of the crew members came in, downcast and somber.

They took tables or stools at the bar, and T J bustled around taking orders and bringing drinks and snacks.

Their voices were low, and there was no laughter.

Maria went off to play video keno. Du Pré drank and looked off into the distance. More people came into the roadhouse.

"Papa," said Maria. "Here."

Du Pré turned round. Ben Burke was standing there, white-faced with rage.

"Hirsch ordered me to tell you your services were no longer needed," said Ben. "He's got Wally Williams advising him, and says we have to shoot a lot of the film over. It's crazy."

Du Pré nodded.

"I can't quit," said Maria. "I signed a contract. I leave, they can sue me."

Du Pré nodded.

"I am so sorry," said Ben.

Du Pré shrugged.

"It makes no sense," said Ben. "We don't have that much left to do. It will cost a fortune. We'll be way over the budget."

Du Pré looked at him.

"Maybe this Hirsch, he is supposed to do this," said Du Pré.

Ben nodded.

"Sink this, the other movie hasn't got the competition," said Ben, "I thought of that. But it doesn't make sense either. How Hirsch got the job eludes me."

"What else?" said Du Pré.

"We could all walk out," said Ben.

"I think I know, what it is," said Du Pré.

"What?" said Ben.

"Lewis and Clark stuff," said Du Pré. "Somebody wants that bad, that Wally Williams, he was screaming about it, remember?"

Ben nodded.

Du Pré sipped more of his drink.

"I take care of it," he said.

Maria grinned.

"You aren't going to give Williams that stuff, are you?" said Ben.

"You got, the telephone," said Du Pré. "I use it?"

Du Pré dialed a number and waited while the phone rang and rang.

"What?" said Bart, finally.

"It is me," said Du Pré.

"Oh, hello, Gabriel," said Bart.

"I need this thing," said Du Pré.

CHAPTER
37

"This dreary business," said Foote, "disgusts me to *read*. Two million dollars offered, no questions asked, for the things which you found. I have no idea who Bob McKenna *is*, other than he made a good deal of money in computers."

"Yah," said Du Pré, into the little phone.

"Fortunately," said Foote, "our security people are quite good. In brief, McKenna bought in to the Lewis and Clark film you are working on, which was over budget, and when the unfortunate Mr. Binder died, he was ready. Hirsch is in some trouble in his profession, and with some pressure here and there, replaced Binder, merely to bring pressure upon you to turn over the Lewis and Clark material. This crap would not do for a bad novel. Most of life would not do for a bad novel either."

"OK," said Du Pré, "so it is what I thought."

"Why," said Foote, "did you think that?"

"The crew," said Du Pré. "I think maybe they see this before, you know, have something ruined. I don't know, just the way they looked each other."

"Well," said Foote, "I expect you have things well in hand."

"Yah," said Du Pré. He shut the telephone.

Bart took the little telephone and put it in his jacket pocket.

Du Pré got in the big green SUV and Bart got behind the wheel and they drove down the loop road that led to the west pastures of the Carbonado. The film crew was there, ready to shoot some footage of the actors slogging along, dragging the pirogues through shallow water near flats thick with willows.

Bart parked atop a low hill, and he and Du Pré got out.

A big black Suburban with deeply tinted windows pulled up to the film crew, and Hirsch and Wally Williams got out, and Maria and Jason Parks and John Thomas Tipton. Sam Smythe's red SUV followed along.

Everyone gathered around Hirsch, in his black leathers.

The huddle broke up and the actors and extras trudged toward the river.

"Hard to do this in those mudflats," said Bart, looking through the binoculars.

"He is trying, get Maria to quit," said Du Pré. "So he make her wade through the mud, there."

"What a bastard," said Bart.

Hirsch and Wally Williams had taken up spots in folding chairs, on a small bump near the river and the willows.

"OK," said Du Pré. "That guy, he know what to do."

They got in the green SUV and drove down toward the film crew. Bart parked near the black Suburban.

They wandered nearer. One of the crew members trotted toward them.

"Closed area," said the man. "You'll have to leave."

"I own the place," said Bart, "so I believe that I will stay."

"Mr. Hirsch said no onlookers," said the man.

"Tell Mr. Hirsch," said Bart, "to kiss my ass."

The crewman trotted off.

"You seen him before?" said Bart.

Du Pré shook his head.

They wandered closer.

Hirsch was standing, screaming at the actors down in the river, all up to their knees in mud and sinking.

Wally Williams lay back in his folding wood-and-canvas chair.

Du Pré looked upstream where the willows were thickest.

Some of them were moving, and not with the wind.

Hirsch was in mid-bellow when the huge pale brown grizzly burst from the willows, roaring, and running directly toward the director.

The bear stopped and stood up and roared again.

Hirsch backed away, and then he ran, flat out, for the big black Suburban, with Wally Williams right behind and the bear right behind them.

Hirsch started the big SUV and he backed furiously away from the bear, and he wheeled the Suburban around in the meadow and he gunned it and he roared over the road toward the movie camp, Wally Williams desperately trying to close the passenger door.

The rest of the film crew was running in any direction they could find.

Maria and the rest of the actors had struggled to the bank. They got out, dripping mud and water. John Thomas Tipton looked terrified.

The grizzly had stopped running after the fleeing Suburban and was shambling back toward the cameras. Suddenly he stopped, stood up, and roared.

"Lester!" yelled a man in faded denim, wearing a tractor driver's cap. "Enough! Cut it out, you big oaf!"

The bear dropped back down on all fours and walked slowly to the man.

The bear yawned and lay down.

Du Pré and Bart walked up to the pair.

"OK?" said the man.

"Wonderful," said Bart.

Lester rumbled happily. His trainer scratched his belly.

"I owed that prick Hirsch one," said the trainer, "which feels damn good."

"Shall I get your rig?" said Bart.

"Nah," said the man. "We can amble up there in a minute. Lester is a ham and he likes people, so he'll want to meet some of the folks here. If he doesn't get to, he'll sulk for a week."

Maria came over, with Ben and Jason.

She smiled at the huge bear.

"He's beautiful," she said.

"Hear that, Lester?" said the trainer. "You ugly hairball."

Lester yawned hugely and sat up. His head was as high as Du Pré's, even slouched and sitting on his butt.

Lester made an odd bubbling noise.

The trainer scratched a huge ear.

"He's sweet," said Maria.

"A nice guy," said the trainer. "It was hell teaching him to *act* like a big mean bear."

"How long did it take?" said Bart.

"Five years, said the trainer.

Some of the film crew had straggled back, and the others were coming.

When they all got there, they applauded.

"Yay, bear!" they yelled.

"Making friends wherever you go," said the trainer. "You can go talk with your fans, Lester."

The big bear ambled over to a knot of worshipers, who petted him.

"Can he have a candy bar?" someone said.

"That fat bastard," said the trainer, "will eat *anything*. When we get to Billings I promised him we'd go to Fuddruckers. He'd like thirty pounds of their chopped sirloin. Loves pickles."

Kit Van Der Meer drove up in his battered old pickup. He was grinning. He got out and he walked over to Du Pré and Bart.

"The idiots in that black SUV?" he said, "drove right through my best wheatfield. According to the contract, they can't do that."

Bart nodded.

"It was the shortest way to the road," he said.

"Suppose no one thought of that?" said Kit.

Bart and Du Pré shook their heads.

"That is one big bear," said Kit. "Glad he's tame."

Lester was rolling on his back.

"Well," said the trainer, "I think we need to go. Back to beautiful Los Angeles. Lester has a role in a soon-to-be-released movie."

"Eating who?" said Kit.

"Various household names," said the trainer, "all terrified until they meet him. What a pussycat."

Lester shuffled back to the trainer.

"Come along, Lester," said the trainer. They began to walk up the hill toward the big green SUV. It had heavy springs and a bed in the back for the bear.

"Couldn't you stay?" said Maria.

"The show must go on," said the trainer. "Say good-bye, Lester."

Lester stood up and he roared, and then he fell back down on his huge paws and shuffled along beside his master.

"I never would have thought of it," said Bart.

"Your idea, Du Pré?" said Kit Van Der Meer.

Du Pré nodded.

"That Hirsch, he is a bully," said Du Pré. "They are cowards."

Ben Burke was standing near, looking pensive.

"Ben?" said Bart, "can you finish this movie?"

Ben looked up.

"Me?" he said. He shook his head, as though he was clearing his ears.

"You," said Bart.

"Yes," said Ben.

CHAPTER
38

"Things sure have got interesting since you came," said T J. "That jerk director came screaming in here, yelling about how the gas pump didn't work. I told him it didn't work until I turned it on. And I wasn't going to turn it on till his manners got better. Then he begged for some gasoline. He was shaking. I pumped him thirty bucks' worth and he threw a hundred-dollar bill on the ground and roared off. Dumb son of a bitch."

Du Pré laughed. So did Bart.

"He ain't comin' back," said T J. "Not in here at least."

"Where are the newspeople?" said Du Pré.

"They all left but two," said T J. "Some asshole's holding his family hostage in Great Falls. The two went after Mr. Congeniality, sensing a story there."

"Oh," said Bart.

"Meant they missed the guy with the bear," said T J. "Nice man. Came in and paid for some gas, and asked me if I would sell him some burgers. All frozen, I said. He said fine, bought a whole box. So I went out, to see what was up. Jesus, what a monster."

"He's a very nice bear," said Bart.

"Big sucker," said T J.

"True," said Bart.

"The guy with the bear was maybe a half hour after the asshole," said T J. "I don't suppose they was connected."

"Not really," said Bart.

"Uh-huh," said T J. "Say, you want a couple of these?"

She reached down behind the bar and fetched up a couple of masks.

Chipmunk masks.

Du Pré choked, and he laughed.

"Picking on him," said Du Pré.

"Uh-huh," said T J. "Anybody got the big head like John Thomas Tipton, we pick on."

"Old tradition?" said Bart.

"Started with Custer," said T J, "you think on it."

"I'd always wondered about that," said Bart.

Du Pré laughed. T J raised an eyebrow, and he nodded and she made up a whiskey and water for him and a soda for Bart.

"So what happens with the movie," said T J.

"They'll finish it now," said Bart.

"We getting another flamer like that clown who was just here?" said T J.

Bart shook his head.

"Ben Burke will finish it," said Bart.

The door opened, and Sam Smythe and Gordon Ketter came in. The cameraman was whooping and laughing.

"Subside, damn it," said Sam, elbowing Gordon in the chest.

"I got it on lovely film film film film," sang Gordon.

"The bear?" said Bart.

"The bear emerging from the willows," said Gordon, "the director, one Hirsch, crapping his pants. He dropped a *load* in 'em, and then he took off. So'd everybody else."

"But not our Gordon of the Carbonado," said Sam.

"Yup," said Gordon. "Saw that big bastard come out of the brush and two thoughts came: I know that bear. His name is Lester."

"Famous bear, Lester?" said Du Pré.

"Yup," said Gordon. "Figured fun was being had right off. Hirsch has a nose problem, and, well, he was not at his best, thinking fast like that."

The telephone rang and T J moved down to the end of the bar and she answered it. She listened a moment and let out a whoop.

"Yes!" she said. She hang up.

Everyone waited.

"Hirsch wrecked the rig he was driving," said T J. "Nobody hurt, but . . . well, they found *drugs*. Lots of 'em I guess. So he's on his way to jail."

"Perfect," said Sam Smythe. "He's toast now. Ben really can do it."

T J looked at her.

"Ben'll finish the picture," said Sam.

"Our Ben?" said T J. "The one with the nice manners?"

"Him," said Sam.

"There is a God," said T J. "Drinks on the house."

"None for us," said Sam Smythe. "We have to get back to work. John Thomas Tipton should be calm enough now to stand in the boat and not shake himself off."

They went back out.

"I," said Bart, "must go home and dig an irrigation ditch for the Martin ranch."

Du Pré nodded.

"I be back soon as the movie, it is done," said Du Pré.

"Playing Friday?" said T J. "Please."

"See you then," said Bart. He left.

Du Pré finished his drink, then he went out to his cruiser, got in, and drove off. He smoked and he kept glancing at the land, and finally he turned off on a dirt track that wound through unfenced scabland, down to the Missouri.

Du Pré parked by the bluffs and wandered down a path into a canyon, a narrow one cut deep by waters from the long-gone ice. At the bottom a small creek trickled, and mosses and ferns grew well in the cool moist shade.

The canyon came to the river, belling out at the mouth.

An old cabin stood back in the cottonwoods, the roof caved in and the logs gone to rot and silver wood. Du Pré looked at the corner joints. Finnish. Cut so there was no place for the water to sit.

He walked down to the edge of the river.

The place where the killer had stood with the rifle, waiting on Rupe and Lee was directly across. Du Pré could see the tree the gunman had used.

The current was slow on this side, and sandbars stuck up through the surface.

Du Pré found a little landing, a broken place in the bank, where sand had gathered. The place was only six or so feet wide.

Wide enough for a canoe.

Rained some, and there hadn't been anyone here for some time.

Du Pré looked up the river. He could see at least two miles, perhaps more.

Du Pré began to cast back and forth across the path as he walked.

He stopped and squatted several times, smoking, looking carefully at the ground.

He got back in his cruiser and drove back to the county road and then west. He passed two old ranch houses, white, simple, set in windbreaks of poplars.

Du Pré stopped and he turned around and he drove back to the roadhouse.

T J was there, and so was Old Harry. Old Harry had a red beer in front of him.

"Fun out at the farm," said Old Harry. "Wish I coulda seen it."

"It was filmed," said Du Pré. "You can see that."

Old Harry grinned.

"They are somethin'," he said.

"I am going back, see they need me," said Du Pré.

"Be along 'bout sundown," said Old Harry.

Du Pré drove back to the Carbonado and down to the movie camp. Everyone was there, laughing and talking and eating and drinking.

Du Pré found Maria and Jason Parks and Ben Burke in the tent, sitting at a table with several other people.

"Got the rest of the day off," said Maria. "Director is a real asshole, first thing in the morning, he says."

"I have studied upon it," said Ben.

"How much longer, the movie," said Du Pré.

"A week," said Ben, "unless there is something unforeseen."

Du Pré nodded.

"You need me?" he said.

"Yes," said Ben, "in case of any trouble with the boats. And we need some shots of you fiddling in the camp."

Du Pré shook his head.

"I am too old," he said. "You get somebody fake it, I play the music."

Ben nodded.

"I am going, Toussaint," said Du Pré. "I will be back in the morning."

"OK," said Maria. "Where is that Ripper anyway?"

Du Pré shrugged.

Snooping around, where Ripper is.

Du Pré went out and looked at the river for a while.

He rolled a smoke and he lit it and he stared at the brown purling waters.

Jack Rupe and Davis Lee had come down the river.

Bill Rupe had never made it out.

Du Pré shook his head, got into his old cruiser, and drove away.

CHAPTER

39

The old woman was in her garden, hoeing weeds with the steady grub-and-chop people get when they do it a lot.

A small yappy rag mop of a dog shrieked at Du Pré when he came walking up to the high mesh fence. The little animal ran back and forth at the base of the wire, squeaking.

The old woman turned, and Du Pré took off his hat.

"Mrs. Leverett?" said Du Pré, "I am Du Pré."

"I see that," she said. She came to the gate, tugging at the stained leather gloves on her hands. They came off and she poked them through the mesh of the wire. She pulled back the bolt and she opened the gate and she closed it.

The fence was twelve feet high.

"Had a damn antelope clear that," she said, pointing. "Dumb thing couldn't get enough speed up to clear it again. Then when I tried to haze him out of the gate he panicked and got his feet through the wire, and so I had to shoot the dumb bastard. Meat was no good, of course."

Du Pré nodded. Panicked animal, muscles are full of adrenaline and sour lactic acid.

"I need a bigger dog," said the old woman. "got half of the antelope in the freezer yet. Noodles here doesn't eat a lot."

Du Pré looked around the little ranch. It still had an old log barn, built about 1885, they must have dragged the logs from the Bear Paw Mountains with oxen.

"My grandfather built that," said Mrs. Leverett. "My dad didn't marry my mother till he was fifty-two. Mother was nearly forty."

There was a tiny graveyard under some Russian olives at the corner of the hay meadow.

Mrs. Leverett followed his eyes.

"Yup," she said, "they're asleep there, close to home."

Du Pré rolled a smoke and lit it.

"Could I have one of those?" said Mrs. Leverett. "I keep tryin' to quit."

Du Pré nodded. He rolled a smoke and he handed it to her and he held out his lighter.

"Come in," she said. "Bad coffee and old stories. Do you like old stories, Mr. Du Pré?"

"Yah," said Du Pré.

She walked to the house, and Du Pré followed. The kitchen was painted in sandy tones, the counters were of strips of walnut and maple glued together and doweled off.

The cabinets had been made by someone who knew wood.

"My husband," she said, "was a rancher and a good one. He would have rather been a maker of furniture. But he was born a rancher, and he died one."

Du Pré touched a door. No shift in the hinges.

Mrs. Leverett cleared some papers from the table and set out two cups and saucers, delicate porcelains with roses on them. She poured coffee from an insulated carafe.

"Cream and sugar?" asked Mrs. Leverett.

Du Pré shook his head.

She sat at the table, and so did Du Pré.

"So," she said. "You have a question?"

"Van Der Meers," said Du Pré.

Mrs. Leverett nodded.

"Kees Van Der Meer came here in 1882," she said. "Old patroon family, some money, not a lot, I guess. He had bought scrubs in Texas, and he drove them north. The Judith Basin was taken, so was the rest of the Musselshell country, most of the good lands were spoke for. He came here. Tough country, but Kees knew if you had enough of it you could make a go of it."

Du Pré sipped his coffee.

"But there were a few others here, too, more than the land could support."

Du Pré set down his cup.

"No one could really ever prove anything," said Mrs. Leverett, "but houses and barns caught fire, cattle were killed, bullets barely missed people. So the rest of them sold out, south of the river. Kees paid a fair price."

Du Pré waited.

"Kees owned all of the lands that became the Carbonado by 1885," said Mrs. Leverett. "That was a real wet summer and the grass was the best anyone had known, better than the old Indians remembered. So everyone went to the bank and borrowed and bought cattle and they all got ready to be rich."

Du Pré nodded.

"Kees was the only one who didn't buy more cattle," said Mrs. Leverett. "He bought fifteen thousand sheep. Railroad wasn't here yet, of course, and so he was going to have to trail them up, couple hundred miles; the line ended at Miles City then. His neighbors got wind of it and they went to Kees and told him if he brought in sheep, they'd shoot 'em all. They meant it, and Kees knew it, so he sold the sheep. Market had gone up on 'em, so he made a lot of profit. And it was too late to buy any cattle that year, so he just waited on the next."

Du Pré nodded.

"Kees didn't like people much," said Mrs. Leverett, "but he did like the Indians. Later on he was one of the people who hid the ceremonial things, the sacred bundles for Sioux and Cheyennes, when the government outlawed their religions. Let 'em do the Sun Dance out on his ranch and flat lied to the feds when they came looking."

Du Pré waited.

"So one of the medicine people warned Kees the next winter would be terrible. Kees bought no cattle. It was 1886."

Yah, thought Du Pré, 1886, winter wiped out the cattlemen in Montana, wiped out the sheepmen, cold and snow for weeks, forty below, in the spring the tops of the trees are full of rotting cows in the coulees, snowdrifts eighty feet deep and the cows sink down in it.

"Kees was sitting pretty," she said. "Money in the bank, competition wiped out, and so he bought up more and more and he brought in Durham cattle, and he made a lot of money and he got married."

Du Pré leaned forward, looking at her old blue eyes.

"They're still here," said Mrs. Leverett, "the only ones from back then. My people didn't come until 1910. Homesteaded. Went to ranching. That story."

"Who is old Harry?" said Du Pré.

"Great-uncle," said Mrs. Leverett.

Du Pré nodded.

A pickup truck drove in, motor grumbling.

Mrs. Leverett didn't move.

"My grandson, Sam," said Mrs. Leverett.

A door slammed.

Du Pré waited. When the screen door opened he got up.

Sam came in. Du Pré had seen him at the roadhouse. Maybe

213

twenty, tough and already weathered, with the squint of people who look a long ways through good country.

Sam stood near the table.

"This is Mr. Du Pré," said Mrs. Leverett.

Sam looked at Du Pré.

"I know who he is," said Sam.

"I am going," said Du Pré. Before I have to hurt this young pup.

"Sam," said Mrs. Leverett, "mind your goddamned manners."

Sam looked at her. He nodded and he got coffee and he found another chair and brought it over.

Du Pré looked at Mrs. Leverett.

"I believe," she said, "that was the genealogy you wanted."

Du Pré sighed.

He nodded.

"Doo Pray," said Sam, "the famous fiddling dick."

"It's no use, Sam," said Mrs. Leverett, sharply. Sam looked at the floor.

Du Pré put on his hat.

He reached in his shirt pocket and he took out the little cassette tape that Bill Rupe had given him and he put it on the table.

"Father, one of the two shot, the river, said give that, the right people," said Du Pré.

Mrs. Leverett looked at the tape, her eyes very old.

"What are you going to do, Mr. Du Pré?" she said.

"I don't know," said Du Pré. "Few days about forty FBIs are here, they do it. I don't know."

Sam drew in his breath sharply and he started to rise, and Mrs. Leverett slammed her hand on his wrist.

"NO!" she said, and Sam slumped back.

"Listen, the tape," said Du Pré.

Mrs. Leverett looked at him for a long time.

She nodded.

"Thank you," she said.

CHAPTER
40

They drove fast through the heavy rain sluicing down. The wipers flung silver gouts of water off and more came.

"God, Papa," said Maria, "what a fucking mess." She was sitting in the backseat of the cruiser with Ben.

"What is this exactly?" said Ben. "I mean I know a little. But if I'm on my way to do something about it, I would appreciate knowing more."

"The kids," said Du Pré. "Maybe they don't kill all nine of the people who are missing, but they sure kill Rupe and Lee."

Ben sighed.

"God," he said. "Why?"

"Papa," said Maria, "what are we going to do?"

"I don't know," said Du Pré.

Du Pré passed a semi, the windshield opaque from water sent up by the heavy tires. Then it cleared and they were past.

"See Benetsee," said Maria.

"I don't understand," said Ben. "This is plain, ordinary, garden-variety murder."

Du Pré said nothing. He rolled a smoke.

"Lots of people there must know," said Maria. "They know and they don't do anything."

"Old Harry," said Ben.

"Yah," said Du Pré.

"Shit," said Ben, "that's scary."

"What is the thing you want me to do, Papa?" said Maria.

"See Benetsee," said Du Pré. "It is that I don't want, start, a war. Me, I don't know what they do, them parents, even the cops. I don't know."

"It's that bad, isn't it?" said Ben. "They are feeling that angry."

"Yah," said Du Pré.

Du Pré slowed. They had come to the east–west road that led to Toussaint.

"Three days of rain like this, you ought to be done with your drought," said Ben.

"It has been going on, ten thousand years," said Du Pré. "Needs more than a few inches of rain."

"Ho, Papa," said Maria. "This is not fun. I think maybe someday I help, get a bad guy, this is not good at all."

"What the hell are you saying?" said Ben. "They murdered *people*."

"He is right, Papa," said Maria.

"Good," said Du Pré, "it is good, be right. Me, I don't know what I do, so I am not so sure I am good."

"What's the problem?" said Ben.

"Something started this, Papa," said Maria.

Du Pré nodded.

"What?"

"I do not know," said Du Pré. "I don't know what to do. So I want to see Benetsee and then I am more confused, his damn riddles."

"You take too much shit from him," said Maria.

"Yah," said Du Pré.

They roared down the highway. The rain had lessened, and the windshield wipers kept up now.

Du Pré smoked and he had a pull at his flask of whiskey and he offered it over his shoulder. Ben took it.

"I wish I knew what was going on," he said.

"Yah," said Du Pré.

Du Pré slowed and turned off on the dirt road that wound up toward the Wolf Mountains, shrouded in gray wet.

There were huge puddles at the bottoms of the hills.

Great gouts of dirty water shot up when the cruiser went through them.

Wet cattle looked mournfully over dripping fences.

Du Pré turned on the bench road and went down and up and down and then he turned left and wallowed through mud to Benetsee's cabin set back in the stand of aromatic cedars and yellow pine. There was smoke purling up from the chimney.

They got out and ran for the porch, and the door opened.

Pelon and Benetsee were playing cards, with a dirty old deck.

"Wine, tobacco?" said Benetsee. He grinned at Du Pré.

Du Pré dashed back out and got the sack from the trunk, cursing.

Pelon took the jug of screwtop wine, opened it, and poured a big glass for Benetsee, who drank it and held the glass out again.

Du Pré rolled the old man a smoke.

"I need help," said Du Pré.

"All the time," said Benetsee. "I don't never see you, you don't need help."

He grinned, his teeth brown stumps in his pale old gums.

"Kids murdering people," said Du Pré, "but me, I don't know which ones, kill who, which ones talk only. And the people there know, they have to, they don't do anything."

Benetsee nodded.

"Bad times," he said. "I don't know times like these, never."

Ben and Maria had sat on the trunk under the window.

"Long way from here," said Benetsee.

"Not for you," said Du Pré.

Benetsee looked at him, and he smiled.

"You come," he said.

He went out the door and through the heavy rain, whistling. He trotted down the path that led west toward the tall rock spire that stuck out from the knees of the mountains.

Du Pré saw something pale through the trees and the rain, and then he bent his head and went on, looking for puddles and things to trip over.

He smelled woodsmoke.

Benetsee went round the little ridge of rock at the base of the spire.

The old Land Rover sat there. A faded and patched wall tent was set up on a mound so the water would drain.

Bill Rupe flipped open the front flap and waved for them to come in. He was sitting in a folding camp chair, reading *The New Yorker*.

"Damn," said Du Pré, "I thought you were dead, in the river."

"Don't think so," said Bill Rupe, looking sadly at Du Pré.

He shut the magazine.

"You talk," said Benetsee, and he was back out in the rain and gone.

Rupe took a small pouch of tobacco from his shirt pocket and expertly rolled a smoke. He lit it, handed it to Du Pré, and made himself another.

"What happened?" said Du Pré.

"Oh," said Rupe, "I spent so long in wars, shooting pictures, I got to be as good at reading ground as any grunt. Downstream from where I left you I saw a flash in the trees, right where the current would bring me close to shore. So I grabbed a dry pack and went over the side. Let the canoe go on."

"Dry pack," said Du Pré.

"Had what I needed," said Rupe, "space blanket, food, compass, map, camera, and film, and so I took up residence, took some photographs of the kid who was going to kill me. Then some others came and I shot them, too. Then I swam the river and hiked out to a road, hitched a ride, and flew home. Got a few things and went to Costa Rica for a few days."

"While you are dead, maybe," said Du Pré.

Rupe grinned.

"Stirred things up," he said.

Du Pré nodded.

"Got back a couple of days ago. My rig was where I had left it." said Rupe, reaching into a leather satchel.

He pulled out a brown envelope with a string tie.

"You know what to do with these," he said. "I truly don't."

"I gave your tape to this woman," said Du Pré. "She was the one I maybe think should have it."

Rupe nodded. He looked drawn and sad.

"Life breaks everybody," he said.

Du Pré sighed.

"OK," he said, standing up.

"Thank you," said Rupe.

Du Pré nodded, and he went out and back up the soggy trail.

Maria and Ben were still inside. The rain was coming down harder.

Benetsee and Pelon were gone.

"Come on," said Du Pré.

They went out to the old cruiser and got in. Du Pré backed fast down the drive and he slid out onto the country road and then he drove off.

"What, Papa?" said Maria.

Du Pré pushed the envelope over the seat to her.

She opened it and then she and Ben looked through the photographs.

"Guy with the rifle and the cell phone," said Ben. "Who is he?"

"Yeah," said Maria.

"His name's Sam," said Du Pré.

CHAPTER 41

"Aunty Harvey is coming this evening," said Ripper. "I have to go and fetch him. His mood is not good. He says you could have fucking well figured things out by now if you had wanted to. He grumbles about Métis treachery. You know."

"It is not like sawing wood," said Du Pré.

"Harvey has faith in you," said Ripper.

"Him don't have to come," said Du Pré. "Nothing for him to do."

"He knows that," said Ripper. "Bill Rupe had a lot of friends. Jack did, too, and Davis Lee is old Boston money. Congressional nuts are being twisted. This travels down the food chain, to lowly folk like me and Harvey, who were friends of the Rupes."

Du Pré nodded.

"You want anything?" said T J.

"Cheeseburger," said Ripper, "heavy on the cholesterol."

"Rare?" said T J.

Ripper nodded.

"Drink?" said T J.

"Iced tea," said Ripper. "My boss is coming, wouldn't do for me to have beer on my breath."

T J went off. A meat patty hit the grill and sizzled.

"You want to tell me anything?" said Ripper.

Du Pré shook his head.

"I don't know about them yet," said Du Pré.

"You're lying, but I don't mind," said Ripper. "I think I got an idea. I may go out in the country, wait."

Hunting, Du Pré thought. I wonder Ripper is any good at it. Probably.

T J brought the iced tea, and Ripper drank it all and held out the big glass for more.

T J filled it.

"Rupe and Lee, T J," said Ripper, "they were good people."

T J looked at him.

"You say so," she said.

Ripper looked at her for a moment. He handed her a bill, and T J walked away with it, on into the kitchen. She looked through the port.

"Where's my change?" he whined, after T J had stuffed the bill in the cash register. "And my receipt."

"Where's my tip?" said T J.

"This is outrageous," said Ripper.

"Two bucks," said T J. She came back to the bar.

"Two *dollars*?" said Ripper.

T J nodded.

Ripper found two dollars in his jeans. He slid them over the bar.

"My receipt?" said Ripper.

T J scribbled something on a green receipt and she handed it over.

Ripper looked at it.

"Aww," he said, "it's only for five bucks."

"You have a plane to catch," said T J.

Ripper nodded and slunk out the door.

"Government," said T J. "Can't trust it."

Bassman came in, wheeling an amplifier. Du Pré got up to help him unload the gear from his van. It took each of them three trips. Bassman set to work connecting the speakers and the board and the microphone lines.

Du Pré paused outside for a moment, and saw a small blue-and-white plane lift off the dirt runway across the road.

He rolled a smoke and just as he lit it Madelaine turned into the parking lot in front of the roadhouse. Her station wagon was full of children.

Du Pré nodded.

Madelaine stopped, and she grinned at Du Pré.

All of the doors opened and Du Pré's grandchildren tumbled out and they ran to him, laughing.

Grandpère grandpère grandpère . . .

Du Pré lifted up each one in turn and kissed them. They hung on his neck for a moment and then it was somebody else's turn.

"Where is Aunty Maria?" said Pallas. "That Ben guy, he is nice to her?"

"Very," said Du Pré.

Save a life, do a good deed.

"OK," said Pallas, "we go and see this movie, Aunty Maria she is a star in?"

"Yah," said Du Pré.

The kids piled into the roadhouse, hollering.

"T J," said Madelaine, "here she is, nice bar, quiet drunks she has known, her life, now this."

They kissed and held each other.

"You be home soon for good," said Madelaine. "This fool movie, it is done then."

Du Pré nodded.

Pallas came back out.

"Where is that . . . Challes Van Dooosen?" she said.

"He heard, you coming, he ran away," said Du Pré.

"He be back?" said Pallas.

"Yah, back this evening," said Du Pré.

"I was some mean to him," said Pallas. "I be nicer this time."

"Ripper," said Du Pré, "likes you very much."

"Good," said Pallas. "When I am eighteen I am going to marry him."

"Good," said Du Pré. "You tell him that, tonight."

"I will," said Pallas.

"Maybe he don't want, marry you," said Madelaine. "He is a lot older."

"He is twenty-seven," said Pallas. "Means he will be thirty-eight when we get married. Not so old."

"What if he don't want, marry you?" said Madelaine.

"It will be good for him," said Pallas. "I will explain, him."

She ran back inside.

"Ripper, he is dead meat," said Du Pré.

"She probably do it," said Madelaine.

Du Pré shook his head.

"Maria she is tough when she is little," said Du Pré. "Not that tough, though."

"Maria don't have eleven brothers, sisters," said Madelaine. "That make you plenty tough, yes."

Madelaine walked to the door and opened it.

"Kids, here," she said, "We are going now."

"Praise God," said T J.

The children piled out the door and they all got into Du Pré's old cruiser. Madelaine and Du Pré got in, with two kids in the front seat and five in the back. The older ones hadn't come.

"Alcide let a fart," said Marisa. "Ugh."

"Hee," said Alcide.

Du Pré sighed and he started the cruiser and they went off toward the Carbonado. He turned off at the main gate and wound down to the camp by the river. There was no one in it but the staff in the kitchen and one assistant reading some papers at a table in the sun.

Du Pré drove on toward the place where they had been filming.

"They are done?" said Madelaine.

"Done here," said Du Pré. "They go, the mountains for some more shooting, then the ocean, but not so many people. Just Maria and that Jason Parks, the Tipton guy, a few others. Take another month, Ben say."

"Maria like it?"

Du Pré shrugged.

They stopped well back from the film crew, who were working on some shots of Maria and Jason and Tipton pushing through the willows with the white pirogue.

The children sat in the car, waiting.

"You get out," said Madelaine, "but don't get, the way of anyone. They are working ver' hard here."

Little heads nodded.

Ben Burke came out of the tangle of cameras and people, smiling.

"Great!" he said. "We just finished!"

Pallas raced over to him and she said something and Ben laughed.

Maria came, in her beaded buckskins, and Parks in his fringed leathers, carrying a Pennsylvania rifle. Tipton was talking to one of the crew members.

The children charged Aunty Maria in a body. She got down on her knees and she opened her arms and she disappeared in the rush of little bodies.

"How is the movie?" said Madelaine, when Ben got near.

"Fine," he said. "We'll finish in a couple more days, maybe early as Monday."

"Du Pré is not going with you," said Madelaine.

"It's going really well," said Ben.

Du Pré nodded, and he rolled a smoke.

CHAPTER
42

The roadhouse was full to bursting with people, and there were many more out in the parking lot, sitting on the tailgates of pickups and drinking beer and talking.

Du Pré and Bassman and Tally, the crippled accordion player, began the music early, as soon as there were fifty people there.

Children darted in and out of the roadhouse, and some were off on the airstrip playing soccer.

Du Pré and the band broke at sunset, and when they did Du Pré went outside and he rolled a smoke and he drank a long tall drink. It was hot in the roadhouse, and the sweat felt good as it wicked away and chilled him.

A small plane flew in from the southeast, and it circled once and parents called their children to get the hell off the runway.

The kids scattered, and the plane came in, the pilot setting it down deftly, rolling to a stop near the windsock, which hung limply on its pole.

Ripper and Harvey jumped out and the pilot taxied to some stakes off the dirt runway and he parked the plane between them and he got out and began to tie the plane down. Harvey fished a duffel bag out of the passenger compartment, and he and Ripper walked slowly to the roadhouse, heads down, talking.

Du Pré went in to get a fresh drink. Madelaine and T J were pulling beers and mixing whiskey ditches furiously, so Du Pré reached over and got the whiskey and he made his own, and then he carried it back outside. People thanked him for his music as he passed.

Harvey and Ripper were standing off in the lot, next to the sedan Ripper had been driving.

Du Pré walked over.

"I get to dance tonight," said Harvey.

"He was very good," said Ripper. "Hardly whined and blubbered at all."

Du Pré nodded.

"What's up?" said Harvey.

Du Pré could see Pallas out of the corner of his eye, bearing down on her fiancé.

"Pallas got to talk to you," said Du Pré.

Ripper looked at the little girl running toward him.

"Christ," said Ripper, "what does the little monster want now?"

"Better, she tell you," said Du Pré. He took Harvey by the arm and walked him away a few steps.

"You find the shooter?" said Harvey.

Du Pré nodded.

"Well?" said Harvey.

Du Pré bent close to Harvey's ear and he whispered.

Harvey looked at him sharply.

"You're *sure*," he said.

Du Pré nodded.

"God," said Harvey, "that's awful."

"After, the movie," said Du Pré. "You see?"

Harvey looked at him, and he nodded.

Then he grinned.

"Why didn't you just tell me?" he said.

"Madelaine wants, dance with you," said Du Pré.

"Yes," said Harvey. He looked off at the rolling endless prairie clear to the horizon.

"This is beautiful," he said. "And if you quote me, I'll deny it."

Du Pré sipped his drink.

"What about the Lewis and Clark stuff?" said Harvey.

"Benetsee took it," said Du Pré.

Harvey nodded.

"I suppose the stuff's safe with him," he said.

"Yah," said Du Pré.

"So . . . after the film crew leaves?" said Harvey.

Du Pré nodded.

"OK," said Harvey. "That's fine."

It was time to play again, and so Du Pré went back in and he got his fiddle and he started "Baptiste's Lament" and Tally and Bassman joined him, and then they played "Black Water" and the crowd began to thin, people going outside to dance in the cool air. Madelaine took Harvey's hand and they went off, and Du Pré laughed.

. . . the woman of the fiddler, she never get to dance . . .

Du Pré looked up, to see Kit and Lou Van Der Meer and their tall children, the two boys and Kelly, the young woman who loved horses. They waved and Du Pré nodded and they went to the bar to get drinks.

Jacqueline and Raymond came late, and they listened to the last of Du Pré's second set and then they herded the kids into their van for the drive home to Toussaint.

Du Pré and Madelaine went outside, and they stood with Raymond and Jacqueline.

Pallas, very tired and sleepy, stuck her head out of the window.

"He said yes," said Pallas, "like I said he would."

"Good," said Du Pré.

"Good night," said Pallas, pulling her head back in and shutting the window.

"Yes, what?" said Jacqueline.

"Pallas say she will marry Ripper, when she is eighteen," said Madelaine.

"That Ripper," said Jacqueline. "He better be some worried, him, my girl she mean what she says."

Everybody laughed.

Jacqueline and Raymond left then, with their tired crew.

Du Pré and Madelaine walked down the road a ways, leaving the people behind.

"You figure it out, Du Pré?" said Madelaine.

Du Pré nodded.

"Not good, huh?" said Madelaine.

Du Pré sighed.

"No," he said.

"Well," said Madeline, "you talk when you want to. Me, I am so lonely, for my Du Pré, I come to stay till we can go home."

"Monday maybe," said Du Pré.

Madelaine looked at him, then she nodded.

Harvey and Ripper were off sitting on the hood of the tan sedan, each with a beer. They raised their bottles when Du Pré and Madelaine came up to them.

"Mighty fine music, Du Pré," said Harvey.

"Good dancing," said Madelaine.

Ripper grinned, and he shook his head.

"I don't want to leave here," he said. "I didn't take any time to look at this country before. But, the light. It makes me want to paint again."

"Ripper was a promising young artist once," said Harvey, "till I got him a job."

"I'll send you cactus," said Ripper, "pots of them."

The sun's last light in the west was a fire of red and purple and white.

A bullbat clacked past, gobbling insects.

Coyotes began to howl in the far hills, the hunting song.

"This will all be over soon," said Harvey. "Right, Du Pré?"

Du Pré nodded.

"Yah," he said.

"Write a song about it?" said Harvey.

Du Pré nodded.

They went back in then, and the crowd had thinned a little as the ranchers had headed home, to sleep till just before dawn.

Du Pré began with a slow waltz.

Couples went to the tiny dance floor and they held each other close as they moved to the music.

I think of them, that Lewis, that Clark, the Métis boatmen, going up the river, young Sacajawea and her baby, the soldiers cursing as they heaved on the ropes, the hills spotted with elk and buffalo, Du Pré thought. I think of them passing here, going west, coming home, hiding the things in the cache, why?

It is in that book.

Cruzatte, his fiddling at night, the men dance, they are a long way from home.

Long time gone.

Long time gone.

The Missouri, flows to the Mississippi, once it went to the Red River.

Ice.

Du Pré fiddled. He played and played, and then he stopped.

The crowd looked at him a moment, and then they applauded wildly.

Du Pré bowed.

"I never heard that before," said Tally.

"Neither did Du Pré," said Bassman. "Heard it now though."

John Thomas Tipton came in, lugging his guitar case, and he stood regally at the bar, swaying a little. He drank a beer. He drank another. He went off to the john.

Dozens of people whipped out chipmunk masks and put them on.

John Thomas Tipton came back from the pisser, rubbing his eyes, and he went back to his beer glass, and it was a moment before he lifted his eyes and looked out on a room full of large chipmunks.

He goggled for a moment.

"Motherfuckers!" he screamed. He grabbed his guitar case and fled into the night.

Sam Smythe went running after him.

The crowd waited, quietly.

Sam came back in.

"He's gone," she said, "solid gone. Ben?"

Ben Burke looked at her.

"Write that idiot out of the script, willya?"

Cheers and more cheers.

The chipmunks all got free beers.

CHAPTER
43

"I want to see where it happened," said Harvey, "and then I will go and take your future grandson-in-law here with me."

"Right," said Ripper. "Get me out of here before that little horror does me in entirely."

Du Pré laughed.

"Little Pallas?" he said. "She scare you some, that is good. She scare me, too. Shitless."

They were having breakfast at Du Pré's camp. Old Harry and his big black dog Lefty were there, and Madelaine.

"I sure sleep well here," said Harvey. "It must be the lack of gunfire in the night."

"Ah," said Ripper. "Ya like it, Harvey, tell ya what, let's get us some prickly pear cactus, take home."

Harvey shook his head.

"It'd just die there," he said.

"Biscuits?" said Madelaine. She lifted the big black dutch oven from the coals and lifted the lid, ashy from the coals that had been heaped on top of it. Puffs of gray dust flew away.

The biscuits were tall and golden brown.

Harvey and Du Pré and Old Harry and Ripper wolfed them down.

With chokecherry jelly and butter.

"So you fellers is going?" said Old Harry.

"Yes, sir," said Harvey. "No need for us here."

Old Harry looked from Ripper to Harvey to Du Pré.

"Movie's done, the one here," said Old Harry, "and I can go back to bein' ree-tired, I guess."

The old man got up and walked back in the cool shade of the cottonwood grove to his bedroll. Lefty went under Old Harry's pickup, but he kept a watchful eye on the table. Scraps could appear at any moment, and a good dog had to be alert.

"Long way to come for a day," said Madelaine.

"Not so long," said Harvey, "For a dance, lovely lady."

Madelaine laughed.

"So smooth talk," she said. "You talk like that, your wife?"

"Every day," said Harvey. "If I don't, she notices."

"You bring her here sometime," said Madelaine.

Harvey nodded.

"Yes," he said.

"If we're gonna make the plane," said Ripper, "and go off to look at the crime scene, we better move."

"It's early," said Harvey.

"Yeah," said Ripper, "but if you don't get your stumps humpin', *I* will drive to Billings, which you will flat hate."

Harvey got up immediately.

They walked to Du Pré's old cruiser and got in and Du Pré did, too, and he drove off on the track that led upriver, to the place where the gunman had stood and waited for the canoe with Rupe and Lee in it.

It took a half hour to get to the flat bench above the grove. Du Pré got out, and he stretched and he yawned and he belched.

He nodded to Ripper and Harvey and he began to walk down the narrow deer path that wiggled down the side of the bluff. It wasn't a long drop, and soon Du Pré was striding through the tall grass, dew soaking his pant legs.

A giant orb spider web had been spun over the trail, and the spider was in the center, holding the guy lines that carried the vibrations of caught insects to her front claws. She was as big as a walnut in the body, yellow and black and white, with two horns on her abdomen.

"Jesus," said Harvey, "I'd hate to get bit by *that*."

"It probably isn't poisonous," said Ripper.

"All them orb spiders, are," said Du Pré.

"Oh," said Ripper.

They edged around the huge spiderweb, blackberry canes clutching at the cloth of their pants.

Du Pré led them through the trees, around another way than the one he had come on before.

A huge cottonwood had fallen, and Du Pré halted and he looked at it a long time. It lay across the path and he had to lead Harvey and Ripper around it, through more brush and thorny blackberries.

"Here," said Du Pré, pointing.

Harvey shook his head.

"Amazing," he said. "I can't see anything but brush and trees . . . all the things that should be here. Course, if we did a grid search we'd find something."

"No," said Du Pré, "you would not."

"So the shooter stood here?" said Harvey, pointing to the tree that hugged the river's edge.

"Yah," said Du Pré. "They shoot, twice, don't eject the second shell, pick up the first."

"A two-seventy?" said Harvey. "That'd go right on through."

Du Pré nodded.

"They go over, into the water, and the river takes the canoe and the bodies go down, catch in the logjam Old Harry knows about."

"He in on it?" said Harvey.

Du Pré sighed.

"No," he said, "I don't think so. But he probably knows, too."

"Hard to be out here, living your life, and then, of a sudden, have a lot of assholes crawling all over it," said Harvey. "But this will just make it worse. Martyrs."

"Yah," said Du Pré.

"That's the canyon over there?" said Harvey.

Du Pré nodded.

"You can see up the river, long way," said Du Pré.

"Not like here. Current is weak here, take a couple of minutes, paddle over here. Then you go home, come back early in the morning, you see them camp."

"What had they done, Rupe and Lee?" said Harvey.

"Upriver," said Du Pré, "other people. They cut some fences, pull them out of the way, so there is maybe a better shot for the camera, look like it did before the cattlemen fence it here."

"Christ," said Harvey. "There's lots of places don't have fences."

Du Pré nodded.

"Yah," he said, "but they want one, does. So the wrong people pay."

"There will be more of this," said Harvey. "I know it."

Du Pré nodded.

"Time to go," said Ripper. "Unless you want *me* to drive."

"I spend a lot of time busting really bad people," said Harvey, "And I like doing that. This is something else."

"Yah," said Du Pré.

"What do we do when there is no place left?" said Harvey. "No place at all where it is simply quiet? I took my family camping, all the way to Maine. Got the tent, the chuck box, the lot. Found a place. Thought my kids could listen to the wind in the pines. Know what we listened to? Air compressors. All those assholes with the motor homes and the air conditioning and the TV and all. The place was bedlam. It's quieter to home in Washington, D.C."

"Modern times, man," said Ripper.

They walked back to Du Pré's cruiser. They got in and Harvey and Ripper looked at the river for a moment and then Du Pré started the engine and they wheeled around.

"Hey look, man," said Ripper, looking out the window to his right. "Stop the car."

Du Pré stopped, and they got out.

A herd of horses was running across the hills, against the sky, forty of them, hooves pounding and manes flying, and they plunged down the hill.

Kelly Van Der Meer was riding after them, her head down on her horse's neck and her hat held in the wind by the chinstrings.

The horses went behind a hill and for a moment they were all out of sight, and then they came up and over, directly toward Du Pré and Ripper and Harvey.

The leader was a huge bay horse, who tossed his head as he ran flat out. The others pounded along behind him.

Kelly came over the hill, standing up in her stirrups, cracking a long whip, and the cavvy turned again, and they thundered by, a river of horses moving like the wind.

Ripper waved, but Kelly ignored him and the horses and the girl flew on, down toward the river. They broke then and milled a moment and Kelly cracked the whip again and they raced down-river and in a moment they were gone, but the drumming of the hooves still echoed.

"Beautiful," said Ripper.

"Yes," said Harvey.

They got in the cruiser and Du Pré drove back fast, the car bouncing on the rutted track.

Madelaine was waiting, with coffee in big plastic mugs.

"You take these," she said.

Ripper and Harvey took the coffee, and they touched their hats, walked to the tan sedan, and were gone.

CHAPTER
44

Lester shambled along beside his trainer, sniffing the wind. The huge bear yawned and chanked his jaws a little.

"Now Lester," said the man, "this is where you shine! You get to do your dying act."

"Places, everybody," said Ben Burke.

The crew took their positions, and Jason Parks and Maria and a couple of extras looked down in the grass for their markers.

"OK!" hollered the trainer, out of sight down in the willows.

"Go!" said Ben Burke.

Jason Parks, carrying the Pennsylvania rifle, walked swiftly over the grass toward the river, Maria and the extras following along.

Parks paused, looking down at the willows, his face concerned. He checked the pan on the flintlock and cocked it.

The willows began to whip around as Lester moved through them, and then the enormous bear, roaring fiercely, burst out of the green bushes and charged at Jason Parks, who threw the Pennsylvania rifle to his shoulder and fired. A long plume of white smoke shot out of the muzzle of the long rifle.

Lester roared and stood while Parks swiftly reloaded and the second time Parks fired the bear bellowed and fell over twitching.

The twitching stopped.

"Cut!" yelled Ben Burke.

"Oh, Lester," said Maria, hurrying to the huge bear prostrate on the ground. "Are you all right, honey?"

Lester sat up and yawned.

"That was wonderful," said Ben Burke. "It's a print. It was perfect. It was great!"

"Lester," said the trainer, "is a real pro."

An assistant brought a two-gallon bucket of strawberry ice cream.

Lester stood up and he yawned happily and he addressed the ice cream, eating huge gulps of the soft pink stuff.

"How long did it take you to train him to do that?" said Maria.

"Trade secret," said the trainer. "But when I started, I hadn't got to puberty yet." He grinned. He was about forty.

"How long have you been doing this?" said Maria.

"Twenty years," said the trainer, "started by accident, sort of. It's a good life. Money's good, and I like my bears."

"You live where?" said Maria.

"Over by Choteau," said the man.

"How did you get Lester?"

"His mother was killed by a semi-trailer," said the man, "and Lester was about dead when I got him. Zoos have been full up for a while. So I fed him and took care of him. Usually these bears get put back into the country, but even there, since all the fires in '88, there are plenty of grizzlies. So they let me keep him. Too, he *likes* people a lot, which isn't that usual, and he probably wouldn't do well there anyway."

"He's wonderful," said Maria. She looked down at her dress.

There were splotches of pink on it, ice cream thrown off by Lester's feeding.

"Come on, you big bozo," said the trainer. Lester licked the last dribs of ice cream from the bucket, and he followed his master to the big green SUV, climbed in the back, and peered out through the window. The rear end of the rig sank eight inches when the bear got on board.

An assistant came and handed the man a check.

"Thanks," said the man. "I better get him home. He needs a little rest. We have to drive to Oregon for another movie day after tomorrow."

The crew waved as Lester and the trainer drove off.

"I wish I was that *professional*," said Jason Parks.

"I made a decision," said Ben Burke. "The bear gets top billing."

"Hooray," shouted the crew.

"That's it for here, then" said Ben Burke, "so . . . we should roll it up and get the wrap party going."

Maria walked off toward the motor home she had been staying in.

"Thanks for finding that bear," said Ben Burke, looking at Du Pré.

"Thanks that Bart," said Du Pré.

The crew was scurrying around, rolling up cables and taking down the portable light stands. They knew what they were doing and they knew they were going home. They moved fast and well.

"I wish Lester could have stayed for the party," said Ben Burke. "Best actor I ever worked with."

"No offense taken," said Jason. "Best I ever worked with. Course, you got shirty with him, he'd eat you, so your direction is *really* good the first time."

Parks grinned and headed off to the costume trailer to shed his heavy buckskins.

"Well, Du Pré," said Madelaine, "you are about through, this Hollywood stuff? Come home now?"

"Yah," said Du Pré.

"Sometime," said Madelaine, "maybe we come, float down the river, I would like to see it."

Du Pré nodded.

A boat motor whined down on the river, and they looked at the noise. A white wake danced behind the craft, as it sped east.

"Canoe," said Madelaine, "not one of those things."

Du Pré nodded.

They walked back to the camp and found Old Harry up, eating some bacon and eggs, with Lefty sitting on the seat beside him.

"Mornin'," said Old Harry.

There was coffee in the blue enamel pot on the small cookstove. They sat in the sun. Grasshoppers chirred and flew past. An osprey sat on a dead snag down by the river, looking at the water.

Old Harry yawned.

"Packing it in," he said. "I kin go back to bein' old now."

Du Pré and Madelaine laughed.

"You got, some miles left," said Madelaine.

"I suppose," said Old Harry. "They's all in a circle though. I done spent my life here mostly, and I like it. Oh, I was in the war and all, and that was time away, and once I got some fool notion I'd like to make more money, so I done moved to the coast to be a cop there. Lasted nine months. Them cities isn't livable, don't care how many folks there is in 'em think so."

"Come to the party tonight?" said Madelaine.

"Be rude I didn't," said Old Harry. " 'Sides I like that Doo Pray's music. Say, that feller plays bass?"

"Yah?" said Du Pré.

"He maybe oughta smoke his mary juanee a little farther from the saloon, there. Now, I ain't sayin' it's him, mind you, but I got a nose and I do really think I done smelled Meskin boo smoke there a few times. You could mention it."

Du Pré nodded.

Old Harry stood up.

"Well," he said, "I expect you done figured it out, so I expect I had best go and arrest her now."

Du Pré nodded.

"Ma'am," said Old Harry, "I'd like to borry your husband here, as I think it would be a little better than I call the sheriff. I can do all the sad business."

"Sure," said Madelaine. "You think they will do something stupid?"

"Never know," said Old Harry, "but if there's the two of us it is less likely."

Du Pré got up and walked to Old Harry's pickup. Lefty jumped in the back.

"You got a gun?" said Old Harry.

Du Pre shook his head.

"Well," said Harry, "go and get it. I don't expect we'll have to use 'em, but they's nice to wave around, certain situations."

Du Pré got out, and he went to his cruiser, got his 9mm, and put the holster on his belt. He put his wallet in his back pocket.

Old Harry pulled up, and Du Pré got in and they drove on to the main house at the Carbonado.

Lou Van Der Meer answered the door. She looked pale and worried.

"Lou," said Old Harry, "I expect you know what we come for."

"They're in the barn," she said. "Let me come with you."

They waited and she was soon there. The barn was a hundred yards away, and they walked quickly.

Kit and Bob and Paul and Kelly were there, all sitting on boxes, near the horse stalls.

"Afternoon," said Old Harry. "Now, Missy, I am afraid I have to arrest you for the murders of Mr. Rupe and Mr. Lee," and Old Harry sighed.

Kelly Van Der Meer stood up, pale and shaking.

The boys looked at each other.

"Fellers," said Old Harry, "I know how you feel. But don't make this any worse. Yer sister's fifteen, and so she gets out when she's either eighteen or twenty-one."

Kelly didn't move.

"You got the right to remain silent," said Old Harry.

"She will," said Kit Van Der Meer.

CHAPTER 45

Du Pré spread the plastic tarp in the trunk of the old cruiser. He had put the tools and boxes that were usually there in the backseat.

A canoe was lashed to the crossbars on the top of the car.

Early morning, and mist and fog had pooled in the low spots along the river. Du Pré left the movie camp and drove west along the track until he saw a few cows and calves down in a patch of grass. They were grazing slowly and did not even look up as he drove in.

He got out of the car and walked over to a calf that weighed about two hundred pounds. He pulled a small .22 pistol from his pocket and he shot it between the eyes. The calf collapsed, dead instantly.

Du Pré dragged the calf to the cruiser, and he opened the trunk and lifted the animal until he could roll it over the lip. The calf flopped loose-jointed onto the plastic tarp.

Du Pré shut the trunk lid, rolled a smoke, and looked out on the river. Twists of gray mist rose from the water.

It was quite cold.

He finished his cigarette and he put it carefully out and he got in the cruiser and he drove on, until he came to the stand of cottonwoods below the place that Rupe and Lee had camped, on the last night that they lived.

Du Pré drove as close as he could to the spot where Kelly Van Der Meer had waited, the rifle in her hands, for the canoe to pass close by the trees that screened her.

Perhaps one of them had never known what had happened.

The other, knew, for a few seconds.

Du Pré opened the trunk of the cruiser and he jerked the calf up and over. It thudded to the ground. He tied light rope around the rear legs and made a large loop in the other end, and stuck his shoulder through it. He dragged the calf along the deer path to the river, twice having to roll it up and over fallen logs. He left the calf on the bank, near where the deep water chewed at the earth.

He went back to the cruiser and he got the canoe down and he pulled it down to where the calf lay.

Du Pré rolled a smoke and he sat on a log watching the water, dark, powerful, alive.

He tossed the butt in the river.

He took the rope from the calf's feet and rolled the dead creature off the bank. The calf sank a little and then came up, barely breaking the surface.

Du Pré waited a few minutes, and then he set the canoe on the water and pushed off.

The calf rode the current, a couple of hundred feet ahead.

Du Pré followed along, using the paddle to correct the canoe's drift. The current wanted it to float down the river sideways.

The river was strong and silent, and the trees and the land rolled past. Deer looked up from their drinking and watched Du Pré with their huge liquid eyes until he moved on.

An osprey flew past, a fish in its talons.

The current moved toward the center of the river's breadth.

The calf went with it.

The water slowed a little.

Du Pré looked toward the sun, coming up, a red semicircle on the eastern horizon. The mist would soon burn off.

The light rose on the river, dazzling, and Du Pré squinted and pulled his hat down. He cursed.

His dark glasses were on the dash of the cruiser.

The river curved round, and Du Pré stroked to catch up with the floating calf, just a black line on the gold water.

The calf rode steadily along, fifty feet ahead.

Du Pré stared at the water, the glare burned back at him.

He glanced over at the south bank. There was a brief flash, the sun had hit the glass of a moving car.

Du Pré looked back at the calf.

It floated on.

He could see a mile or so down the river, and the logjam that had held the bodies of Rupe and Lee was a jumble of black and gray on the right bank.

Hole in the earth under that.

The trees rose up, tall old cottonwoods, the rotting limbs they had shed silver lines in the shadows.

Fragile trees, but fast-growing. They could be eight feet through in eighty years, if the soil was right.

Du Pré looked ahead and he couldn't see the calf.

He scanned the water.

There it was, moving to the left.

The current picked up, and the calf sailed on.

Du Pré calculated a little.

Maybe, maybe not.

He went round the last slight turn and the calf slowed a little and Du Pré pulled up so he was only about thirty feet from it.

The brush and logpile reached about a quarter of the way across the river over on the right.

Du Pré stared at the calf.

The glare was softening as the sun rose higher.

Du Pré glanced back at the movie camp.

People were stirring, walking here and there.

A mile or so to the logjam.

The current was maybe seven miles an hour.

"Less than ten minutes I know,"Du Pré murmured.

The calf began to move toward the right bank, very slowly.

It moved more.

Du Pré relaxed.

The current speeded just a little.

The calf moved farther to the right.

Du Pré nodded.

He looked down the river and frowned.

No line, where a rock pushed the river over. Should be a huge purl there, the river going to the right of it.

The calf moved, this time to the left.

"Son of a bitch!" said Du Pré.

He dug in the paddle.

Something burned across his chest and then he heard the rifle.

Du Pré went over the side then, and a bullet went overhead.

CRACK!

Du Pré swam, keeping the canoe between him and the gunman.

Thwap.

Another bullet went through the fiberglass, and bits spalled off and hit Du Pré's face.

He stroked hard. The canoe began to turn broadside to the river's current.

Du Pré grabbed the gunwale and he kicked to swing it around.

A bullet passed inches from his left hand.

No more fiddling he shoots any better, Du Pré thought.

The water began to pull at his legs, drawing them down.

Bad water here.

Du Pré cursed and he grabbed the gunwale of the canoe and he slid over and flattened himself. He was barely below the line of sight of the rifleman, and it was a small canoe and he would be hit now.

Son of a bitch.

The canoe began to swing broadside again. Du Pré cursed and he sat up.

The current was strange, a jumble of waters, little waves dancing on the surface.

He was headed for the logjam.

He dug at the water with his hands, trying to swing the canoe around.

He was headed right for the logs at the far left, and the water was white and dancing there.

Goddamn! Du Pré thought.

I am not shot yet.

I should have been dead by now.

The weird current turned the canoe.

Du Pré looked at the logjam.

Son of a *bitch!*

He looked down at the water. It was full of bubbles.

Hydraulics they are ver' bad here.

The canoe was pulled around, as though hands were grabbing at it.

Du Pré kept the canoe balanced.

It swung quickly broadside, and hit something out of sight in the water and Du Pré was tossed out. His knees banged a sunken log.

Du Pré felt the pull, down and down. The water had met a great obstacle, and wanted to chew a hole under it to escape.

He lunged for a thick tree trunk and he got his hands over the top and he held on while the river pulled hard on his body.

He could hold on a while, but the pull was too strong for him to draw his legs and body up and away.

He could hold on.

For a while.

Then the river would eat him.

CHAPTER
46

Oh God take care please of my Madelaine and my daughters and
my grandchildren . . . Oh God . . .

Du Pré could feel the exhaustion building in his straining muscles, a rising aching heat.

The river pulled relentlessly.

Oh God . . .

Du Pré felt something on the back of his neck.

He had been wearing his cowhide jacket.

Someone had grabbed his collar.

They were pulling, hard.

He moved up a half inch.

He strained.

Two inches.

He slid up, and got a new grip on the log. There was the stub of
a branch on the far side and he gripped it and pulled and whoever
was holding his collar pulled and he inched up.

The river was letting go.

Du Pré could move his legs now and he bent them and rolled them up and the river's grip broke.

He dropped over the log, gasping for breath.

Water sluiced out of his jacket and pants.

His boots had been sucked off.

He breathed for a moment.

He choked and coughed and spat.

His whole body trembled.

Thirty more seconds, and he would have been down there forever.

"Du Pré!" said a voice.

Du Pré turned his head and he looked up.

Ripper. Squatting on his haunches. His face was daubed with charcoal and he was dressed in camouflage. Duck hunter's stuff. Like the reeds on the banks of the river.

"Good morning," said Ripper. "Nice day here in beautiful Montana. I am from the Tourist Bureau. We like it here, the Last Free Range of the Brown Recluse Spider, the Place of Unprecedented Meteorological Horrors."

Du Pré coughed and gasped. He'd swallowed water and breathed some, too.

"It was Old Harry," said Ripper. "I have been out in the country, living off the odd lizard and small stones. Saw you with the calf. Harry was back in the trees there, and he hotfooted it back to his truck and got his rifle and headed down for a good spot to kill you from. I ran like hell. Not fast enough though."

Du Pré nodded.

He turned and sat with his back against one log and his butt on another. The river was making the whole logjam vibrate.

"We got to get out of here," said Du Pré.

They made their way toward shore, stepping on slimy wet tree trunks an inch underwater, and then a foot.

"Move!" said Du Pré. The whole jam was going to shift.

They crawled and grabbed and cursed.

248

Du Pré glanced down.

Sand dancing. Quicksand. A spring under there.

And then a little gravel bar.

They stepped off the logjam, and it crunched and ground, branches and whole battered trees lifted up and settled down, water bashed and foamed.

"Son of a bitch!" said Ripper. "That is ugly."

Du Pré bent over. His head was spinning. Ripper helped him to dry ground and sat him on a tussock of grass.

"Where is Harry?" said Du Pré.

"Back there," said Ripper. "I shot him in the chest. Old bastard got off two rounds at me. Only thing he hit was my cell phone. But I thought you needed me more than he did, so I came for you."

Du Pré nodded.

Ripper pointed to a path. He went down it, a stainless-steel 10mm Magnum in his hand.

They walked for perhaps five minutes and came to a little open patch.

Harry was leaned up against a stump, his head down, but Ripper stepped on a stick and the old man lifted his head and swung his right hand up.

He held a small pistol in it, and he pointed it at his right temple.

"Stop there," said Harry, his raspy old voice strong, "You got some questions, but you come near me and you ain't gonna get no answers."

Ripper started to move off, to get behind the old man, but Du Pré grabbed his arm.

"Siddown, ya little shit," said Harry. "Doo Pray knows I mean it."

Du Pré nodded.

He sat on his haunches and pulled Ripper down with him.

Old Harry coughed.

"Doo Pray," said Old Harry, "you take care of Lefty, all right?"

"Sure," said Du Pré.

"Can't keep him yourself you find him a good home. He loves kids."

"Yah," said Du Pré. "Done."

"All right then," said Old Harry. "Thought I had you fooled."

Du Pré shrugged.

"You're right," said Old Harry. "There's a place farther out, got 'em all in it. Some of 'em still got the slugs in 'em."

Du Pré nodded.

"Why?" said Du Pré. "Why you do this?"

Old Harry coughed.

"I been here in the West, Montana, man and boy my whole life. It's good country, good people. Then these goddamned environmentalists show up, and after a while I figger 'em out. They's just greedy little shits want the place for theirselves. They get that chickenshit in the White House, raise the grazing fees, any damn thing drive these folks out, so they can watch the goddamn buffalo roam."

Du Pré nodded.

"Who else is with you?" said Du Pré.

"Yes, ma'am," said Old Harry. "And I hung 'em all myself."

Du Pré laughed. Ripper looked puzzled.

"Tell the pup," said Old Harry. "I hate to leave him out of the conflab we's having."

"Granville Stuart," said Du Pré. "He was the first white settler here. Cattleman, lots of rustlers. So he and his friends ride, hang thirty-seven of them. People still bitter about it. Years later, he is in Miles City, woman comes up to him, says, you hung innocent men . . ."

Old Harry wheezed and nodded.

"So Granville, he tips his hat, and he says, yes, ma'am, and I hung 'em all myself," said Du Pré.

Ripper looked at Old Harry.

"You evil old son of a bitch," said Ripper. "You got those half-wit kids together and you got them to commit murder. Murder is a crime, Harry, the worst of all."

"They's killin' us," said Old Harry, "the bastards."

Ripper looked at the ground.

"We got to fight," said Old Harry. "We got to fight."

Ripper shook his head.

"It never works, Harry," he said. "It just doesn't."

"Feels good, though," said Old Harry.

"How many?" said Du Pré.

Old Harry laughed and laughed, and shook his head.

"Doo Pray, Doo Pray," he said. "Pull 'em up and count 'em."

He put the pistol to his head and pulled the trigger and the gun popped and Old Harry jerked once and fell to the side, quivering.

Du Pré sighed and he stood up and he walked over. He put his foot on Old Harry's wrist and he reached down and got the pistol.

"Watch the woods," said Du Pré. "Those kids are there, they might shoot."

But Ripper already was, his gun up.

"Let's go," said Du Pré. He began to walk down the path. Ripper followed, moving from cover to cover.

"They are not here," said Du Pré, over his shoulder. "No birds are complaining. No squirrels."

Ripper trotted up closer.

"That old shit," he said. "I doubt we can make cases now, unless one of the kids talks."

"They will all have lawyers before I have dry clothes," said Du Pré.

"This is no good at all," said Ripper.

A dog barked, frantically. Lefty was in the cab of Old Harry's truck, jumping from side to side.

Du Pré opened the door and the dog got out and he whined and he sniffed the wind. He ran down the path.

Lefty howled, a long scream of pain and loss and bewilderment.

Du Pré nodded.

"Yes," he said, "that is about right."

CHAPTER
47

"That's awful," said Ben Burke. He looked distraught.

"Yah," said Du Pré.

"We can't have the wrap party here," said Ben. "God."

"Come, Toussaint," said Madelaine.

"Yes!" said Maria.

"Right," said Ben. "I'll go and tell everyone. They're about all packed anyway. These days, it doesn't take what it used to."

He left the big tent, running.

"Most of them come there anyway," said Maria. "Some had to leave before, they have another movie."

Like them wheat combiners, Du Pré thought, heading on.

After a moment, Du Pré and Madelaine left, too, and they went back to Du Pré's camp and they put the few things he had there into the trunk of the old cruiser.

They drove back to the movie camp. The big green tent was

coming down, and what had been there was disappearing into the motor homes and the single eighteen-wheeler very quickly.

"I come up with Ben," said Maria.

Jason Parks was walking toward them, dressed now in jeans and a soft blue shirt and a Panama hat. He leaned down to the window.

"Would it be all right for me to come there?" he said. "I don't want to cause any trouble."

"Nobody bother you, Toussaint," said Madelaine. "They don't hold it against you, you are famous."

"I have about an hour's work left," said Jason. "Well, it's not *work*. I need to thank everyone, I think some of them won't be coming to Toussaint."

"I got something, to do," said Du Pré. "With that Maria and my Madelaine, we come back, you follow us."

Maria was talking to one of the extras, and shaking his hand.

"Can you come now?" said Du Pré.

"I got to talk, these people, Papa," she said. "They work very hard, this."

"OK," said Du Pré.

Du Pré drove off, up the same route he had taken the day before with Ripper and Harvey. He parked on the flat above the big grove of cottonwoods, and he and Madelaine got out.

Du Pré opened the trunk of his cruiser and he got out a chain saw and he checked the gas and oil and they were full. He picked up the axe in its leather sheath.

"Oh, hoh," said Madelaine, "Du Pré knows something."

They walked down the path and into the cool shade of the cottonwoods, and to the tree lying across the path. It had been dead for many years but still was sound in parts. It had been huge and very old.

Du Pré pointed to the forks, halfway up the length of the fallen tree. They looked like a hand now, with a jagged break, a line across what would be the flesh between finger and thumb.

"Benetsee say there," said Du Pré. "I try it. Maybe this is not the tree."

A kingfisher flew past, screeching.

"Ho," said Madelaine, "it is the tree, Du Pré."

Du Pré nodded and he started the chain saw and he cut through the trunk high up, a foot or so below the forks, and then he cut the big branches away. He then had a section of the tree four or so feet across, and he stopped the chain saw and he got on the other side and he lifted it and rolled it out and it fell flat.

He looked carefully. He started the saw again and he cut away a big chunk of clean wood, leaving some gnarled sections where the old branches had come off the bole.

There was a thick brown line in the middle.

Du Pré got the axe and he struck it hard near the edge and the wood popped and the chunk came apart.

"God*damn*," said Madelaine.

An elk skull was there, stuck in the wood, and something else, a rotted bundle, which was orange and shredded.

"Old leather," said Du Pré. He took his knife and he dug at the wood around the bundle. There was sap-sodden wound wood there, but it peeled away like a shell.

Du Pré tugged, and the long package came out.

Du Pré grunted.

"Shoot him in the ass, he take Cruzatte's fiddle away, hide it somewhere, punish him," said Du Pré.

Madelaine laughed, and she clapped her hands.

"They don't write that in that journal," said Du Pré. "Dumb shit thing to do, take Cruzatte's fiddle."

But Lewis had, and he had stuck it in the high fork of a tree here and the tree had grown, and it had flooded and an elk, drowned, had got stuck there and the tree had grown around the skull, too.

And then it died and it fell over.

"Benetsee tell you?" said Madelaine.

"Yah," said Du Pré.

He cut away the rotted leather.

The fiddle was chalky white with age and rot, made, probably, of pine. But the bone bridge and the pegs were fine, and the fingerboard of polished chokecherry.

The box had been crushed, and the ribs showed, and the knife marks that Cruzatte had put in them when he whittled them from the maple.

"Son of a bitch," said Madelaine. "That is Cruzatte's fiddle!"

"Yah," said Du Pré.

"Them people want the stuff from the cache, they want this, too," said Madelaine.

"Yah," said Du Pré.

"But you don't give it to them, Du Pré?" said Madelaine.

"No," said Du Pré. "It is mine."

Du Pré and Madelaine walked back to Du Pré's old cruiser and he opened the trunk and he took out a two-foot square of brain-tanned elk skin, and he folded the old ghost fiddle in it and he tucked it in a corner of the trunk.

"Maria, she have the things from the cache," said Madelaine. "They are hers, yes?"

Du Pré nodded.

"Benetsee, him giving gifts, always," said Madelaine.

Du Pré nodded. Long ago, a coyote show me where my father buried things, Catfoot, he kill Bart's brother, long time gone.

"You make some new songs, Du Pré," said Madelaine. "You make one for them dumb kids and that old fool Harry. Him old enough know what he is doing it is wrong."

Du Pré nodded.

"Harry, out of another time," said Du Pré. "People out of the time they know, they go crazy. Sometimes. Thing I am mad about, him, he drag those kids along."

"Yah," said Madelaine. "It is not right."

"Jack Rupe, Davis Lee, they are writing a good book, this place, but they are on the river right after some bastards cut the fences. Like many grandpa Louis, Englishman he is killed, posse hang old

Louis, he don't have nothing to do with it. But he is a Métis, and he is near, so he is guilty."

"Ah," said Madelaine, "You don't tell me that before."

Du Pré looked at the bundle in the corner of the trunk.

Madelaine touched his cheek.

"Crying, Du Pré," she said. "It is ver' sad, yes."

Du Pré nodded.

He sighed and he wiped his eyes and he shut the trunk lid.

"They come, build a coffer dam, dig out those other people," said Du Pré. "Push the river over awhile, bring up the dead, take them to the morgue, dig out the bullets they got them, try to find the guns they came from. But them kids. They are like stones. Their lawyers are with them cops talk to them, they say nothing. Ripper, he knows this. He says they will never, get tried. Never pay nothing, never know how wrong it is."

"Pret' strong kids," said Madelaine.

Du Pré looked over the river, to where the old cabin was.

"There is stuff over there, I don't understand at first. Old candles. What you do with a candle, in the wind? There is this rock, black from little fires. Round it on the ground, dog's teeth."

"Ah," said Madelaine.

"Dog soldiers," said Du Pré. The crazies who fought with a hide rope around their chests, run to a stake in the ground.

Never retreat. Die, but never retreat.

"Gonna get worse, eh, Du Pré," said Madelaine.

"Yah," said Du Pré. "Me, I do not think this is the only place in Montana got dog soldiers in it."

"Bad times," said Madelaine.

Du Pré nodded.

"People don't talk to each other," he said. "Then they fight."

Madelaine looked over the river.

She put her arm around Du Pré.

"Du Pré," she said, "see over there, where there is that eagle in the tree? Little steamboat there, taking on wood."

CHAPTER
48

The saloon in Toussaint was filled with people from the movie crew and Du Pré's friends and enemies. Most of the movie people had come, Jason Parks was the first to arrive, in his little black pickup, wearing worn old Levi's and running shoes and a cap that said INSTANT ASSHOLE, JUST ADD WHISKEY.

"Fine hat you got there," said Madelaine, looking at it.

Jason took the hat off and he looked at it.

"Um," he said.

Madelaine handed him a TOUSSAINT SALOON hat, blue with gray lettering and piping.

"Much better," said Jason. He handed his old hat to Madelaine, and she put it in the trash.

A couple of reporters came in, looked around, and goggled at Jason. They looked at each other.

"*You!*" said Madelaine. "You bother him one time, out of here!"

The reporters looked at each other again.

"OK," said one, "we're looking for . . . Gabriel Du Pré?"

Du Pré didn't turn around.

"Du Pré," said Madelaine. "Him in jail, that drunk driving."

"Oh," said the reporter.

They left.

"They be back," said Du Pré.

Madelaine nodded.

"I still be here," she said.

Madelaine went to the end of the bar to take orders from some of the movie people.

Nepthele and Bassman and Tally arrived, all laughing.

Bassman got them some of that good weed, thought Du Pré, I can smell it from here. Sweetgrass, my ass.

"Du Pré!" said Bassman. "Some man, ask me you are in jail that drunk driving. I say yes. He ask where, I say that Great Falls. They look ver' sad."

Du Pré nodded. He got up and went to help them bring in all of the sound gear. It didn't take very long, but the three were clumsy from the cannabis. They would stumble and then roar with laughter.

"Jesus," said Madelaine, "they should stick, that whiskey."

Du Pré nodded, and he had some.

The movie crew was happy. Another job completed, another story on film. They laughed and chaffed each other.

Susan Klein came in from the big barbecue pit out behind the saloon. She smelled of woodsmoke, oranges, and pepper.

"An hour," she said, "and we will have beef. Made up my special sauce.

"They gonna drink a lot of beer," said Madelaine, "try to cure that sauce of yours."

"Uh-huh," said Susan.

The reporters came back in.

Du Pré turned and he looked at them and he sighed. They came over.

"*Seattle Post-Intelligencer,*" said one, "Polson and Phibbs, and we wondered . . . ?"

Du Pré shook his head.

The reporters looked at each other.

"We'll have to use other sources," said Polson.

Du Pré shrugged.

"He's supposed to be difficult," said Phibbs.

Du Pré turned back to his whiskey.

"She walked," said Polson, "that girl up on the river. Shot two men," and they had to let her go."

Du Pré sighed. He turned around.

"You got to write something?" he said, "you write, it is better to behave, the river. Don't bother them people. You write that."

The reporters scribbled.

"What about the Lewis and Clark stuff?" said Polson. "Where is it? I hear there are about forty lawsuits headed your way."

Du Pré shrugged.

People outside the saloon began to yell.

"Now what," said Madelaine, "is the hell going on?"

She went out from behind the bar and to the front door and she looked out.

She waved to Du Pré.

Du Pré got up and he carried his glass to the door and he looked out.

"Good," said Madelaine. "This party would be no good without him."

Lester the movie star grizzly bear was shambling across the parking lot with his trainer ambling alongside.

A woman screamed.

Madelaine glared at her.

"You don't be rude, Lester," said Madelaine. "He is a ver' nice bear."

Lester came up to Du Pré and Madelaine and he sat down and he yawned. He had a lot of big white teeth.

"Jesus," said the woman, "is that somebody's *pet?*"

"Lester," said Madelaine, "is everybody's pet. Hi there, big guy." She scratched Lester's giant ear. Lester chuffled happily.

"God," said Polson, "that is one monster."

"Mind your own business," said Madelaine, "we maybe don't feed you to him."

"A reporter," said Polson, "minds everybody else's business. It's what we *do*."

Du Pré laughed.

"You stay," he said. "Eat some barbecue, listen to music. It is all in the music the story, you hear it there."

"OK," said Polson. "Beats feeding the bear."

Madelaine went back inside.

Du Pré and Lester looked at each other and they nodded.

The big van that Jacqueline and Raymond had to move their throng of children in one mass drove in and the doors opened and kids shot out, laughing and shoving each other.

Little Pallas, who had stumbled and fallen, got up and she ran and came to Du Pré. Her knee was bleeding, but she ignored it.

"Ah, bear," she said. "Maybe I can ride him, yes?"

"Sure," said the trainer, "but you have to ask him nice."

"Lester," cooed Pallas, "I maybe ride your big strong back."

Lester chuffled and he nodded.

The trainer lifted Pallas up and sat her on Lester's neck.

Lester stood up and he shambled off, Pallas clinging to his long ruff hair. The huge bear tried to walk softly, hard to do when you weighed a thousand pounds.

Du Pré's grandchildren shoaled around him for a moment and then they raced off to other things.

Maria and Ben Burke arrived. Maria was beautiful in her costume, the long beaded buckskin dress. Ben was wearing a sport coat and a tie.

"Papa," said Maria, "I feel silly."

Du Pré put his arm around her.

He shook his head.

"You look good," he said. "You can wear that dress."

Maria blushed.

"What happens now, Papa?" whispered Maria.

Du Pré shrugged.

"Benetsee has those things," said Maria. "You got the fiddle. Kelly, the police let her go, she is silent."

Du Pré nodded.

"We rode some," said Maria, "she is a good rider."

Du Pré looked at his daughter.

"Rode after the horses," said Maria. "It is a game, they run over the country, ver' fast. I tell her that Bart is a good man, he won't mess up the Carbonado. She was worried."

Du Pré nodded. He waited.

"She don't say nothing to me about that," said Maria, looking at Du Pré's face. "I don't ask either."

Du Pré nodded.

"They will be all over, down there," said Maria. "All over up here, too, the Lewis and Clark stuff."

Du Pré nodded.

"What are you going to do?" said Maria. "I will be back in England."

Du Pré laughed.

"They want, talk to Benetsee," he said, "that is what they can do."

Maria laughed.

"OK," she said, "that don't work for sure."

"What will you do?" said Ben Burke. "It'll be mad here."

Du Pré rolled a smoke. He looked at Lester and Pallas, off on the grass.

"They don't be here in the winter," he said.

CHAPTER
49

The wind was howling and snow blasted hard against the windshield of the big SUV. The man on the radio said all roads in eastern Montana were closed by the Great Blizzard.

Du Pré and Ripper were headed west, into the storm.

"You swear there is a road out there," said Ripper.

"Yah," said Du Pré.

"The weather's bad if you won't take your cruiser," said Ripper, "Du Pré driving this yupmobile. So they are good for something after all."

"Yah," said Du Pré, "but this is the only time in ten years this piece of crap is good for anything. Spend fifty thousand dollars, drive one day in ten years."

"We could have waited," said Ripper.

"Miss all the fun," said Du Pré. "We maybe get stuck. Call up Chevrolet, say, we are stuck, TV crews coming, how much you pay for us to shut up?"

"That's extortion," said Ripper.

"So is fifty thousand dollars," said Du Pré.

"It all worked out like we thought," said Ripper. "They fish out the other six people. Seventh one the river probably did take. All shot with the same gun. Harry's rifle. His little myrmidons paid close attention to Harry. They got lawyers, they clammed up, and we didn't have shit. So Harry killed them all."

"Maybe he did," said Du Pré. "Maybe they just kept watch for him. Maybe. I am dreaming one time, I dream that Kelly Van Der Meer and her brothers, that Sam kid, couple others are at the old cabin. They are pissed off, going to do something, they are talking. Harry, he has smelled them, he is in the shadows, listens, comes out, says, you are kids, fools, this is how we do it."

"Could be," said Ripper.

Du Pré accelerated downhill and smashed into a deep drift. He bulled out the other side and fishtailed up the hill for a time until the snow thinned.

"Harvey thinks I'm skiing," said Ripper. "This is highly irregular. Going to chat with criminals."

"Harvey," said Du Pré, "is smarter than that."

Ripper looked at the air outside, all white.

"How the hell do you even know where you *are*?" he said. "It's a fucking whiteout."

"My country," said Du Pré.

They were silent then, for a long time, until Du Pré turned off the road under the snow to another road that was invisible, too.

Du Pré stopped the big SUV and he shut it off.

The wind was screaming.

"Ok," said Ripper, "if you say so."

Du Pré buttoned his cowhide jacket, jammed his hat down over his head, and opened the door. Stinging snow swirled through the car.

He waited for Ripper, who had trouble with the zipper on his fat down parka.

Du Pré led him along a faint trail and lights appeared, a house, a warm yellow glow in two windows.

Du Pré pounded on the door, and it soon opened.

He stepped in and Ripper followed.

"We have a little weather," said Mrs. Leverett. "I've seen worse."

"Worse?" said Ripper, from the depths of his vast coat.

"Who is this?" said Mrs. Leverett.

"Charles Van Dusen," said Ripper, from somewhere in the folds.

"It is all right," said Du Pré.

"He's OK," said a voice from the other room.

They shed their coats and went to the kitchen table.

They sat. Hot coffee appeared.

Bill Rupe came in, smiling.

He sat down, and put a small tape recorder on the table.

Mrs. Leverett came and took another chair.

Rupe pressed the PLAY button.

In the late afternoon Du Pré and Ripper were bashing through drifts, headed for Toussaint.

Du Pré rolled a smoke, and Ripper had one, too, and the snow rattled on the glass.

"You know," said Ripper, "I spend my time going after bad folks. I like it. Nothing I like better than seeing bad folks off to the goddamn can. And that was wrong, wrong, wrong. But Old Harry there, he was really smart. He kept those young fools out of it but took them far enough in so they knew where they were."

"Yah," said Du Pré.

"They really do want to destroy the ranchers," said Ripper.

"Yah," said Du Pré.

"The guy who's toughest, though, is Bill Rupe. Incredible, absolutely incredible. His *son* is murdered, by mistake. The guilty people are the ones he helps."

"He is a good man," said Du Pré.

"That's what Harvey said," said Ripper.